Bought By Three Men

A BILLIONAIRE ROMANCE

CALLIE SKY

Bought By Three Men

Copyright (c) 2023 by Callie Sky

For more information contact:

authorcalliesky@gmail.com

Cover Design by : PC Designs

To My Husband John, for being my possessive man but helping me write about women getting banged out by multiple men.

Trigger Warnings – These may contain spoilers

If any of these are a trigger for you don't read this book. There are so many other amazing books out there. No book is worth it.

Violence, Death, Homelessness, Throat grabbing, Sex scenes, Sex scenes with multiple partners, Backdoor play, Stabbing, Death Threats, Blood, Suicide, Drug Abuse, Overdose, Domestic Violence, Rape, Abusive Ex, Torture, Mental Health Issues, Unprotected Sex. Fire. Child abuse.

CHAPTER 1

Ava

I PUSHED UP ON MY TOES TO SEE THE NEXT PERSON I would be fighting. My right eye had swollen shut, but I could still see clearly through my left. The last girl sucker-punched me. Not that I blamed her. I would have done the same thing to her. A lot of money went to the winner.

Each match won was three grand. Getting in the ring was only two hundred. Barely enough for a decent meal. Yet, it was enough to get people to fight in the underground bunker. Years ago, someone made this place in preparation for World War 3. That war came and went, along with some others.

The bunker remained intact. Then, Von found it last year and turned it into a women's boxing club. Since I was always in some scrap or another, he asked me to fight for him. He said it was also because of my bubbly personality and love of pink. It made me stand out, and people who didn't know me always bet against me—their loss.

"Ava, are you sure about this?" Dottie, my little sister, wiped the blood off my face. She hated that I did this. I probably wouldn't spend my Friday nights fighting if my family didn't need the money.

1

My stomach turned. I looked again at the next fighter. The crowd cheered, which consisted primarily of Rich men. Some Elite were also there, but only a few. They bored quickly, and watching the Homeless beat each other up was beneath them.

Three classes of people made up New Boston; the Elite: who ruled, the Rich: who prospered, and the Homeless: who barely survived. I was lucky enough to be part of the bottom economic class.

"Dottie, I can take her." I grabbed her by the shoulders and looked her in the eyes to try to be more convincing.

"That's Big Booty Judy!" Dottie pointed to the ring.

Judy bounced from foot to foot. Her hair was in a tight red bun, and it didn't move as she jumped. From a distance, she appeared small and fragile. Well, aside from her plump ass. That bubble butt had its own zip code. Everything about her gave you a false sense of security. She was all muscle and well-trained, and her size made it better to get up close and attack.

"I'm like half a foot taller and have long arms. Don't worry, I'll knock her out and won't break a nail doing it." I flashed her my perfectly polished razz nails. Two fights and none of it had chipped.

Dottie crossed her arms and looked down at me. She was five-nine, only two inches taller, but she towered over me when she gave me the disappointed mom look. Since our mom lost her mind, Dottie took over. She did the maternal instinct thing better than I did. She was only seventeen, and I was twenty-five, but she was more mature than me in many ways.

"In this corner, standing at five foot even, one hundred twenty pounds, we have the undefeated champion of The Underground, Big Booty Judy!" Von waved his bony hand at her. Judy grunted.

It was my last chance to back out. We could have left. Von would have understood. I could only see from one eye, had a

2

broken nose, and various parts of my body ached. I had already made decent money for food and my mother's medication.

"Will anyone challenge our champion?" Von peered out into the crowd.

The chatter stopped. Everyone looked around to see if anyone would be brave enough. Of course, the Rich dipshits didn't know this was all part of the act. Von figured they would be more interested if they didn't know who was fighting. He was right. The Rich came from all over New Boston to watch. His club was the most popular in the country.

"No one?" Von hobbled over to the edge of the rink. He was pretty young, but an accident left him with a limp. Rumor was the accident was him not paying a loan shark.

I was supposed to challenge Big Booty Judy. Von never told us who we were fighting, only which matches we were in. He claimed it made the whole act more authentic. This was my match—the last one of the night. I shouldn't have agreed to three, but we needed the money. Now more than ever.

"Ladies and Gentlemen, it appears no one wants to fight Big Booty Judy." Von looked into the crowd and shook his head.

"Boo!" a man shouted.

Then the crowd erupted, they screamed and shouted, demanding a fight. Had it not been the night's last match, Von would have skipped to the next one.

"Let's go home," Dottie whispered. "You can fight again next week. We have enough money for Mom's meds and food."

She was right. Big Booty Judy fought dirty, and I was in no condition to attempt a fight against her. "Okay."

"Well, it looks like the crowd really wants a fight." Von waved his hands around.

The crowd cheered and pumped their fists. Judy crossed her arms, looking bored. I picked up my speed before he forced me into the rink.

"Okay, Okay!" Von waved his hands down to calm the crowd. "I will double the winner's prize."

I kept walking. I didn't have a chance against Judy.

"Still nothing?" Von asked. "Okay, I will triple the loser's money."

I stopped.

Dottie grabbed my arm and tried to pull me toward the doors.

Triple.

I turned.

"This is a bad idea," Dottie whispered. "I'll pick up extra shifts at the shop."

Dottie had a gift for computer technology. She would dig around in trash cans of the rich and refurbish old computers and anything with a motherboard. Because of that, she had a part-time gig fixing them. It wasn't the best-paying job because rich people would buy another one, and most homeless couldn't afford them.

"There aren't extra shifts," I whispered to her. "I'll do it!" I shouted to Von.

Everyone turned to me. Dottie groaned beside me. I slapped Dottie's back. She crossed her arms and shook her head.

"We have an opponent!" Von pointed at me. The people parted to allow me access to the ring.

I adjusted my pink wig and walked toward the ring. It was part of my persona, which made total sense because I was all about pink. I mean, who wouldn't be? A splash of color made everything better.

Two men in suits stood off to the side. I probably

wouldn't have noticed them, but they were half a foot taller than everyone around them. One had tattoos peeking out of his sleeves onto his hands. The other looked like he had never smiled.

They were both staring at me. Mr. Tattoos looked like he wanted to eat me, and not in a good way. Mr. No Smiles gave me a death stare. He probably had a burial plot in his basement waiting for some random girl to stumble into. *Not me, mister. I would scratch your eyes out first, even if you are the sexiest man I have ever seen.* Both of them were.

"You are too pretty to be stepping into that ring." Mr. Tattoos winked.

I opened my mouth to reply when Dottie pushed me. She was the level-headed one. I swore Dottie took all the responsibilities, so I didn't have to. She would make a great mother someday. Not me. I babysat once and lost the kid for two hours. But thanks to me, she had a killer manicure and eyeliner so sharp it could slice someone. It didn't matter. Her mother was not happy.

She legit attacked me. I broke a nail, but I also broke her tooth. That's when I learned I could fight.

"Now, entering the ring is a fan favorite. Five foot seven and one hundred forty pounds of pure pink happiness." Von waved his hands at me.

I climbed under the rope and got into my corner.

"Gentlemen and the few ladies here. I see you, Greta." Von winked at a lady in a bonnet and red dress. "I present to you, Pink Puncher!"

Cheers and hoots swam through the crowd. I soaked it all in. Yeah, Big Booty Judy was undefeated, but the people loved me.

I weaved and bobbed as she came at me. My fist got her square in her unglossed lip. In response, she grinned, showing bloody teeth, and approached me again. The fight lasted thirty-seven seconds.

Blocking her hit would have been helpful. I tried, really. She was fast. Her punch caused stars, and I hit the mat.

CHAPTER 2

Ava

DOTTIE WAS THERE PULLING ME UP BEFORE I COULD get my bearings. I reached out to grab the rope and missed. Before my face could slam into the mat again, two strong arms wrapped around me.

A man lifted me and carried me away from the ring. The crowd was cheering for Judy. It was a good hit, but damn, it hurt. Luckily, my wig was still on my head. The thing cost an arm and a leg and was one of my favorite things I owned. At least I got six hundred bucks, which took less than a minute.

"There is a room in the back," Dottie whispered to whoever was carrying me.

I tried to open my eyes to see who it was, but my head was pounding, and the lights were bright. Honestly, I was grateful someone was carrying me. I didn't want to walk. It would take me a week to heal from this. Which meant I would be suitable to fight when the club was open next week.

We entered the dressing room, and someone placed me on the bench. Dottie grabbed a cup of water and held it to my lips. Most of it dribbled down my mouth.

"Told you, you are too pretty to be in that ring," someone said.

I looked up and saw the fuzzy image of a tall man covered in tattoos. It was Mr. Tattoos, and right next to him was Mr. No Smiles. What the heck were they doing in here?

"Fuck off," I mumbled. I just wanted to get my money and get out of here.

"Seems dangerous for pretty girls to be beating the crap out of each other. Why do you do it?" Mr. No Smiles asked.

Von hobbled into the room and slapped me on the back. It wouldn't have hurt so bad if I had not been in three fights. The damn man hit like a small child. "Nice job out there. I almost thought there wasn't gonna be a fight."

"There shouldn't have been," Dottie snapped. "You gotta stop putting her in so many fights."

"Everyone loves her. If she isn't in a fight, I don't get nearly as many bets." Von reached into his pocket and handed me two bills.

I stared down at the two hundred dollars. I knew I had taken a brutal hit to the head, but it wasn't adding up. He was short on my money, and I was in no mood to argue with him. "Von, I'm not doing this today. Where is the rest?"

"I gave you the money for the other fights." Von looked genuinely confused.

"Right, and this fight was triple. Where is the rest?" Dottie stepped in front of me and got in Von's face. She wasn't a fighter, but she was protective over the people she cared about, which was a concise list.

"Oh," He waved his hand dismissively. "That was part of the act. Ava knows that."

My mouth dropped. That jerkass was trying to swindle me.

Mr. Tattoos grabbed Von by the throat and slammed him into the lockers. He moved so fast I hadn't even realized it was him. The crash from the lockers made Dottie squeal. Violence always bothered her, yet she came with me every week to the club.

"You aren't trying to cheat this little lady out of money?" Mr. Tattoos slammed him again. "Are you Von?"

The way he spoke to him was as if he knew him. The tone of his voice made it sound like he didn't like him very much. As much as I loved someone giving it to Von, I had to step in. It wasn't Mr. Tattoos' place to defend me. It was no one's but my own. Plus, I needed Von. He paid the most out of any fight clubs in New Boston.

"Get off of him," I demanded. My voice came out squeaky and strained, entirely unlike how I intended.

Dottie tried to keep me from getting up. I waved her hands away and only swayed a little.

The men completely ignored me. Mr. No Smiles glared at me while the other two men had a stare-down contest. To Von's credit, he kept his ground as he stared into the eyes of Mr. Tattoos. Well, Von tried to. He was much shorter and smaller than the other man. It looked like a child being defiant against his dad.

"Let go of him." I grabbed Mr. Tattoos' arm. Okay, no one should be that muscular. I may have given it an extra squeeze, totally on accident.

"Would you rather I grab you?" Mr. Tattoos looked me up and down. He spent a little too much time on my chest. I was rethinking the low-cut pink tank top and hot pink mini shorts.

"I would rather you leave." I pointed at the door.

"Ava, it's fine. Mr. Moore and I are just having a little chat." Von whispered. His face was getting redder by the second.

Moore? The name sounded familiar, but I couldn't place it. He was rich, and they weren't as well known as the elite.

Maybe he had shown up here before, and I had heard his name. Doubtful. Someone like him would be hard to forget.

"Moore? Like Moore Tech?" Dottie bounced on her heels. "That means you're Mitchell Moore's kid. Ahh, you're Ethan Moore. Ican'tbelieveitsyoucanItalktoyouIhavesomanyquestions." If she didn't take a breath, she would pass out.

Moore Tech. That meant he was elite. What was he doing in a club like this?

The arrogant asshole released Von and smiled at Dottie. "That's me. If you wanna come by my office, I would happily show you around."

Dottie squealed.

"The fuck you will!" I snapped.

Mr. No Smiles grabbed his shoulder and whispered something in his ear.

"Dude." Mr. Moore took a step back. "I'm offended. I know she looks like a teenager. I was trying to be nice."

"She is a teenager. She's seventeen." I pushed on Mr. Moore's chest. He didn't budge.

"She shouldn't be around a place like this. Where are her parents?" Mr. No Smiles asked.

The question stung. It may have seemed like a simple enough question. Although asking the way he did implied she needed parental supervision or had no parents. That was only partially true. Our mother lost her grip on reality a long time ago. As far as our father, he was dead, and that was my fault.

"I look out for her when she's here." Von rubbed his neck.

What? He was full of shit. Von looked out for himself, and that was it. Besides, Dottie didn't need anyone to look out for her.

"Anyway, the offer stands." Mr. Moore handed Dottie a business card.

Her smile reached from ear to ear. It wasn't often she looked so happy. Dottie was always worried. I wanted to keep that smile on her face. She deserved happiness, but not from an elite.

I grabbed the card from her hand, ripped it into tiny pieces, and tossed it at Mr. Moore. Dottie stood there with wide eyes, and her mouth dropped open. I had ruined her happiness, and I hated myself for it. I had never acted like a parent, treated her like a child, or upset her. She would hate me for this for a little while. One day she would understand elite were dangerous.

Tears swelled in her eyes. My heart crumbled. I grabbed her arm and pulled her out of the club.

CHAPTER 3

Ethan

SHE WAS GETTING CLOSER. HER PUSSY CLENCHED around my cock. I had fucked Tasha enough times to know when she was about to cum.

She gripped the countertops as her moans increased. I pounded harder. She wasn't the sweet, gentle kind when it came to sex. She would bend over and lift her skirt when she was in the mood. No foreplay, it was my favorite part of sex.

I usually didn't mind the get-to-the-point attitude she had. I would fuck her, and then we would go about our business. Two years ago, I thought maybe she was the one for me. Boy, was I wrong.

"Harder!" she screamed.

Was the girl from last night the same way? I could practically see her pink hair sway as I set her on my bed. Would she let me kiss every inch of her? Even with her bruises and swollen eye, I could tell she was beautiful. It was in the way she walked and the way she protected her sister from me. I wanted the Pink Puncher. I had to have her.

"Where are you?" Tasha twisted to look at me.

"Huh?" I blinked.

She stepped away from me and pulled up her underwear. "Ethan, what's going on?"

"Why aren't we together?" I wanted to ask her why she didn't want to be with me, but it would sound like I was whining.

"We have been through this. Elites get together to strengthen their empire. We don't need to." She crossed her arms.

"She was right. We were some of the wealthiest Elites in New Boston. It gave us a unique opportunity. We could marry for love. Ha. What a joke of a concept, love. Marriage was for one of two reasons. Strengthen our empire or continue your line.

Yet, I couldn't help but ask. "What about for love?"

She laughed. Shit, I shouldn't have asked that. Tasha stopped laughing and stared at me. It wasn't often I felt small. Not since I was a child. It was how she looked at me as if she pitied me.

"Are you serious? You don't even believe in love. Neither do I. It's a concept poor and homeless people use as an excuse for everything." She stared at me as if trying to determine if I was joking.

"I got you." I pointed at her and laughed. "Just making sure you weren't falling for me."

She let out a sigh of relief. "Never. Now can you fuck me? I was about to cum."

I bent her over the counter again and slid her thong to the side. The sight of her pink pussy dripping made me hard again.

As I rammed my cock inside her warmth, she bucked against me. *How would Ava feel?*

Two quick coughs sounded behind me. I wasn't sure who it was, so I didn't look. If Tasha heard it, she didn't move. She continued moving her hips and moaning.

"Son, a word," my father's voice echoes through the kitchen.

I turned my head but continued to fuck Tasha. "Go ahead."

"Now!" His tone was even more demanding than it usually was.

I pulled out of Tasha and zipped up.

She stayed bent over the counter, exposing her pussy to my father. Looking back, she winked at him. "When you're done with Ethan, maybe you can help me finish, Mr. Moore."

His cheeks reddened as he turned. My mother left him years ago, and he hadn't been with another since. He always said he was too busy, but I believed she broke his heart. Love was a joke.

Moore Mansion was large enough to fit all the Moore's and our staff. We all had our own wing and avoided each other most days. I followed my father down the hall and into his office.

My grandfather stayed to himself on the east wing enjoying his retirement. My father lived in the west wing and ran Moore Tech. As for me, I had the south wing, and I lived the life they should have. We had money, so why not enjoy it?

My father closed the door and sat on the sofa. That's when I noticed his face. His eyes were bloodshot. What I had thought was him blushing now looked more like he had been wiping away tears.

I had only ever seen him cry twice. The day my mother left and the day my sister died. Fuck. This was bad. My stomach turned.

"When?" I asked, knowing what he was about to say.

"A few minutes ago. Heart attack. He placed his hand on my shoulder. "They tried to save him. Your Grandpa was a fighter."

He continued to talk as I got up and stormed down the

hall. My gramps had a room turned into a makeshift hospital room in case he got sick. He was always prepared. There had been no need for it until now. He would still be in there.

I stepped into the room. My gramps was lying on the hospital bed with a sheet covering everything, including his face. A tiny nurse was shutting off the monitors with tears pouring down her face.

At one point in my life, all I had was him. When I lost my sister, my dad shut himself down. He stayed hidden with his grief. My gramps helped me through it. Now he was gone. Fuck.

I grabbed his hand with my tattoo-covered one. He was still warm as if he was sleeping. I could still hear him. *Another tattoo? What are you thinking? How will you ever find a wife?*

The room was cold, even though the fireplace was going. My father sat next to me on the sofa. Across from us was Mr. Benny, our lawyer.

It had only been three days since my gramps passed away, but Mr. Benny insisted on seeing us. My gramps wasn't even in the ground yet. It took time to plan a funeral with thousands of attendees. Everyone would show up to pay their respects and try to make business deals. Everything was business.

"I know you two are grieving, but we must discuss the will." Mr. Benny opened his briefcase.

"Shouldn't Tristan and Joseph be here?" I asked. Tristan was married to my late sister, and Joseph was their son. Even if my gramps didn't plan on giving Tristan anything, he wouldn't leave his great-grandson out of the will.

"Not for this." Mr. Benny rifled through papers. Sweat poured down his temples. The room was freezing, so the perspiration had to be from his nerves, not the temperature.

"What is this about?" My dad leaned forward to appear more intimidating. "My father isn't even cold yet. The will is not to be read until after the funeral."

"Yes, but this is of importance." He pulled a piece of paper out and adjusted his glasses. He cleared his throat. "My dearest Ethan, seeing you so closed off has always pained me. Losing the only two women in your life has made a serious negative impact on you. I mean, look at all your tattoos."

I chuckled. Only my gramps would find a way to bring up my tattoos, even after he died. He was wrong about losing two women. I lost my sister, but I didn't lose my mother. She left.

"I needed to find a way to unfreeze your heart. Well, at least show you the importance of love. As I am writing this, you are about to turn twenty-eight. It's time." Mr. Benny wiped the sweat from his forehead. "Um. Um. Before I read this part, I want you to know I'm checking the legality of this."

"Read it," I demanded.

"Yes, sir. Ethan, I have changed my will. All of Moore's assets are frozen except enough to pay my funeral and for you and your father to survive for one month."

"What?" my father and I said simultaneously.

"There's more." Mr. Benny quickly continued. "At that time, everything will be donated to various foundations across New Boston unless you, Ethan Moore, are married."

I snatched the paper from his hand. My gramps was sneaky, but this? I had to have heard that wrong.

"I'm gonna need you to explain that." My father raked his hand across his face.

"Ethan has one month to get married, or your family will lose everything." Mr. Benny wiped his forehead again.

"Fuck!" I ground my teeth.

CHAPTER 4

Tristan

THE SUN SHONE IN MY EYES, PREVENTING ME FROM adequately seeing Joseph. He was on his fifth or sixth lap. The swim team at his school noticed he was fast in the water and scooped him up. As long as it didn't distract from his baseball, I didn't mind.

One day, he would be on the New Boston Red Sox. Of course, I still had to bring professional baseball back, but I was working on it. After the economic crash, they canceled all professional sports. Damn shame. Years later and football was back and doing well. Now it was time for my favorite sport to shine.

"Uncle Ethan!" Joseph jumped out of the pool.

I turned to my left, and sure enough, my brother-in-law was right there. Well, ex-in-law. As a widow, I didn't have in-laws anymore. The thought of my wife made my stomach sour. No amount of time would heal that pain.

"Hey buddy, nice swimming." Ethan high-fived Joseph. "Your dad let you take a break from baseball?"

"No, I gotta do both and keep my grades up. It's bogus." Joseph rolled his eyes.

"You want to get into the best schools, right?" I narrowed my eyes at him.

"Yes, Dad, but I'm in second grade, and we are elites. I could buy the school." His kid logic never ceased to amaze me.

"Uh... speaking of being elites. Joey, can you give your dad and me a sec?" Ethan chewed his lip.

Joseph nodded and dived back into the pool.

My servant CeCe must have seen Ethan because she came outside with a tray of whiskey for both of us. When my brother-in-law was around, drinking was a must. Especially after the week he had. Losing his grandfather was rough on him. The funeral was filled with tears and business deals. I still couldn't understand why people thought funerals were a good time to discuss a merger or, worse, a loan. Ethan handled it by getting blackout drunk and puking in his hot tub.

How he was functioning today was beyond me. I hit twenty-eight last month, and a hangover now lasted days. Part of me expected him to turn away the whiskey. Nope, he downed it and asked for more.

"What's up?" I sat down on a nearby lounger. Ethan paced near me, making me nervous. I knew he was upset about his gramps, but this seemed excessive.

"Gramps. I mean, what is he thinking? He can't be serious. Bro, what am I gonna do?" He was talking as if the man was still alive.

I knew the feeling. After I lost my wife, I would still think of her in the present. There were still times I forgot she was gone. I would turn a corner and expect to see her. Shortly after she passed, I even called out, asking if she saw my keys.

"You own a few law firms. You gotta do something." Ethan's voice came out as if he was begging. He never begged.

"Slow down and tell me what the fuck is going on." I looked over to make sure Joseph didn't hear me swear. He was doing his laps while Diego, one of my servants, timed him.

"Sorry, bro." He pulled a piece of paper from his suit jacket and handed it to me.

I scanned the handwritten letter, trying to decipher it quickly. The words Ethan and married stuck out. I stopped and reread the letter. The whole time, Ethan paced and chewed on his lip.

Once I read it for the third time, I placed it on the table. Ethan stared down at me. He raised his eyebrows and pointed at the paper. He was waiting for me to reply.

"Haha, that's gold." I burst out laughing. I tried to contain the laughter, but I couldn't. His gramps told him for years to find a nice girl and stop getting tattoos. In the afterlife, he found a way to get Ethan a wife.

"Dude, stop laughing. This isn't just about me. All the Moore money will be donated." Ethan started counting with his fingers. "My father, me, Joseph, and probably you. We will get nothing."

"Four people. Take away the fact that Joseph and I don't need a dime, and that's two. You guys will be fine. You can stay here." I waved my hand toward the mansion.

Even though Ethan wasn't my brother-in-law anymore, he was family. As funny as I thought his Gramps' clause was, I wouldn't let anything happen to him or his dad, Mitchell. My ex-father-in-law was a good man and did everything for Joseph.

"I don't want a handout. Not to mention all the billions of dollars that would go to New Boston, it would crash the economy again." Ethan's voice quivered at the word billions. I didn't blame him, that was a lot of money.

"Crash the economy? It would help build the country." America had ten countries since the crash. There were fifty states, but now they divided themselves to create their own countries. New Boston was the most prosperous out of all of them. It thrived because the elite put so much money into it.

Billions would help. Economics was always my favorite subject in school. Part of what helped an economy grow was taking care of the bottom class. They thrive, and we thrive.

"Stop with the economics lesson. We donate enough to the Cartright foundation." Ethan grabbed another glass of whiskey from my servant and downed it in one gulp.

The Cartrights started a non-profit to help the homeless. They were building apartments and creating jobs. It was making a population that was ready for baseball. Our country was rebuilding.

"Hello! Help me!" Ethan waved his hand in my face.

"I'll look over everything. Not that it will do any good." I glanced over the paper again.

"What do you mean?" He scrunched up his face as if I had just shit on his foot.

"I mean, if you want your inheritance, you better get married." I leaned back and interlaced my fingers behind my head.

"Fine, I want that pink girl!" He slammed his glass on the table.

"Pink girl? You mean the fighter?"

He nodded.

My stomach sank.

I wasn't jealous or anything. It was just something about Ava that drew me in. I had planned to return to the club, but I had the funeral.

None of that even mattered. Ava would never be with an elite. I could tell by the way she looked at us. She hated us for having everything and her having nothing.

"She's perfect. Hey, we could both marry her. She would fulfill my gramps stupid clause and be a mother figure for Joseph. Don't look at me like that. I'm not talking about replacing Ash. Come on." Ethan was practically begging.

I shook my head. How was I considering his idea? Joseph

did need a mom figure. Not that anyone could replace my wife, Ashley. It would be nice to have a woman around again. I had servants, but I meant someone to really talk to. Discuss life with. Be a friend. Ethan's idea did kind of make sense. If we both married her, we could split the time. I wouldn't have to be a husband to her, I could leave that to Ethan. If we managed to do this, I would have to establish some ground rules with her.

There was one major problem. "Even if I agreed, she would never go for it."

"So, we make her." Ethan grinned.

CHAPTER 5

Ava

THE DOOR FLEW OPEN AS FELIX RUSHED INTO MY apartment. My best friend was more like a brother than a friend. We grew up together on the streets. His tent was right next to ours. He had no family. His parents died when he was little from some terrible accident. He doesn't talk about it.

He was there the night my dad died. I pushed the thought aside. No sorrow. Tears would ruin my mascara, and I just applied it.

I didn't need to look behind Felix to know his girlfriend was there. The ying to his yang, or was he the ying? I wasn't sure. Sandy always wore dark colors, never smiled, barely spoke, and was the kindest person I knew. Since Felix never stopped talking, it was the perfect match.

Plus, it was adorable that they were both short. Dottie measured them once. They were both five-three.

Felix grabbed my arm and pulled me toward the kitchen. I would have protested, but he looked scared. Dottie followed, but Sandy stopped her and pointed to our mother. Whatever they had to say, they didn't want my mom to hear. This was bad. Like no nail polish, runny makeup bad.

"You should sit. Wanna sit?" Felix asked. "Maybe we could go pilfer some makeup for you. Sandy said you could do her nails. As long as you remove the polish right after."

"Slow down. What's going on?" Obviously, I would love to toss some raspberry red polish on her chipped nails. If whatever they had to tell me wasn't that bad, I was totally gonna take advantage of the offer. Who was I kidding? I was taking advantage of the offer, no matter what.

"I'm just gonna do this fast, like a bandaid. Rip it off. Right. That's the best way." Felix rambled. Sandy grabbed his hand to comfort him.

"Spit it out," I demanded.

"Okay. They closed down all the fighting clubs, like all of them. Don't know why. Sandy and I went to Mastro's for my fight, and there was a sign on the door. Closed. So we stopped by Von's, same thing." Felix ran his hand across his face.

Fighting was how we made a living. Once I realized I was good at it, I got Felix into it. I looked down at my outfit: bubblegum shorts and a too-tight pink top. No, I wasn't hoping to see those two elite men again. I just wanted to look my best tonight. Nothing wrong with that. Now it was for nothing.

Closed. Fuck! How could they be closed? How? It could only be for a week. There was no way it would be for longer. How would I get my mom's meds? Or food? Or makeup? I had been planning on one day opening up a little shop. I knew fighting wouldn't last forever, but I never expected this. No, it couldn't last.

"Well, maybe it's for a week." I paced. "It can't be for longer."

"We checked. It's permanent." Felix dropped his head. "There's more."

"More?" What else could there be? "They closed, end of story."

"It's not about the clubs," Felix whispered.

Sandy shuffled through the kitchen drawers and pulled out a nail file. She had been over enough to know I kept a nail file in every room.

She handed it to me and gave me her hand. I quickly began filing her nails. It kept me distracted enough not to cry. I spent hours on my eye makeup. The bruises from last week had faded, but not enough. It took a lot of concealer and glitter to make my face presentable. It absolutely had nothing to do with the man with the tattoos and the one who didn't smile.

Sandy's nails were atrocious. The ones that weren't chewed up were broken and jagged. I filed, waiting for whatever Felix had to say.

"We were on our way over here. We took the long way through the park. I was nervous about telling you about the fights. Figured you would be upset. Sandy said you would handle it well. You always land on your feet." Felix glanced at Sandy, and she nodded.

Ding. Dong.

My stomach tightened. Felix flinched. Sandy looked down.

"I think we were followed," Felix whispered.

I glared at him. "If you know who is at the door, you better say something now."

He opened his mouth and shut it again.

Dottie answered the door. She kept the chain on so it only opened a crack. She took something from whoever was there.

"An envelope? Mail?" my mom asked from her chair. Her body was so frail. She barely ate. Her clothes always hung from her bones. Her eyes sunk into her face. She had a few teeth remaining. What was once a curvy, beautiful woman was now barely a shell of a person.

"I remember when we never had mail. Those were the days." My mom began rocking. "Your father would say..." The tears started flowing. "Your father..." She rocked harder. "Your father..."

Dottie dropped the envelope and ran to our mother. She wrapped her arms around her and squeezed. I grabbed the shot from the counter, we always had one ready to go. As Dottie tried to calm her, I jabbed her in the arm and pushed on the plunger.

We carried her into the bedroom and set her down. She continued to rock and mumble. Dottie waved me off. She would stay with her until the sedative ran its course. Until then, our mother would be in a loop, it happened every time she mentioned our father.

Felix and Sandy waited for me in the kitchen. They saw it happen so many times they didn't even blink. It was more complicated when we lived in a tent. There was nowhere to take her when she had an episode. Felix would come to wrap her in his arms and rock her until she fell asleep.

"Oh, an envelope. I wonder who it's from." Felix picked it up and spent too much time inspecting it.

"Tell me." I raised my brow.

"It's for you." Felix turned it over. "Want me to open it?"

"Not that. When the doorbell rang, you said you thought you were followed." I pointed at him with every word. "Who did you think was gonna be there?"

Felix let out a deep sigh. "Brad."

Mothballs erupted in my stomach. My vision doubled. My heartbeat increased or slowed to a dead stop. I wasn't sure.

"When we were heading over here, we noticed a new tent. It looked familiar. I mean, we see thousands of tents, so it coulda been a coincidence. Then I saw the pi symbol stitched on the back. Always trying to look smart, so we knew it was him." Felix continued to fidget with the envelope.

Three years of my life were wasted on Brad. Brad Busby. I did everything for him. He had a hold on me that I couldn't explain. Everyone said it was love. 'We were so in love.' Gag me.

Brad had everyone fooled that he was a great guy. What no one saw was how he controlled my every move. He picked out my clothes right down to what bra I could wear. He decided everything for me.

He even became my manager so he could control my fights. I was in a silent hell. Then he got a job offer to manage a female fighter in Tentokesee. He left without a word.

Once he was out of my life and the fog cleared, I realized how controlling he was. Without him, I could make my own decisions, like what to eat and how much to spend on pink pucker lipstick.

If he was indeed back, I was in trouble. He would come for me. I knew it. Tears fell from my face. I was screwed.

Sandy took the envelope from Felix and handed it to me. I pushed her hand away. She tapped on the corner of it, then slapped my arm.

Ugh. She was insistent on whatever it was.

My life was crumbling around me, and she was concerned with mail, why? It was silly, actually.

"Um, Ava. Sandy's right. Look at who it's from," Felix squealed.

wiping away the tears, I finally looked at the damn thing. It was powder blue with gold lettering. It looked very official and snazzy.

In the upper right corner, in swirly letters, was The Marriage Auction Association.

Dear Miss Ava Palmer of Kira Heights,

You are invited to the Fifty-fourth annual Marriage Auction. This year will be monumental in many ways. This is the first year we are allowing *Homeless to enter.

To accommodate the influx of expected entrants, we have a new automated system for bidding. No more waiting days to find out if someone purchased you! Lastly, Elites will be able to purchase two total entrants. You could share your spouse with your best friend. How fun!

To enter, please respond with your name, age, height, pronouns, and list of previous sexual partners.

Having children or previous marriages makes you ineligible to enter.

*Homeless must have a residence with a mailing address to be eligible.

The Marriage Auction Association

"Helping populate New Boston one marriage at a time."

Dottie entered the room, and I handed her the letter. None of us spoke while she read it. Maybe she could shed some light on this insane invite.

For years, there had been rumors that the rich and elite had so much money they even bought their wives. Apparently, it wasn't a rumor. They really did. And now I had an invitation.

"Oh, it's okay for you to get sold to a rich or an elite, but I can't take a business card from one?" She flicked her curly brown hair out of her face.

So, she was still mad about Moore Tech. I had tried to talk to her about it, and she refused to listen to me. "That's different. I tried to talk to you about that."

"Yeah, like always, you are the one that gets to make the

bad decisions, while I have to be the cautious one. I know." Dottie rolled her eyes at me.

"Every bad decision I have made has been to protect you and mom." I tried to push away thoughts of the past, they always had a way of sticking around.

"Ava, I'm sorry. I didn't mean." Dottie wrapped her arms around me. "I wasn't talking about that night."

"Um, can you ignore the invite?" Felix asked, trying to bring us back to the present.

I shrugged.

"Of course she can," Dottie snapped. "They can't force you to marry someone."

"Are you sure? It looks like it was sent to every eligible homeless person that was given housing. Maybe this is like a quid pro quo." Felix smiled at Sandy. Even if it was a demand, they were fine. They still lived in a tent. I had offered them to stay here, but they refused.

"Is there more with the invite? Like a pamphlet or something?" Dottie checked the envelope and pulled out two more pieces of paper.

One was more of a small card where I put my stats (age, sex, etc.). The next was a bullet point list.

Marriage Auction Rules and Regulations.
-This is not mandatory.
-You receive twenty percent of your bid. You can choose to give it to your family or place it in your bank account.
-If purchased, your new spouse will take care of you financially.
-If not purchased, better luck next year.
-You have one week from purchase to exchange vows and consummate the marriage.

-Once a week, on the day of your choice, you must have sexual intercourse with your spouse.

-All parties involved in the marriage are under no circumstances to be physically abusive.

-Once purchased, you are to immediately live with your new spouse and start your new life. So cool!

-This is a five-year contract. At which time, all parties may decide to renew or not.

-There will be no penalty for not renewing at the five-year mark. Unless a child has been created during the marriage.

-Early termination will be granted if either party is infertile.

-If purchased, you must abide by all rules of the Marriage Auction. If either party violates the contract, they will be punished up to and including termination.

Sign, date, and send this in with your statistics card.

"Good, it's not mandatory." Felix wiped his forehead.

"It seems safer than fighting. Look, no physical violence." Dottie pointed to the rules.

I looked at Felix. Fighting was out of the question now, anyway. It was odd that the invitation came right after the clubs closed. Or was it a sign to do this? Twenty percent of what I was sold for had the potential to be a lot of money for my family. I only had to deal with the rich person who bought me for five years. I could do that.

"This is another one of these bad decisions you are gonna do, isn't it?" Dottie asked.

"You did just say it's safer than fighting." I turned to Felix. "I need a favor."

"Anything," Sandy replied.

"You two must move in here and care for my mom and Dottie."

"You can't really do this. This is your worst decision so far." Felix crossed his arms.

"It's only five years. I grabbed a pen and signed the rules and regulations. "It can't be that bad."

CHAPTER 6
Ava (Day 1)

SOMETIMES I MADE TERRIBLE DECISIONS. EVEN WHEN I knew it was a stupid idea, I would do it like when I fought Big Booty Judy and when I entered the marriage auction.

As I sat in the back of the room of the auction house, I realized it was my worst idea to date. Honestly, I did it for two reasons. I told my family it was so they would get my cut, but that wasn't the only reason. There was another reason—a big one.

Brad. He would find me and try to control me again. He knew my secret and would use it against me as he had in the past. At least if I were in a marriage, I would be safe for five years.

"Ladies and Gentlemen." A skinny man with a bowtie stepped before the entrants.

Metal chairs were spewed across the room. People sat in groups and chatted. One glance, and you could tell who was rich and who was homeless. Aside from me. One glance at me, and you couldn't tell. I was homeless, yet I wore makeup and clothes like I had money to spare.

"We are pleased to have one hundred and twenty-three

31

entrants. Everyone was given a card with a number on it. Pin it to your shirt. If no one bids on you, take a seat, and we will recall you at the end. Sometimes purchasers don't get their first pick, so they will go with someone else. How exciting!" He clapped his hands together.

A wiry woman raised her hand. She wore ripped jeans and a hoodie so big it stopped at her knees. Clearly homeless. The man with the bowtie pointed at her to speak.

"Can more than one elite purchase us?" She was smiling from ear to ear.

"Oh no. That wouldn't be fair for the elites to share one of you." He shook his head and practically spat at the ground.

I opened my mouth to argue. They could purchase two of us to have orgies with, yet it couldn't work the other way around. Hypocrites.

Five years. I had to keep telling myself *five years.*

"Well, as long as there are no more questions, shall we begin?" He walked over to entrant number one and escorted her out the doors.

Three minutes later, she came back and ran over to a big screen. It wasn't on before, so I hadn't noticed it. The size alone should have stuck out to me, but I was nervous.

On the left side, it said entrant number, bid amount, and purchaser number. On the right of the screen was entrant number two, walking onto the stage. He did a little twirl and blew a kiss to the crowd.

Number one screamed and jumped.

On the left side of the screen, her information showed up.

Entrant Number: 1
Bid Amount: $100,000
Purchaser Number: 54

One after another, men and women were ushered to the stage. The rich went first. My number was ninety-nine, so I had a while to go.

The girl in the oversized hoodie walked onto the stage and danced while taking off her hoodie. She stood in ripped jeans and a bra. The crowd hooted and hollered. An elite would definitely buy her.

Bowtie man grabbed the next entrant, so she was ready when the bra girl returned. My heart sank, I hadn't noticed her before. My observation skills really needed some work.

I should have known she would be here. It didn't matter that she was here. Unless they purchased us together, then I would be stuck with someone who hated me for the next five years. Ugh, I wasn't even sure why she hated me so much.

Big Booty Judy flicked her red hair back and turned to me. She winked, then walked onto the stage.

There were still ten entrants between her and me. This meant she would come back and talk to me or find a way to ruin my day. It was no secret she didn't like me, shit, she didn't like anyone. I just assumed I was at the top of her list for most hated.

I moved chairs and tried to hide behind a pole in the middle of the room. It looked more like it was used to twirl on than structural support. It wasn't much of a hiding place, but it was better than nothing.

Like clockwork, three minutes later, Judy came back and walked right over to the screen. She grunted, and I was almost positive steam flew out of her ears.

I peeked over.

Entrant Number: 89
Bid Amount: 0
Purchaser Number: 0

A smile spread across my lips. I had to suppress it. It must have hurt so badly, even if she did deserve it.

"You!" Judy stormed toward me.

The pole didn't hide me very well. "Me?"

"Yes. Who else has a little sister who can hack the system?

You had her do this because I kicked your ass!" She was shouting so loudly that the entire room fell silent.

"It was a fair fight. I wouldn't do that," I whispered. Having this negative attention made me feel small.

"Ladies," Bowtie's stern voice cut through the shouting. "If you can not behave yourselves, I will ask you to leave. Miss Eighty-nine, I can assure you no one can hack our system."

I slumped into my chair. Judy almost got me kicked out. My family needed this money. Even if I got the same bid as the lowest one, they would be set for a while. Plus, I could try to convince whoever had to marry me to send them money.

Judy pouted and stormed away. Of course, there was always a chance no one would buy me.

Bowtie came over and put his hand out for me to take it. *Fuck.* It was my turn.

The stage had red curtains that were pulled back to reveal the audience. I was an ant being observed under a magnifying glass. I usually loved the attention during a fight. These people were looking for my faults and deciding if I was worthy.

Dottie tried to tell me to smile, wave, and be appealing. All of her coaching faded away as I stared into the spotlights. I did nothing, I just stood there. Bowtie grabbed my hand and escorted me off the stage.

Shit, had it been three minutes already?

Like everyone else that went before me, I went over to the screen. My number popped up, and I gasped. There had to be a mistake.

Entrant Number: 99
Bid Amount: $1,000,000
Purchaser Number: 1

Ahh! Someone bought me for one million dollars. That was the highest bid so far. I hadn't done anything but stand there. Wow, my family would be fine. This was all worth it. I turned to have a seat and waited for my purchaser to collect me.

Some purchasers came right away, others waited until they purchased two people. It didn't matter to me. I would wait all night for my purchaser. It was worth it to know my family had money. *What's five years?*

Bowtie came and yanked me out of my chair. Had I not seen him, I would have crashed into him when he pulled me up. *What the heck?* He pulled me toward the screen and pointed. I knew a million dollars was a lot, but geez.

"Did your sister find a way to hack our system?" He rattled me.

"Huh...no," my voice trembled.

"How?" Judy shouted.

"Ask the purchaser if they bid a million. It's easy to confirm." I blinked away tears.

"Which one?" He shook me again.

I looked at the screen. My entrant number flashed.

Entrant Number: 99

Bid Amount: $1,000,000

Purchaser Number: 72

I blinked, and it flashed again.

Entrant Number: 99

Bid Amount: $1,000,000

Purchaser Number: 63

"Three!" Judy shouted. "How did she get bought by three?"

My head spun. Was it real? The screen flashed between the three purchasers. It had to be a mistake. They couldn't expect me to be shared. Bowtie said that never happened.

"Ladies and Gentlemen, due to this um...this glitch, I need a moment." Bowtie bowed. "I shall return. Ninety-nine stay here."

I didn't move as the screen flickered between the three

bids. My stomach turned. This sucked so much. I would rather give up make-up for five years than be shared.

Judy snickered in the back. "They will discover her sister did this. You all read the rules. They will kill her for this."

Murmurs spread across the room. Some agreed, others said they would ban me. Was Judy right? Would they kill me? Dottie didn't do this. She would never risk getting me in trouble.

This was so bad. Take all my lipsticks and nail polish. I would rather give up the color pink. No, makeup ever again. No wigs. No, nothing. This was the worst decision of my life. They were gonna terminate me for this, and I didn't do anything.

Moments later, Bowtie reentered the room. Two very tall men flanked him. They looked familiar. Crap. It was Mr. No Smiles and Mr. Tattoos. They stood there, arms crossed, looking sexy as hell. The other entrants all whispered and pointed at them. Yea, they were hot.

"Ninety-nine, excuse my earlier outburst." Bowtie bowed. "I have conferred with the board. It seems it was a simple glitch. Since rules are rules, all three men can purchase you. Since it's a glitch, you can walk away. But if you do, you will not receive twenty percent of all three bids."

I choked on my spit—so much money. I tried doing the math in my head. My brain was floating—twenty percent of three million. I couldn't say no.

Mr. No Smiles and Mr. Tattoos tapped their feet. They must have been on the board awaiting my answer. No Smiles, even yawned.

"It's still only five years? All the rules apply?" I asked.

Bowtie looked at the other two men. They nodded. He turned back to me. "Yes."

"Okay. I'll do it." I turned to go back to my chair and wait for my purchasers. At some point, all three of them would come to collect me.

"Ninety-nine, where are you going? Mr. Miller and Mr. Moore have purchased you. They request you leave immediately." Bowtie waved at the two men.

Fuck, I thought they were on the board, not my purchasers. "Hold on, what happened to the third?"

Bowtie handed me an envelope and walked away.

I looked up at two of the men I would be spending the next five years with. I was royally fucked.

"Last time we met, it didn't go so well. I'm Ethan." Mr. Tattoos stuck out his hand.

"I'm Tristan." Mr. No Smiles kept his arms crossed.

This was gonna be a long five years.

CHAPTER 7

Purchaser 63 (Day 1)

I tried to run to her. Heat and smoke were so intense I could barely see her. The flames licked the walls, threatening to get me as well.

She sat in the middle of the room, legs crossed, watching the flames go higher. I tried to call out to her. If she heard me, she didn't move.

The walls caved in, I screamed.

Sweat dripped down my face as I woke. It was always the same nightmare. Well, more like reliving the same night over and over.

Six years ago, a house caught fire. I happened to be walking by and noticed the woman in the window. I couldn't reach her. I didn't even know who she was. Years later and I had a reminder of her etched down to my soul.

"Adam. It's two in the afternoon." My best friend/butler barged into my room.

He was a beast of a man. I was confident he was part giant. His hair was stringy and stuck out all over his head. Some even came out of his ears. Most people were afraid of him. Me? I hired him.

"Do you have a point, Bri?" I got up and stretched my sore muscles.

"The nurse is here for your physical therapy." Brian picked up my dirty clothes and tossed them in a nearby hamper.

"I don't need PT." I flexed my legs, bending at the knees as best as possible. The fire caused permanent damage to my legs. I still walked just fine.

"Your limp is getting worse. How are you ever gonna find a wife?" Brian continued to tidy up my room.

"I don't want a wife. Plus, it's not my limp that would bother a woman. It's this." I pointed to my face.

Bri waved me off as if I hadn't said anything, then turned and left the room.

I sighed and hopped into the shower. Sometimes arguing with Bri wasn't worth it. After I was fully awake, I would call and cancel PT.

When I reemerged, the nurse was sitting in my desk chair. Before I got dressed, I stood there naked. I was so mad at Bri for not dismissing the nurse. I didn't need PT.

"Your limp has gotten worse." Nurse Damar pointed at my leg.

"You're not gonna leave, are you?" I asked.

He shook his head and started pulling equipment from his bag. I sat on the bed, and he began with the massage. After that, it would be stretches and then exercise. He was predictable.

Right after the fire, Bri hired all female nurses in hopes I would fall in love. I sent them all away, refusing to let them see my face. Then he found Nurse Damar. A tiny little man that gave killer massages.

Halfway through, Brian barged into the room, he never knocked. The noise bothered him. He was wheezing and panting, and sweat poured down his forehead.

"Boss, I fucked up." He flapped his hands. He only called me 'boss' when he was distraught.

"Calm down. What did you do? There is nothing we can't fix." I had enough money to buy my way out of anything. It was the only perk of being an elite.

"Not this. Oh, you are gonna kill me." He started pulling at his hair. "Unless they kill you first."

Damar and I grabbed his hands to stop him from ripping out his hair. Tears dripped down his face. He was on the verge of a meltdown. Fuck.

"It's okay. Whatever it is. I would never be mad at you." I pulled his head into my chest.

"I... uh..." Sobs made it impossible to understand. "Auction... didn't think..."

"What could have possibly happened in an hour?" Damar asked. It was a good question. When he had come into the room earlier, he was fine.

"The Marriage Auction," Bri whispered.

My heartbeat raced. Realization hit me harder than my parents used to. 'Unless they kill you first.' Those were his words.

The Marriage Auction Association had rules. Break one, and you paid the penalty, up to and including termination. Which meant they would kill you. I should know. My grandparents founded the damn auction. And yes, they would terminate you. It was their way of making sure no one broke the rules.

"You entered me in the auction? That's five years. Bri, who bought me?" If I knew who it was, maybe I could get out of this.

"No, Boss. I bought someone for you." Brian's words were barely above a pin drop.

That did make more sense. How would he have put me on

display like a farm animal? The whole thing was atrocious. Because of Brian, I was now a part of it.

"You bought me someone?" I released him and stepped back. Anger vibrated through my veins. I wanted to scream and yell at him, but that was a terrible idea. Loud noises bothered Bri.

"I got you a wife." Bri looked at me and smiled. He may have been scared of my reaction, but he was proud of himself.

Damar burst out laughing. Bri flinched. I dug my nails into the palms of my hands.

"Aren't the rules you have one week to consummate the marriage?" Damar asked through fits of laughter.

"Boss should have no problem with that. She is hot." Bri pulled a paper from his pocket and handed it to me.

It was a screenshot from the auction. A woman stood in the middle of the stage. Long brunette hair flowed down her back. She wore a pink outfit and no smile. She actually looked shocked to be up there. And yes, Bri was right, she was hot. A woman like that came along once in a lifetime. Not that I cared, I had no time or want for a woman.

"See hot. And so she doesn't think you are some weird recluse, I gave her a letter from you." Bri wiped away the last of his tears.

"Huh?" I asked.

"The letter you wrote to that woman who died in the fire. It was so beautiful. The woman I bought you, Ava Palmer, is gonna love you." Brian beamed at me. All signs of his near meltdown, gone.

Fuck. I would have to have a meeting with my grandparents and find a way to get out of this.

CHAPTER 8
Ava (Day 1)

I don't know you, but I see you every night. When I close my eyes, you are there— standing among the flames. I try to reach you.

When I was little, I would dream I was floating. The trees would reach for me pulling me down. I could never get out of their grasp. Now instead of trees, it's fire. No matter how hard I try, I can't reach you.

I imagine what you must be like. What type of person are you? Do you have loved ones? I could look you up, but I never will. Some things are too painful. Instead, I'll just imagine you. I know it's silly to imagine a woman I have never met. Yet, I can't help it. You are seared into my soul. Like the flames, you have scorched me.

Adam Gould.

I READ THE LETTER MULTIPLE TIMES ON MY WAY TO my new home. As beautiful as it was, it confused me. He had just purchased me, and yet he acted like he had thought of me for years. Or was it a metaphor? Maybe he hoped for a particular type of woman. Perhaps I was a replacement for someone he loved.

"Is that from the third purchaser?" Mr. Ethan Moore, tattoo guy, held out his hand.

I folded it up and shoved it back into the envelope. "That's none of your business."

"If we have to share you with him or her, it is our business." Mr. Tristan Miller, no smiles snapped.

They had a limo pick us up from the auction. The thing was so long. I had never been in a car, yet alone something like this. Felix would love it. He had a thing for vehicles. Totally fascinated by the whole concept.

"You say that as if I am a piece of property," I snapped back.

"You are ours. Have been since we saw you fight." Ethan clasped his hands together.

I ignored the way my stomach fluttered at his words. His possessiveness gave me a feeling I had never had before: being wanted. It was an odd thing to feel wanted, and I liked it. All the years I wasted on Brad, he never made me feel that way. *Maybe I could last five years.*

"Now give us the letter!" Tristan demanded.

Maybe I wouldn't last.

"Two conditions." I might as well get what I could from them.

They both nodded, waiting for me to continue.

"One, if you know him, I want to know everything."

43

They nodded in unison.

That was easier than I thought it would be. Hopefully, the next would be as well. It was what I really wanted. "Two, I want my family to be at our exchange of vows."

"Done." Ethan reached out with his tattooed hand.

I gave him the letter. Both of the men quickly scanned it. Ethan then folded it up and placed it in his pocket.

"Hey, that's mine," I pouted.

"Come get it." The bastard winked at me.

I debated it. Climbing on him, squirming around while I tried to reach into his pocket. Maybe he would tickle me. Maybe both would join in. I shook my head, trying to dismiss the images.

"So, Adam Gould?" I crossed my arms.

"Don't know much." Ethan shrugged. "He's a recluse. Rumor has it he is deformed, some accident or something."

That would explain the letter. Adam was worried about being seen. Maybe I would write him back, let him know something like that would never bother me. We had a week to consummate the marriage, I would see him at some point.

The limo rolled to a stop in front of a massive mansion. It looked freshly built or at least remodeled. Homeless usually stayed away from this side of town unless they worked there. I never had a reason to come here. Being this close to a pristine structure was breath-taking and scary. To know someone owned all of it and lived there was insane.

"Welcome home, Peach," Ethan whispered in my ear, sending chills down my back.

This wouldn't be so bad. My biggest issue would be missing my family. I was sure I would get to see them throughout the five years, but it was different. I spent every day for the past twenty-five years of my life with them.

A little boy in swim trunks with sopping wet hair ran out of the house. Oh no, I wasn't good with kids. If one of them had kids, I was screwed. The invite said you were ineligible if you had children. Maybe that only applied to entrants.

I climbed out of the limo. Ethan and Tristan were already out, waiting for me.

The little boy kept running. He had to have been going to one of the men. As he got closer, I realized he was looking right at me. I stepped back, the limo pressed into my back.

He jumped on me. His sopping wet hair slapped my face, clearly screwing up my makeup. Little arms wrapped around my neck. The kid wrapped his legs around my waist. What was going on?

"Mommy! Mommy! You guys bought me a mommy! This is so great. We are gonna play all day, and you can cook all my meals." The kid was shouting into my ear.

I froze. This was not what I signed up for. I could barely take care of myself. Cook? Not a chance. My arms stayed by my side. What was I supposed to do?

"Alright. Enough." Tristan peeled the kid off me. "You are gonna scare her."

The kid laughed. So did everyone else. I was shocked, and they thought it was funny.

"You should see your face." The kid pointed at me. "I'm Joseph Miller, that's my dad." he pointed to Tristan. "And that's my uncle." he pointed to Ethan. Then he stuck out his hand.

I shook it. "Sorry. I'm not good with kids or being a mom."

"No worries, I had a mom. She died. I was just messing with you. We have a surprise inside." Joseph put his tiny hand in mine and pulled me toward the mansion.

I followed, ignoring how my heart gave an extra beat for this tiny human. He was yanking me so fast I could barely keep up.

Doing a little jog, we reached the front doors.

"Okay, Ava, close your eyes." He stopped.

"How did you know my name?" I scrunched up my face.

"Uh, you'll see. Now do it," Joseph huffed.

Reluctantly, I closed my eyes. The kid guided me inside. A few times, I almost tripped, and strong hands wrapped around my waist, holding me steady. I didn't know which one of the men it was, and I didn't care. His touch sent tingles through me.

After what felt like forever, but was probably only a few minutes we stopped. The strong hands turned me around to face the way we came. At least, I thought that was the way I was facing. It was a shame I hadn't gotten to see any of what the place looked like. Although the kid was giggling so loudly, it seemed like the surprise was worth it.

"Okay, open!" the kid yelled.

A wall. A giant boring white wall was in front of me. I mean, I didn't want to seem ungrateful. It was just, well, I kinda thought people with money went big with surprises. Like every color of pink polish available. Or a brand-new wig. Nope, I got a wall. Granted, at one point in my life, I would have killed for a wall. So, yeah, I changed my mind. It was a perfect surprise.

The giggling grew louder. It was as if the kid and the two men were giggling. No, wait—a woman's laugh. I continued to stare at the wall. Why? I didn't know.

"Turn around," the kid giggled.

I obeyed. A huge banner that said 'Welcome home, Ava' was in clear view. It had bright pink lettering with glitter, so much glitter. I was so distracted at first, I didn't notice the people holding the sign. No, not people. My People!

Dottie, Felix, and Sandy were holding it. Tears welled in my eyes, I couldn't breathe.

"H...h...," I stammered.

They dropped the banner and engulfed me in a massive

hug. I had seen them this morning, but that felt like saying goodbye. This was, well, it was hello.

"How?" I finally managed to get out.

"Ethan and Tristan. They picked us up. Well, not them, their driver," Dottie squealed.

"You should have seen the car. It was awesome." Felix waved his hands around.

I turned to the two men. They were leaning against the wall, hands in their pockets, grinning at me. I mouthed 'thank you' to them. They both gave me a nod as if this wasn't a big deal.

"Tell her the best part." The kid poked Dottie.

She ruffled his hair. She was so much better with children than me. "We get to stay."

"Stay?" I scrunched up my face.

"Yea, stay. This is Tristan's house. He has given us all rooms. You should see them. They are the size of your apartment. It's so amazing. Sandy and I were gonna petition to stay with your sister and mom to take care of them while you were gone. Now, we don't need to. How cool." Felix bounced on his heels.

"Mom?" I didn't see her. Not that I thought she could handle this much commotion.

"Didn't do so well in the car. She's sedated now," Dottie said.

"So all four of you get to stay?" I asked. I needed all the facts before I got too happy.

They nodded.

I turned and ran at the two men. I jumped on Ethan first. He must not have expected me to do that because he stumbled back into the wall. He quickly righted himself and wrapped one arm around me. I could stay like this forever, but I knew people were watching. I wiggled out of his grasp and gave Tristan a quick hug.

"Thank you," I whispered through tears.

"No problem, Peach," Ethan replied.

"Thank Joseph too. My son couldn't believe you were gonna come live here with us without your family." Tristan pointed at his kid. When he looked at his son, he actually smiled.

I scooped up the kid and hugged him. Ugh, I forgot he was still wet from the pool. No matter, nothing could ruin this. I was with my family, and they had the money. Yeah, I could last five years.

CHAPTER 9

Tristan (Day 1)

I PLUCKED JOSEPH FROM AVA'S ARMS. THE KID WAS still soaked from the pool. Not that he cared.

"Thank you again." Ava grabbed my hand and shook it. Her hands weren't what I expected. They were soft, and her nails were pink. I expected them to be rough from the fighting and her nails to be broken.

I released her hand and shoved my hand back into my pocket. I made this arrangement for Ethan and Joseph, not for myself. There was no way I would be mesmerized by her skin.

Ethan had been so insistent on this, he said Joseph needed a mother figure, and he was right. Joseph was so excited when we told him we were buying Ava. He wanted to know everything about her. He was fascinated with having someone live with us. Joseph loved people, he got that from his mother.

"Now to business. Ava, Ethan, if you two will join me in my office." I ruffled Joseph's hair. "Why don't you show our new house guests around?"

Joseph grabbed Dottie's hand and guided her along with the other two out of the room. I didn't like the idea of Felix being here. When we sent for Dottie and her mother, she

49

insisted Felix and his girlfriend Sandy come along as well. They weren't blood-related, but according to Dottie, that didn't matter. She said if we wanted to make Ava happy, then they came too.

Once we were in my office, I took a seat at my desk. Ethan and Ava sat across from me. It was good to have separation from her. I didn't need her peach-scented skin distracting me.

"I'm just gonna get to the point. We are going to need you to sign this contract." I slid the paper across to her.

"Wow, that's fast. I thought we had a whole week to exchange vows. This is so soo..." Ava inspected her nails as if that would help her think. "Well, not what I expected. What's next, you guys bend me over the desk and take turns consummating the marriage?" Ava clamped her hand over her mouth as if she couldn't believe what she said.

My dick twitched. I pushed aside thoughts of burying my dick inside her tight, wet pussy. *Focus!*

"No. This is something else. The auction has certain rules to follow, or they will kill you. I'm sure you got the rules and regulations." I rifled through my desk for that. Maybe she hadn't been given it.

"Kill?" She grabbed her throat. "Kill? It said nothing about killing."

"It does here." I pointed to the bottom of the page. "Up to and including termination."

"Yeah, termination. Like fired from the marriage auction. Never to enter again." She looked back and forth from Ethan to me. Her face dropped. "Mr. Miller, Mr. Moore, you guys have to do something. What if I mess up? What if the other guy is a recluse and I can't get him to..ya know...consummate?"

"It's Ethan and Tristan, stop with the formal shit," Ethan sighed. He hated being called Mr. Moore, that was his father's name.

"Ava, relax. Nothing is gonna happen to you. This contract is for our safety. It's a non-disclosure. As for the other guy, we will take care of that." I tried to use my calming but stern lawyer voice. It usually worked on my clients.

She just blinked at me as if she didn't understand.

"We bought you for two reasons, to be a wife for Ethan and a mother figure for Joseph. None of which include me. I will provide financially and give you and your family whatever you guys may need. We exchange vows next week, and that's it. Do you understand?" I asked because she just stared at me.

"No, I'm gonna need you to be blunt." She clasped her hands together.

"You and I will not be having sex, ever. This contract states that you will never speak of this to anyone." I handed her a pen.

"You don't want to sleep with me, that's fine. I don't want to sleep with either of you." She snatched the pen and signed without reading it.

I would have to teach her that in the future, she was only to sign something after reading it.

"Peach, I doubt that. You wouldn't have agreed to this. They gave you a chance to walk away." Ethan raked his hand down her arm, leaving a trail of goosebumps I could see across my desk.

My phone beeped.

SECRETARY

You have to get here fast.

Why? Did the deal with Aiden fall apart?

He was selling me land that would one day be Miller Stadium and house the New Boston Red Sox. I couldn't lose out on that deal.

SECRETARY

No, she's here.

Who?

Lisa.

I kindly excused myself and left. Ava still looked confused and almost like she was upset that I wouldn't be having sex with her. She was insanely attractive, and the thought of having her got my dick hard. I wanted her, but this was for the best. Since I lost my wife, I couldn't. It was like I was cheating on her.

Lisa was in my office pacing when I got there. Her hair hadn't been combed in weeks, maybe months. She kept her arms crossed and scratched at her forearms. I didn't think it was possible, but she lost more weight.

I saw pictures of her when she was younger. She was so much more put together. I wouldn't say she was pretty, but she was healthy, happy, and a mother. She was no longer any of those things.

"Sir, I did like you said." My secretary, Lynn, stopped me before I entered my office. "I tried to give her the money. She said she needed to see you. That this was bigger."

"You did just fine. Thank you." I guided her to the side so I could walk past her.

Lisa had been coming around for years, six to be exact. I tried multiple times to set up a deal where I would send her the cash. Since she didn't know where she would be sleeping from day to day, she said no.

Instead, she would come to my office when she needed a fix. We came to an agreement, she would come in the back door and only approach my secretary. Lynn or whoever was working that day would give her the petty cash. If she saw my family, she was to leave immediately. Her standing in my office was never part of the deal.

"Lisa!" I snapped as I slammed the door. "What are you doing here?"

"You thought I wouldn't find out!" she shouted at me. Her body smelled of sour milk and burnt plastic.

"Find out what? Lisa, we have a deal. Are you backing out?" I pointed at her. She knew if she stepped out of line, the money would stop.

"Ha. You owe me so much money. I saw the newspaper. Mr. Moore died. I want my cut." She twirled around as if the money would fall from the sky.

Fire ran through my veins. My vision darkened. She had no right to a dime of that money.

"Lisa, are you kidding? You walked out on them twenty-five years ago!" I knocked a statue off my desk. It shattered on the floor. "Your daughter was one! Your son, three! Mitch had to raise them by himself." I knew the story all too well.

My late wife cried to me many nights over her mother. She could never understand why she had left. It was one of the many things that plagued her. She was terrified she would end up like her mom. In a way, she did. She willingly left our son.

Lisa left Ashley and Ethan at the park. A few people saw her get up and walk away as they were playing in the sandbox.

Terrified that someone coaxed her to do it, Mitchell hired an investigator to find her. He found her in an abandoned building high out of her mind. Mitchell tried to get her to leave with him. He would get her help, stay with her, do anything for her. She refused. Said she wasn't fit to be a mother. She told him the demons in her mind told her to leave.

I had never met her until a few weeks after my wedding.

She showed up here. Our wedding was covered by every news station, so she found out. She begged me not to have children with Ashley. Lisa claimed the same demons that haunted her got ahold of her daughter. I thought she was a crazy drug addict and sent her on her way.

After Ashley's death, she came back to tell me she was right. The papers had called Ashley's death an accident. There was no way she could have known the truth. Yet, she did.

Part of me felt guilty for not listening to her and getting Ashley the help she needed. The other part feared she would come around Joseph. I would never allow her to be a part of his life. So, I started giving her money.

"They were better off without me. My poor Ash." She wiped a fake tear from her face.

That's when I noticed what she had been scratching at. It was a tattoo that looked fairly fresh. Down her arm in black ink was 'Ashleigh.' I grabbed her arm and pulled her to me.

"That better be a different Ashley," I roared.

"Nope. It's my baby. Mitch chose the spelling of her name. I never liked it." She smiled at me. Most of her teeth were missing.

"You show up thinking you have a right to any Moore money, and you have a tattoo of my wife's name spelled wrong." I glared down at her. She didn't flinch. "You have a lot of guts. I'm going to say this once. Leave, stop at my secretary's desk and get your money. That's it. If I see you again, I will cut that tattoo from your arm."

"Always so serious, Tristan." Lisa pulled away from my grasp, turned and walked away.

CHAPTER 10

Ethan (Day 1)

When I was little I was better at getting into fights than making friends. It was easier to punch someone for looking at you than to ask them to share their crayons. Maybe that's why I was so attracted to Ava. She had a great right hook.

As far as Adam Gould was concerned, I would not be sharing my crayons with him. Ava was mine. Even Tristan, who technically owned part of her, didn't mind letting me have all of her.

Damn it, he couldn't have her. I punched the door in front of me. My knuckles split open smearing blood. Good. This wasn't my house. I wanted to burn this whole thing down. Ha, that wasn't a bad idea and it would solve my problem.

The door flew open. A big burly man with crazy hair stood staring at me. I was pretty sure he was part giant. At 6'2", I never felt short. Next to him, I was tiny.

"What do you want?" he roared.

"I'm here to see Adam Gould." I stared him down.

"He doesn't see people." The giant pushed the door.

I slammed into it with my shoulder, preventing him from closing it. Fuck that was gonna bruise.

"Stop it," he whined. "Boss hates people, and I already made him mad."

"If he hates people, why did he buy a wife?" I was trying to distract him, so I could push past him.

"You know about that?" The man stepped back and started shaking his head. "I messed up."

Tears swelled in his eyes. He was shaking so badly I thought he was gonna fall over. Mumblings fell from his lips. The tears turned into a rainfall.

Shit, I had to do something. He was off balance, so I was able to sneak past him. The foyer had very little in the way of furniture. I grabbed a bench that didn't look strong enough to hold the man. *Well, it's this or nothing.*

I set the bench behind him and eased him backward. He wrapped his arms around me and continued to sob. Tears, snot, and drool soaked through my suit jacket. Even his snot was giant-sized.

The man's ass hit the bench and kept going. The legs gave out. He kept his grip on me. We both crashed into the ground.

"Let go of me." My words were muffled into his chest.

He squeezed tighter and rocked. I was like his oversized teddy bear. How did I get myself into this situation?

"Should I even ask?" Laughter came from above us.

I turned my head to see a man standing above me. He had shoulder-length curly blonde hair that hung over parts of his face. His sweatpants and t-shirt clung to his frame as if he purposely bought them a size too small. I had met him once before, time did not do him well.

"Boss, I'm so sorry," the giant sobbed.

"Let the man go," he chuckled.

The giant finally released me. It took a second to get up and regain my balance. Then it took both of us to help the giant up. Once I was up and everything was good, I took off my drenched suit jacket.

"Ethan." Adam stuck out his hand.

"Adam." I shook his hand.

The giant continued to sob. "I'm Brian."

I nodded to him. We were already close enough that a handshake was past us.

Pointing at the broken bench, I said, "Sorry."

"It's only from the twenty-first century." Adam shrugged. "Bri, go take a few minutes. I can deal with this."

Brian mumbled as he walked away. His sobs were still heard down the hall. I wanted to follow him and make sure he was okay. He broke my fall, so I knew he had to be in pain.

"Ethan Moore, what can I help you with?" He tucked his hair behind his ear. That's when I saw it. Burn marks ran down the length of the right side of his face.

"You can help me with a recent purchase of yours." I tried to avoid looking at his scar while looking him in the eyes.

"Sorry, I don't do much business with Moore Tech. I'm into publishing. Tech is destroying books." Adam turned as if to dismiss me. "Even if I did, given our history, I would find somewhere else."

"I'm talking about Ava Palmer," I said.

He slowly looked back. His cheeks reddened. Anger flashed across his face. I blinked, and he had already composed himself.

"Listen, I need you to explain to the board it was a mistake. The glitch in the system had you purchase her with two others." I assumed he would want someone all to himself. It was an easy fix.

"Rules are rules." He waved toward the door. "Now, if you will excuse me."

"Your family owns the auction. Tell them there was a glitch," I growled. No way would he have her.

"Which is why I know the rules and the consequences." He stepped closer to me. "You know why the auction is so successful? The first year a man put himself up for auction. His aunt bought him. He refused to marry her. My grandparents tied him to poles on the auction stage. They invited all the purchasers and entrants. In front of two-thousand people, they cut his balls off and let him bleed out. Termination."

My balls flinched. There was no way I would allow that to happen to me. A quick suicide would be better. I had heard the story. Since then, not a single person had tried to defy the auction.

"So, how do you think this is gonna play out? You get custody of her on the weekends? I know you. It's been years since you left your mansion. How do you plan on fucking her? She is gonna see your face and run." It was a low shot. I didn't care. There had to be a way to get her all to myself. Not to mention if he got involved, the plan with Tristan would be fucked. Tristan would have to perform his duties, so this asshole didn't rat him out to his family.

"My dick works just fine, and it'll be in Ava's pussy. I will be around to collect her. If you stop me, it'll be you bleeding from your nuts." Adam practically foamed at the mouth.

She was mine. I clenched my fist and swung. I made contact with his jaw. My knuckles were already split open, so blood smeared across his face.

Adam grinned at me. His lip split open. Blood poured. I should have kept going, but he didn't hit back. I ground my teeth and left.

There had to be a way to get him out of the marriage. Killing him would be an option if his family didn't own the fucking auction. The backlash would be too severe.

. . .

I had one option. If I had to share her, I would be the best husband she could ever want.

After some recon, I found out some things she liked. I had never tried to romance a girl. None of them stuck around long enough. Well, except Tasha, and she just wanted to fuck.

On my way to Ava's room, I ran into Tristan. He saw me and hurried off his phone.

"Hey bro, everything good?" I asked. He had been acting strange since our meeting with Ava. I wasn't sure if it was her or whatever text he got.

"Business stuff. How'd it go with Adam Gould?" He averted his eyes. Something was going on with him.

"He wouldn't back down, so I hit him." I shrugged.

"Don't worry. It'll work out." He slapped my shoulder and kept walking.

I shook my head and headed to Ava's room.

She laid on her stomach, swinging her legs back and forth. She was heavenly. I wanted to climb on the bed and claim her as my own. Would she allow it? At some point, she would have to let me, but I wanted her to want it. I wanted her to beg me to fuck her.

"Hey." I knocked on her doorframe.

She jumped, spilling nail polish on the sheets.

"Get ready," I demanded.

"For what?" She fumbled with the nail polish. "I'm so sorry about this."

"Leave it. It's a surprise." I waved my hand in a come-on motion.

"I need to know what to wear, and I need to clean this up," she huffed.

"You would look good in a garbage bag. Now leave the mess. CeCe will clean it." I grabbed her hand.

CHAPTER 11

Ava (Day 1)

Salt filled the air. Wind carried the mist off the ocean. A lighthouse shone in the distance, its beacon guiding ships home. Sand squished between my toes.

Ethan hadn't let go of my hand since we left the house. It was as if he was afraid I would float away. I could have told him not to touch me, but I liked the way my hand fit into his.

I pulled his hand closer. The entire top was covered with a skull and snakes. It was what I imagined Medusa's bones would look like. Each snake ran the length of his finger. A vision of him sliding one of those fingers inside me flashed in my mind. I quickly pushed the thought to the side.

"What did you hit?" I asked. All of his knuckles had been recently split open.

"A door." He shrugged. "So why do you wear all pink?"

We walked along the shore, both of us left our shoes by a few chairs. Hopefully, we would be able to find them if it was dark before we got back. The tide was getting closer and closer to our feet.

"It makes my mom smile." I kicked at some sand. "While dumpster diving one day I found a fluffy dull rose colored blanket. I cleaned it and wrapped her in it to keep her warm. It was the first time she smiled since my father died."

"Color in a dark world. I like it." He smiled at me.

"Why did you take me to the beach?" It was such a perfect first date. Could I even call it a date? We were to be married in a week. Was dating a thing?

"To be honest, I talked to your sister. She told me you like walking around the beach." He bent down and picked up a seashell.

"But why take me?" I couldn't help it. He had no reason to be nice to me, let alone romantic.

Brad would have never done something like that. He was only nice when there were witnesses. He always wanted people to know how great he treated me. I bit my lip, there was no reason to think about him.

"You are gonna be my wife. That doesn't just mean I take care of you financially. I will take care of all your needs." He turned to me and tilted my chin up to him.

I had been so enthralled by him I didn't realize we were under a pier. Barnacles crawled up the rotting wood. Seaweed piled up around the poles. It all looked as if no one had been here in years. Maybe they hadn't. I had never been to this beach, so I didn't know if it was popular or not.

Ethan and I could have been the only people here in a long time. At that moment, I would have guessed we were the only people to exist. His blue eyes glowed brighter than the ocean. I fell into them, into him. I didn't know how long we stood there staring at each other. I did know the tide came in. Water covered my feet. It was freezing, yet I couldn't move.

He stayed still. One hand under my chin, the other intertwined with my hand. He licked his lips. Was he going to kiss me? Could he hear my heart beating in my chest?

My stomach turned. There were a million reasons not to kiss him, not to fall for him. He was an elite. No matter how much I tried to ignore that fact, he was. He lived a lavish life. Completely different from my own. I wouldn't let Dottie take his business card, yet here I was, alone with him under a pier staring into his eyes.

Fuck this. How could I hate him without knowing him? He has been nothing but nice to me. Here's to another bad decision.

I grabbed his hair at the nape of his neck and pulled him down to me. Our lips crashed. Sparks flew. The world stopped.

He wrapped his hands around my waist and pulled me closer. I opened my mouth to allow him access. He massaged his tongue with mine.

Warmth pooled between my legs. My body was on fire. I'd never been kissed like that. He kissed me as if I was everything. As if I was his everything.

"Fuck. I want you right now, Peach." Ethan growled against my lips.

"So take me," I moaned. He was the gasoline to my fire. I would burn down the world if it meant he would continue kissing me.

"I want you pure for our wedding night." He pulled away.

"Pure?" I laughed. "I'm twenty-five. If you wanted a virgin, you should have bought someone else, someone younger."

"Who have you been with? How many?" He grabbed my hair and pulled my head back. Anger scorched his eyes.

"Did you even read my stats card?"

"Why would I? I didn't give a damn about your preferences and weight. You are mine!" He emphasized each word.

"Technically, I'm yours, Tristan's, and Adam's." He was starting to piss me off.

He was acting foolish. We barely knew each other. I got the feeling he thought I was some bubbly, happy, innocent girl. I wasn't.

"Tristan won't touch you, and I'm dealing with Adam." He released my hair.

A fish rubbed against my leg. I was so jarred I screamed, "A swimmy!"

Ethan laughed. And laughed. He tried to compose himself several times. He couldn't. His laugh was contagious. I started laughing too. A swimmy? I couldn't think of the name of them.

"You mean a fish?" He continued to laugh.

"I had a slight brain fart," I chuckled.

That's all it took. The tension dissipated. Ethan grabbed my hand and led me back to our shoes. The sun was setting. Had it only been this morning that I was up for auction? It seemed like so long ago.

Ethan walked me all the way to my bedroom door. He didn't bring up the fact that I wasn't a virgin again. Actually, he didn't talk at all. Whatever was on his mind kept him occupied. Maybe it was the kiss. I hadn't stopped thinking about it, so maybe he hadn't either.

"Well, goodnight." I turned to open my door.

He twisted me around and slammed me against the wall. My heart pounded. His hand traced my jawline. His lips grazed mine.

I opened my mouth to kiss him. He moved quickly. Ethan was on my neck kissing, licking, nibbling. I was instantly wet. He kissed a trail down my chest, and I was suddenly glad I had on a low-cut top. He pressed against me. His dick was pushing at my stomach.

I was dizzy. He was so close. I needed him. Needed his touch. Ethan's hand grazed the waistband of my shorts.

"Ethan," I moaned.

"Yes, Peach?" His fingertips played at my stomach.

"Please," I begged. I needed him to touch me.

"Say it." He nipped my neck again.

"Touch me." I was so wet I was afraid I would drip down my shorts.

He cupped my pussy through the outside of my shorts. I ground against his hand. I knew he could feel my dampness through the clothing. I didn't care. I needed to cum.

"Remember, you are mine." He kissed my lips and pulled his hand away. Ethan then turned and walked down the hall.

I tried to call out to him. Anything I wanted to say got caught in my throat. I had already begged him to finger me, what else was there to say?

I looked up and down the hall to ensure no one was around. Once I knew it was clear, I shoved my hand in my underwear. Fuck, I was soaked.

It took no time at all. The orgasm floated through me. It was quick and relieved the throbbing in my clit.

Once the effects of the orgasm left my body, I went into my room. Ethan had me so flustered it hadn't crossed my mind to play with myself in my bed.

I flopped down on the bed and rolled over. I should have changed, but it wasn't like I was gonna fall asleep. Sleep was for people who weren't riddled with nightmares.

A piece of paper was on my pillow. I grabbed it and realized it was a letter.

Ava,

I realize our engagement is unconventional. You must have so many questions. Like why I didn't come to collect you. I wish I could explain. Maybe someday I will.

For now, know that I will hold up my end

of the contract. It appears you already have a place to stay, so I will not interfere. I will make arrangements with Mr. Miller to exchange vows and consummate the marriage. Decide which day of the week you would like to have sexual intercourse, and I will send for you.

If you need anything, my butler Brian, will be more than happy to help you.

I suggest you start birth control, so this contract ends in five years.

Best,
Adam Gould

Uh, what the heck? It was so formal, completely unlike the other letter I received from him. The latest letter was like a robot sent it.

I tossed it aside. That was when I noticed the envelope. Oh, maybe he sent two letters.

I ripped it open, excitement spread across my face. This one had to be better than the other one. Maybe it was a poem of some sort or another metaphor.

My heart dropped.

Red.

Blood.

The page was smeared with blood. Words were scribbled across the page, barely legible.

Your blood will splash the walls.

CHAPTER 12

Ava (Day 1)

I PACED THE ROOM. MY HEART SLAMMED INTO MY chest. I couldn't calm down. He found me. Not only did he find me, but he got into the mansion. When Felix and Sandy told me they saw his tent, I knew it wouldn't be long before he came for me.

I thought I was safe here. One of the reasons I put myself into the auction was because the rich and elite have body-guards. There was security outside the mansion, yet somehow he got past them. Motherfucker was clever.

My hand went to my hip. He was clever and cruel. On my hip were his initials, BB. I tried to leave him once. It was the first time he swung at me. I knew I wasn't one of those battered women, so I told him we were over. He held me down and carved his initials into me. He marked me as his.

I thought when he left, I was free. I would never be free of him. He was back. What would he do to me now? Exactly what the letter said. He would splash the walls with my blood.

Shit. What was I gonna do? Could I run? No, I wouldn't leave my family behind. Should I hunt him down and kill him? It wouldn't be the first time I took a life. The letter was probably a trap. If I hunted him down, I would make it easier for him to get me.

Fuck. I clenched the letter. Tears crept down my face. I dropped to the ground and let it out. He would find me and either kill me or worse, make me stay with him.

The lights in my room were too bright. I crawled over to the bed. Instead of climbing in bed I went under it. They said children were afraid of monsters under the bed. My monsters weren't under the bed, or maybe I was the monster.

The tent was smaller than normal. Everything was black. Dottie was in her sleeping bag. Her snores filled the air.

I clamped my eyes shut. Tonight would be the night. I was ready. The knife was clenched in my fist.

My parents rustled. It was the same thing every night. Tonight would be the last night.

"Please, no," my mother cried.

"You can't tell me no," my father slurred.

The struggle began.

I had to wait until he was occupied, so he didn't hear me. My stomach twisted. My father's breath filled the tent. He was panting. The vodka was so strong it stung my nose.

I slithered out of my sleeping bag.

My father was on my mother. Tears poured down her face. Fresh bruises were already forming around her eye. He had her dress up around her waist.

"Please stop. The girls are in here," my mother begged.

"Keep it up, and they'll be next." he pushed down on her.

I plunged the knife into his back. He screamed. I did it again and again. Life was flowing from his body, but not fast enough.

"Daddy!" my sister cried. She was seven. Too young for this.

"Dottie, close your eyes!" I demanded.

My father turned and grabbed my neck, stealing my life. Air! Air! I couldn't breathe.

Dottie crawled out of the sleeping bag and grabbed the knife. I kicked at my dad. He released my neck only slightly.

Dottie was so close.

The knife was in the air.

"No!" I screamed.

Hands clamped my arms. I fought. Someone was dragging me. I bit down on the hand. Blood. I opened my eyes and looked around.

It was dark. I was still half under the bed. Whoever I bit stopped pulling at me. I was pushed further under the bed. What the heck? They needed to make up their mind. Whoever it was crawled under the bed next to me and remained silent.

We stayed like that for a while. I stared into the darkness. My nightmare was the same every night. Could I call it a nightmare? It was a replay of real events. I killed my father. The only difference was in real life, it didn't end. The vision continued to play. Everything that happened that night played in my head even when I was awake.

Because of my actions, my mother lost touch with reality. We kept her medicated, so she didn't hurt herself. I wasn't sure if she was upset I killed her husband or upset I made her help me bury him. She was too far gone to tell me the actual trigger. No matter what it was, it all led to me.

"Thank you," I whispered into the darkness.

"Joseph always thought the boogie man was under his bed," Tristan replied. "Still does sometimes."

"Maybe I am the boogie man." I wiped a tear away.

"That would explain the bite," he chuckled.

"Sorry about that," I mumbled.

"Don't be. I heard you screaming. When I came in here, I couldn't find you. Your arm flopped from under the bed. Scared the crap outta me. I grabbed at you. Had I realized it was you at first, I would have just got under the bed with you." His fingertips grazed my leg. He pulled back.

"Why?" I didn't mean to flinch at his touch, it was the after-effects of the dream.

"To keep you company. You aren't the only one with nightmares."

"But the whole non-disclosure." I shouldn't have been so bitter about that. It just made me feel unwanted by him.

"That's different. Now come on. You'll sleep better on the bed." He started scooching over.

"No thanks."

"Okay." he came back.

His body was pressed against mine. This time he didn't try to touch me. A small part of me wished he would have. I had never fallen asleep in someone's arms. Brad said cuddling made him sweat.

What was wrong with me? I was next to a super hot guy that was about to be my husband, and I was thinking about Brad. My stomach clenched.

The letter. I had fallen asleep holding it. I felt around for it. Nothing. Tristan snored lightly beside me. Hopefully, he was laying on it, and I could grab it in the morning before he saw it.

I snuggled up next to him. The smell of citrus and bark filled my nostrils. Listening to his breathing, I fell asleep.

CHAPTER 13

Tristan (Day 2)

I sat up. Well, I tried to. My head slammed into a metal bar. What the? Rubbing my head, I realized I was still under the bed with Ava.

Last night I couldn't fall asleep and found myself outside her door. Instead of doing the normal thing and knocking, I stood there.

At first, I thought her grumbles were moaning. There was no way I was going to listen to her please herself. No matter how many times I told myself to leave, I stayed there.

Then the scream came. I barged in and scanned the room. Nothing. Where was she?

A piece of paper was next to the bed and covered in what looked like blood. I picked it up.

Your blood will splash the walls.

Fuck! It had to be Lisa. After our meeting, she must have found out I was getting married. This was her way of getting back at me for not giving her part of the Moore inheritance.

Not that I could have if I wanted to. She didn't realize that. Lisa was too lost in the drugs.

An arm flopped from under the bed. Fuck. Did Ava do something stupid? My heart sank. I grabbed her arm and pulled. She bit me. Phew. She was alive. I crawled under the bed with her.

It was something I learned from my late wife. When battling demons, silent company was sometimes the best.

While she was still sleeping, I crawled out from under the bed. My body ached. I wished she would have slept on the bed. Maybe I wouldn't have woken up like I got trapped inside a coffin.

I crept out of her room. Hopefully, it was still early enough that everyone was still asleep.

Joseph came barreling down the hall. Guess I wasn't that lucky. He had on his swim trunks. That kid would live in the water if I let him.

"Daddy!" He wrapped his arms around me for a quick hug.

"Don't you have school?" I asked.

"Yea. Dottie woke me up early. She said we could do a few laps, and then she would take me to school. Can you believe she never went to school? Ava taught her." Joseph was smiling from ear to ear.

I would have to remember to thank her later. She seemed like a good kid. She would make a good aunt for Joseph.

Joseph was down the hall before I could tell him to have a good day. A second later, Dottie was running past me. She waved and kept going.

The house had never been so lively. I kept a minimal staff and didn't have too much company. It was only the second day, but I enjoyed the noise and the smile on Joseph's face.

Ethan was coming down the hall. I dipped into a nearby room. He knew something was up with me. How could I tell him it was his mother? He hated the woman. Only mentioned her once. His dad kept a picture of her. Ethan used to stare at it, deciphering if he got her eyes or hair. Then one day he thought he saw someone that looked like her, but she was a junky. He never looked at the picture again. I didn't have the heart to tell him it probably was her.

He walked down the hall toward Ava's room. He was probably on his way to see her. The moment he saw her fight, he fell for her. Had the circumstances been different, he could have pushed his feelings for her to the side. Instead, his gramps forced him to marry someone. He chose her. I didn't blame him, she was perfect.

Once Ethan was past me, I snuck out of the room. CeCe and her husband Daryl worked for me. She took care of the house, and he drove me around. I should have driven myself to find Lisa, but I didn't want to leave my car unattended.

I found Daryl in the kitchen with CeCe. He was helping her prepare breakfast.

"Sir, can I help you?" CeCe flipped a pancake. They were Joseph's favorite.

"No, thank you. Daryl, I need you to drive me somewhere." I turned to walk away, then turned back. "Can you grab some of your worst clothes? Like the ones you fix the car in."

He nodded without asking any questions. I trusted him not to say anything to anyone about what we were about to do. Not even his wife. He wouldn't risk getting them both fired.

A few minutes later, we were both in the car heading to Poortown. I changed in the back while Daryl circled around. If anyone really looked at me, they would know I wasn't homeless. Hopefully, this wouldn't take long.

"Sir, where would you like me to go?" Daryl asked.

"Not sure. I'm looking for a woman named Lisa." I peered through the window, hoping she would appear.

"I could get you a different woman if you are just looking for practice." Daryl winked at me.

I scrunched my brow.

"Ya know, since you have to consummate the marriage next week, and it's been a while." He pulled over. A group of hookers lined the street.

"My dick works just fine." I got out of the car and approached them.

Big mistake. They surrounded me. All of them were licking their lips and purring at me.

"You pretending to be homeless, Big boy? I can help you live out your fantasies. Wanna fuck me next to a dumpster?" The hooker grabbed my hand.

I pulled away. "I'm looking for a woman named Lisa. Older. Skinny."

"I can be anyone you want." Another one bit her lip. If she leaned over any further, her chest would fall out.

The only woman not crowding me nodded for me to follow her. I pushed past the others who were still begging me for money and sex.

"Tell me more about this woman." She chewed on a toothpick. She had on jeans and a t-shirt, indicating she either wasn't a hooker or was their pimp.

"Her name is Lisa. She has the shakes. There is a tattoo on her arm. It's Ashley spelled wrong." I ground my teeth. The thought of her tattoo pissed me off.

"Shakes? From drugs?"

I nodded.

"More than likely, she'll be on drug alley. It's five or six blocks up. You'll know when you see it." She held out her hand.

I placed a fifty in her hand.

"Word of advice. Homeless don't smell like they just ran through an orchard." She sniffed the air and walked away.

Daryl parked two blocks away from where I thought drug alley was. I didn't want them to see the car.

The first street the woman said it might be, had a few people mulling around. Nothing that indicated it was the right place.

Before I hit the next street, burnt plastic crawled up my nose. It had to be it. I turned the corner. Definitely the place. Garbage overflowed in the dumpsters. People littered all over. A cloud of smoke hovered above.

I didn't blame any of them. When I lost my wife, I wanted the pain to go away. I went through a lot of bottles of rum. Until one day, I crawled my way out of the sorrow.

I stopped the first person that looked somewhat coherent. "I'm looking for Lisa. Older. Skinny."

"Lisa Addy?" he leaned against the wall.

"Maybe. I'm not sure what last name she goes by these days." I shrugged.

"That's not her last name. It's Addy for addict." The man chuckled, then pointed further down the alley.

Searching for her, I stepped over people. When I got my hands on her, I was going to strangle her. Threatening Ava like that. No wonder Ava slept under her bed.

Lisa was curled up next to a dumpster. Her misspelled tattoo had a rope tied around it. The needle was on the ground. Fuck. I didn't have time for this.

"Lisa. We gotta talk." I untied the rope.

Nothing.

"Lisa!" I shook her.

Nothing.

Fuck.

I scooped her up. She weighed less than my son. As I ran

down the alley, people shouted at me. I couldn't hear what they said, my heart was pounding in my ears.

Daryl must have seen me running. He was out of the car with the back door open.

"NB General!" I shouted as I jumped in the back.

"Sir, you can't." Daryl's words were strained.

"Go," I growled.

Daryl stepped on the gas. He swerved in and out of what little traffic there was. As he sped, I tried to find a pulse. Nothing. Shit. If she died in my arms, I would kill her.

We pulled up to the emergency room entrance. I jumped out with Lisa and ran inside. Everything was silent. The nurses turned and stared at us. Security slowly approached us, hands on their guns.

Dr. Scario, a man I highly respected, walked toward us, hands in the air. "I'm going to have to ask you to leave."

"She's dying. Help her!" I nodded toward Lisa. Why was he doing nothing?

"There is a free clinic a few blocks away. If they aren't too busy, they will help with your kind." Dr. Scario pointed toward the door.

My kind? Oh. The clothes. Lisa's appearance and smell. He thought we were homeless. I went to many charity events with him, and he didn't recognize me.

"This is Lisa Moore of Moore Tech. You're gonna deny an elite?" Most doctors and nurses were rich, which meant we were above them. I tried not to push my status around, but desperate times.

"Oh." Dr. Scario jumped. The atmosphere changed. Everyone started moving. Lisa was taken from me. Security took their hands off their guns. Someone yelled for a crash cart. Within seconds she was being wheeled away.

"Are you her butler?" A nurse with a clipboard came over to me.

"No. I'm Tristan Miller of Miller Law Firm." I stuck out my hand. "I was uh...changing the oil on my car."

"Right." She handed me the clipboard. "You need to fill this out."

Three hours later, Dr. Scario came out to the waiting room. "She's stable and awake if you want to see her."

I stood up and started walking.

"Hold on. We need to discuss something. She had a lot of drugs in her system. We were lucky to get her back." He looked down. There were plenty of the elite and rich on drugs. He acted like this was something new.

"But you did. Nice job Doc." Maybe he wanted praise.

"I had a conversation with her. The Carolinas have a very nice rehab center. High success rate." He shoved his hands in his pockets.

"Good. I'll pay." This could have been the wake-up she needed.

"Great. One problem. She said the only way she will go is if you take her." He handed me a brochure.

Fuck. That asshole. She said that on purpose. She probably figured I would say no. That Bitch.

I pulled out my phone.

ETHAN

> I need you to look out for Joseph for a few days.

Done. What's going on?

> Nothing.

Sure. Don't forget the wedding this weekend.

> How could I?

I clicked on CeCe's name.

CECE

> Pack me a bag for three days. Then come to NB General. You'll take Daryl home. Tell no one.

Yes, Sir. Anything else?

> A few meals would be nice.

Yes, Sir.

CHAPTER 14

Ava (Day 2)

I CRAWLED OUT FROM UNDER THE BED. SLEEPING next to Tristan was the best sleep I had gotten in years. I was able to close my eyes without seeing my father's face.

Tristan was gone. I didn't know what time he left. I was just grateful he willingly slept under a bed for me. My cheeks burned, I could not be falling for him and Ethan. Could I?

Knock. Knock.

I scrambled around, looking for the letters. I didn't want anyone to see either one of them. The one from Adam was still on the bed. The threatening one was on the floor near the bed. Hopefully, Tristan didn't see it. I shoved that and the other one in the nightstand.

Knock. Knock.

"Come in." I hopped on the bed like I had been there the whole time.

Ethan entered, taking up way more space than necessary. He wore jeans and a tight t-shirt. The tattoos on his upper arm were colorful and bright. The largest was an aqua-blue squid that wrapped around his elbow. One day I would map out every one of his tattoos.

"Get ready. I have an exciting day planned." He clapped his hands together.

"Are you gonna tell me to wear a trash bag again?" I rolled my eyes.

"Correction, I said you would look good in a trash bag." He pointed toward the bathroom. "I would suggest a shower but don't wash your hair. Then clothes that come off easily."

"It's hot water day!" I jumped off the bed.

"What?" He scratched his head.

"The day of the week when we get hot water to take showers." I averted my eyes. Did they not have a hot water day?

"We have hot water every day."

"Oh. Cool. Yeah. That makes sense." I shuffled my feet, kicking at the air. Hot water day was such a big deal in the apartment. Dottie and I would give mom a bath, which seemed to relax her. It was always her better days. If they had hot water daily, could she take baths every day? It would help her.

"Anyway, hurry up. We leave soon. If you need any help in there, let me know." He grinned, then left.

It was the best shower of my life. The water was so hot the mirror steamed. I danced around as the water hit every angle of my body. I sang the few songs I knew, not well, but it was fun. He told me not to wash my hair, I did it anyway.

There was no way I would ever leave the bathroom. Whatever Ethan had planned, it couldn't be this amazing. My skin was red and pruney, I didn't care.

When I got tired of standing, and my whole body was washed twice, I laid down. The water caressed my body. My hands traveled down my stomach. I couldn't help myself.

I thought of kissing Ethan. The way my pussy was soaked from his touch. I imagined his hand between my legs. He was the one rubbing my clit.

"Ethan," I moaned.

I rubbed faster. So close.

Then visions of Tristan played in my head. *They were both there. Both teasing me. Both bringing me closer.*

"Tristan, Ethan, let me cum," I moaned. The vibrations came. I orgasmed from my own touch again. I would really have to get one of them to give me an orgasm. Fuck, I wanted them.

"Uh, Peach," Ethan called out.

Shit. I scrambled in the tub. Water sprayed my face. It took a few times to get up.

"Almost ready," I called back. Maybe he didn't hear me.

"It's been an hour. We are gonna be late." His voice was muffled as if he was on the other side of the door. No way he heard me.

I did a quick rinse and hopped out of the shower. Fresh towels were on a rack next to the sink. I grabbed one, wrapped it around myself, and opened the door.

Ethan stared. His eyes dropped to the towel. Would he take me right here? I wanted him too. Shit, I was getting wet again.

"So much for not washing your hair," he chuckled.

"It'll dry quick." I shook my hair.

"The blow dryer is under the sink. That'll be faster." He pointed.

I blinked. No way.

"You had to have heard of a blow dryer. No? Get dressed, and I'll show you." He stepped out of the way.

Yeah, I had heard of them. I read enough to know of what is referred to as modern conveniences. I just never owned one. Even if I could afford it, they took up way too much electricity.

I tossed on hot pink leggings and a white t-shirt. After I did my makeup, I would change my shirt. No need to do it now. Especially since he was gonna let me use a blow dryer.

I went back into the bathroom, and Ethan already had it plugged in, along with a brush in his hand. Surely he didn't plan on doing it.

He pointed to the toilet seat for me to sit. I flicked my hair back, exposing two wet spots on my chest.

His eyes grew wide. "You are not wearing that."

"Yes, I am." I hadn't planned on it, but he would not dictate my wardrobe.

"Then you won't leave this room. I can see your extremely perky nipples." He licked his lips. "Now sit, and you can change after, I like the view."

With a huff and a puff, I slumped onto the toilet seat. I would argue with him after.

Ethan was gentle. He brushed out my hair, starting at the bottom, and working his way up. Any time he came across a knot, he slowly worked at it. Although he said he liked the view, not once did I catch him looking. Instead, he brushed my hair.

Once my hair was detangled, he turned on the blow dryer. I jumped a little. How was I supposed to know it would be louder than a club full of drunks? Ethan chuckled and pointed it at me. Hot, and I mean hot air slammed into my hair. I was afraid my hair would burst into flames. It didn't.

Ethan brushed out my hair again after it was dried. Which only took a few minutes.

"Do you always blow dry your woman's hair?" I knew I sounded jealous, I couldn't help it.

"You're the first. Unless you count my sister, she had episodes. During them I would take care of her." He looked anywhere but at me.

"Where is she now?" I would love to meet the woman who taught him about hair.

"Dead. Now let's go." All signs of emotion gone. "Change your shirt."

I went into the bedroom to change, but not before I got a glimpse of the mirror. Damn. My hair was wavy, thick, and had volume. *Get it, Ava.*

Ethan had me out of the house and in the car a few minutes later. I tried to protest that I had to do my makeup. He didn't care. Wouldn't even let me bring it with me. He could be very bossy at times.

"What's up with the makeup? I would think someone in your position wouldn't waste money on it. How do you even get it?" Ethan was back to his curious self, tossing questions at me.

"So what if I'm homeless? How I choose to make myself happy is my business." I took a deep breath. "Sorry, that came out harsh. I just love it. Goes with my whole persona. I fight and everyone is cheering me on because I'm the fan favorite. I know why that is. It's because I wear tight clothes, put on makeup and do my nails. I love when the crowd goes wild. As for how I get it, that's complicated. I do what I can. Some I make, others I trade for. A few times, fans have gifted me some."

"Fans? Like those men that were watching you?" Ethan sucked his teeth.

"Yea, so?" I shrugged. "Why are you so interested in my makeup?"

We pulled in front of a building and he ran around the car to open the door for me. The building looked brand-new. There was even a man outside washing the windows. Across the top was a big sign that read Weekday Spa.

I practically hopped inside. It was perfect. Every color of nail polish I could imagine lined the walls. Glass cases with more makeup than a girl could dream of spread across the room. Comfy seats were everywhere. I wanted to live here.

A woman in a white outfit sauntered over with a tray of champagne glasses. Another woman came over with grapes, cheese, and crackers. My stomach rumbled. I hadn't realized I had forgotten to eat.

"Mr. Moore, Mrs. Palmer, come with me. You're a little late but no worries. We can still do everything." The woman with the champagne glasses bowed to us.

"Everything? Like what?" My cheeks hurt from smiling so much.

"The full bridal package. Mani, pedi, facial, hair, seaweed wrap, waxing, and a massage. Mr. Moore said you would like everything." She walked us to the back of the building.

"Bridal? Wax?" I didn't know what she thought she was waxing.

"Well, yes. You two are getting married this weekend. No one wants a hairy vagina for that. Guys like it smooth." She turned and winked at me.

"Better for eating," Ethan whispered in my ear.

Instantly wet.

The woman brought us to a locker with a robe and slippers in it. They waited outside while I changed.

The next few hours were magical. Women pampered every inch of my body. I had no idea a place like this existed. Instead of just a makeup store, I wanted this.

Body hair I didn't know I had in places I couldn't reach was removed. My nails were filed and painted. Everything was scrubbed and made to feel new. I was new. It was perfect. Then we got to my hair.

"Oh, Ethan did it." I told the man. I wanted to keep it like this forever.

"I just figured you might want it pink. Like the wig you own." Ethan stood behind me.

He had been by my side the whole time, except when they waxed my private area. I enjoyed his company and the endless amounts of food he had the workers bring. After a few glasses of champagne, I had switched to water. I didn't want to be drunk or even buzzed.

"Really? I can do that? Like fluorescent pink?" My hair was a muddy brown. There was no way dye would stick.

The man nodded and went to work. The whole time he asked me about my life before. He was rich and did hair for fun. Homeless people fascinated him. Especially one with a love of the spa.

I told him the big picture stuff, leaving out all the trauma I dealt with. Then we got to the marriage auction. Apparently he found his husband that way. Some rich CEO that he loves, but was boring in the love making department.

Ethan smirked and winked at me. It was like he was saying I didn't have to worry about that. I couldn't wait to find out.

I was nervous about the wedding night, I didn't have to sleep with Tristan, but I did have to sleep with Ethan and Adam. How would that work? One at a time or both at the same time? I had to admit I was a little turned on by the perspective of both ways.

Ethan looked down at his phone and sighed.

"Everything okay?" I asked as the hairdresser was finishing my hair.

"Yeah, Tristan took off for a few days. Don't worry, he'll be back for the vow exchange." Ethan shoved his phone back into his pocket.

My heart sank. I was kinda hoping he would be around for another sleepover. I slept so easily next to him.

"Do you not like it?" The hairdresser fluffed my hair.

I peered into the mirror. He put different shades of pink in my hair to mimic highlights. It flowed down my shoulders and stopped at my breasts. I moved my head around to see every angle possible. Tears swelled in my eyes. I grabbed the man and pulled him in for a hug.

"Thank you. Thank you." I sobbed.

"No problem. By the way, my name is Jack. If you want, I can do your hair for your wedding." He stepped back. I didn't think he liked being hugged. I made a mental note not to do that again.

Ethan nodded, answering for me. Then he was pulling me toward the back of the building again.

"Are we leaving?" I didn't want to complain, but I never wanted to leave.

"Do you still want the massage?" he asked.

"Yes, please." It was the one thing that hadn't happened yet.

"One condition."

"Anything."

"I give you the massage." Ethan pulled my hand up to his lips. "No one touches your body but me."

I giggled and didn't mention that various people had their hands on me all day. Instead, I nodded as he brought me into a room with a table.

He directed me to remove my robe, lie on the table, and cover myself with a sheet. I directed him to turn around. I grabbed a towel and wrapped it around my waist. If the sheet slipped I didn't want him to see the scar Brad left me.

Ethan turned on a sound machine that mimicked a thunderstorm. Then he flicked a switch and the lights dimmed. The anticipation alone was driving me wild. I laid there watching him, waiting.

Finally, he walked over to me. My stomach fluttered. This was really about to happen.

He grabbed the sheet. "Roll on your stomach. I'll start with your back."

As I rolled, I noticed he didn't look. Totally respectful.

His hands were on my back before I could properly settle myself. I knew he had strong, large hands, but damn. One hand took up half my back.

He immediately went to work. "Peach, why do you have so many scars?"

"I'm a fighter." *And I was in a nasty relationship.*

"You were a fighter. You will never do that again." He put pressure on a particularly painful knot that I had since the night Judy knocked me out.

"Still am. Once they open the Underground back up, I'm gonna sign up for some fights." I pushed up to argue.

His hand pushed me back down. "No. You have all the money you will ever need. Why risk yourself?"

"It's a part of me. It's not just about the money."

"Well, the Underground may remain closed forever." He went back to gliding his hands across my skin. "Now, shush, and let me work my magic."

I fell into a trance. His hands were incredible. At some point, he grabbed an oil that smelled of peaches. The warmth and the way his hands slid was encaptivating.

Every time he finished with an area, he put a heated cloth over it. He massaged my arms, hands, and scalp. I melted under his touch. His hands stopped at the top of my ass. *Don't stop!*

"Can I remove this towel? I won't touch you inappropriately." he asked.

"Yes," I moaned. He could have asked for the world, and I would have handed it to him.

Never had I been so relaxed. Never had I felt so comfortable being so exposed. He had me. Had all of me. It started the moment I walked past him the day of the fight with Big Booty Judy. The fact that such a strong, badass man could be so gentle with me was a miracle. He treated me like an egg he was afraid to drop.

I was worried he would ask me to flip over. As much as I wanted him to massage my front, I didn't want him to see the scar. With the towel gone, the BB would be visible even in the dim light.

He moved onto my feet. At first, it tickled, and I tried hard not to laugh or flinch. He must have noticed because he started rubbing harder. His fingers pushed into my heel. Damn, it felt so good.

Then his hands glided up my calves. My pussy throbbed. I needed his touch. At this point, I was pretty sure the sheet was gone. His hands moved up closer.

A small moan escaped my lips, then another. I spread my legs ever so slightly. Maybe if he saw how wet he was making me, he would touch me. His hand went all the way to my center, stopped, and went back down.

I moaned louder trying to get his attention. My pussy ached from need. Ethan went right past my center and grabbed my ass.

His hands kneaded my ass. He pulled my cheeks apart, exposing my hole then pushed them back together. Ethan was torturing me. He had to see how wet I was. He had to hear my moans. Shit, he had to feel the sexual tension in the air.

I spread my legs further apart. He growled. *Finally, touch my pussy.*

"Peach, you are making it difficult to be professional." He squeezed my ass.

"Then don't," I moaned.

"Say it," he demanded.

"Say what?" I asked shyly.

"Say you want me to touch you. Beg me to make you cum. Demand I lick that tight cunt of yours." He separated my ass cheeks. His fingers were so close to my asshole. Fuck I wanted him to play with it.

"Please, Ethan. Please touch me. Make me yours. Lick this cunt and claim it as yours." I was barely breathing. At the moment, he could have told me to say anything, and I would have. I knew my pussy was dripping all over the table, and I didn't care. I just wanted to cum.

His finger grazed my asshole, making its way down to my pussy. He swirled his finger in my juices and went back to my asshole. With his wet finger he slide the tip into my ass. Fuck, I had never experienced something so wickedly delicious. He slowly fingered my ass, each time going a little deeper.

Without warning, he climbed onto the table with his finger still in my ass. Had I not felt the weight distribution I wouldn't have realized it. His tongue ran down my slit.

"Fuck," I moaned. My body was on fire. I needed him.

"You like that, Good girl?" He continued to finger my asshole.

"Yes, Ethan." I grabbed at the table. I was so close.

He licked my slit. I quivered. Then he dove in. He ate me like he was starving. I was melting into him.

Every part of me called out for him. The vibrations started. He sucked my clit bringing me over the edge. I exploded. My orgasm ran through my entire being. All of me was in that explosion. Then I came back to reality.

He continued.

"I came." Maybe he didn't know.

"And you will cum again." He went back to licking.

I tried to tell him I had never had more than one. He sucked my pussy and fingered my ass. Then with his other hand, he fingered my pussy. There was so much happening.

I loved it. I raised my hips to give him better access. He sucked harder.

Shit. The vibrations again. I. I . I. Wow. I was shaking. I fell apart and was brought back together.

"Ethan, I'm coming!" I shouted.

He rode out my orgasm. Licking me as I came back down to Earth. With the last of the vibrations, he stopped.

I sat up, grabbing at my chest. That was incredible. I tried to tell him and couldn't. Every time I tried to talk, I couldn't.

His eyes grazed down my body. I realized I was naked. Like, no sheet or towel. He was seeing everything. All of me, all the scars. Shit.

He stopped at my hip. "What is that?" His jaw twitched.

"A long story." I grabbed the sheet and wrapped it around myself.

CHAPTER 15
Adam (Day 2)

I TRIED TO RUN TO HER. THE FLAMES LICKED THE walls threatening to get me as well. Heat and smoke so intense I could barely see her.

Walls crumbled. Beams fell. I called out to her. She reached out her hand to me. My fingertips grazed hers. The smoke dissipated. It was the girl from the picture, Ava Palmer. She screamed for me to save her.

Ethan Moore appeared behind her. Had he been there before? Ethan grabbed Ava. She smiled. Was she okay? The flames engulfed them. I turned to leave. The walls caved in.

"Adam, It's two in the afternoon. I dropped off the letter like you said. It was very nice of you. Get up for PT." Bri walked in carrying a tray.

"No physical therapy today." I crawled out of bed. The letter wasn't nice, it was straightforward.

"You need it." Bri placed the tray of food on the desk. Since he bought me a bride, he had been trying to make up for it. Yesterday he made me dinner and went out to buy me wine.

This morning he brought breakfast and mimosas. Yea, he was trying to ensure I wasn't mad at him.

90

"You don't have to keep feeding me." I sat at the desk and dove into the food. It was only waffles and cereal, but I appreciated it.

"My mom said food will make you feel better." Bri smiled. When he wasn't sure how to behave in certain situations, he would ask me or call his mom.

"Yes, if I was sick." I shook my head. "You know what. Your mom is right."

Bri smiled at me. When I first hired him, his mom was worried sick. She stayed with us for a few weeks to ensure he was okay. Finally, I had to let her know it was time. He had to grow up. Be his own man. He still called her daily, and they visited each other once a week. Part of me couldn't wait to find out what she thought of him buying me a person.

"Nurse Damar will be here in one hour." Brian checked his watch. "Well, fifty-seven minutes."

"Cancel. We have other plans." I hadn't planned on bringing Brian with me, but this was his mess.

"Plans? Who is coming here?" he asked.

"No one. We are going somewhere," I replied.

Brian opened his mouth and closed it. He did that three more times. I just grinned at him. It had been six years since I left the house.

I adjusted my mask several times. After the fire, I had it made. It covered the right side of my face, conformed to my face and moved with my movements. It was creepy. You could tell it was fake. It was like one of those AI dolls. I hated it.

I walked into my grandparent's house without knocking. I lived with them periodically over the years. When my parents would decide they didn't want to be bothered with me, they would drop me off.

Their butler Corbin ran over to me. "Master Adam. Oh

my. It's been years." He flung his arms around me. Since he was a little person, it was somewhat awkward.

"Are my grandparents home?" I asked, stepping back.

"Yes. They are entertaining on the patio." Corbin gave a little bow.

"Entertaining? Who?" If it were my parents, I would turn and leave.

"A young lady." Corbin winked at me.

My stomach turned. Could it be Ava Palmer? How would she know to come here? Did they send for her? I told her in the letter I would send for her. She could have thought it was me.

I wasn't ready. Shouldn't, couldn't meet me like this. I had on jeans and a t-shirt. My hair hung in my face. The mask. Fuck. She couldn't see me. Not to mention, what if I didn't like her?

"Could you tell them I need to speak with them? It's imperative. I'll be in the family room waiting." I turned and walked away. Bri followed without a word.

Their family room was unlike any I had ever seen. They took the word literally. Pictures of the Gould family littered the walls. Our family was bigger than most. My grandparents had eight children. Their children had multiple children. I was the only one out of all the cousins that didn't have any kids. I intended to keep it that way.

I tripped over a box of legos. Those things were evil. Some of the great-grandchildren must have been here or still were. I didn't know most of them. When the accident first happened my cousins and siblings wouldn't bring them by. My nephew cried when he saw my face. I stopped letting them in.

"Darling." My grandmother pulled me into her embrace. Her floral perfume tickled my nose.

"Hey, Grandma." I kissed her cheek. I hadn't realized how much I missed her until now.

"Sit, sit." She waved at the sofa. "Do you need food? Corbin! Corbin! Ah, there you are. Please bring some food. Adam and Brian are wasting away."

It was hard to believe this was the same woman who once castrated a man. There were rumors and whispers that she had done worse to many people. It was possible, I guessed, everyone had their dark side.

"Where's Grandpa?" I sat down across from her.

"With our guest. What a lovely woman. Anyway, what do you need?" She pursed her lips.

"How did you know I needed something?" No use beating around the bush.

"You haven't been by in six years. You barely take my calls. Now, what is it?" She lit a cigarette and took a long drag.

"Brian bought me a wife at the marriage auction. I don't want her." I cut my eyes at Bri, please *don't have a meltdown.* Not like he could control that.

"Brian, Margie and Betty are upstairs. Why don't you see if they need any help." Grandma smiled at him. She knew how he got, and he loved my cousins. They always kept him busy.

Corbin scuttled back into the room with a tray of sandwiches. Brian grabbed one and headed upstairs. I waved Corbin away, I had already eaten.

"You know I love you. Adam, you hold a special place in my heart." She flicked her cigarette. "I would do anything for you, but this is out of my hands."

"You and Grandpa own the auction. Fix this," I pleaded.

"Rules are rules," she shrugged.

It was the same saying I had heard my whole life. Break a rule and pay the consequences. Simple as that.

"Change the rules. I can't marry her." I ground my teeth. I couldn't understand why she wouldn't help me. Ethan could have Ava. I only told him I was gonna fuck her to piss him off. Then I wrote her a letter to anger him further.

"As your grandma said, rules are rules. Lucky for you, we may have a solution." My grandpa entered the room.

"Grandpa." I pulled him in for a hug. That's when I noticed the woman behind him. She was a tiny, frail thing. She was barely five feet tall and had her red hair in a tight bun. This wasn't the girl from the picture.

"Adam, I would like you to meet Judith Blackwell. She may be able to fix this." He waved at the tiny girl.

"Pleasure." I shook her hand. For someone so fragile looking, she had a mean grip.

"So you're one of the schmucks that bought Ava." She rolled her eyes at me.

"Not intentionally." I released her hand. "How can you help?"

"Ava's little sister is a tech genius. She rigged it so three people would buy her, and no one would buy me. Jealous Bitch." Judith foamed at the mouth.

I stared at my grandparents. I wasn't sure how that would help me.

"We have been looking into it since the glitch. So far, all we know is the system was set to allow all one million dollar bets on Ava Palmer." Grandpa sat and pulled out a cigar.

"So if you have proof, why can't you cancel the contract?" It didn't make sense to me.

"The board ruled in favor of Ava and two of her purchasers. We have to treat it lightly if we are to pull the contract." Grandpa lit his cigar.

"Plus, there is nothing linking Ava and her sister to the glitch." My grandma lit another cigarette.

"I'm telling you it was them," Judith whined. "I'm a witness. They did this to me."

I didn't like her. Maybe it was the way she complained or that her nose was too pointy. Maybe it was the way she was snitching. It didn't help that she kept staring at me.

"Child, we can not hang two people based on your accusation." My grandma blew smoke in her direction.

"Hang?" I grabbed my throat. I didn't want someone to be killed. I just didn't want to marry her.

"Yes. Rules are rules. Break them and pay the consequences. If she is killed, the contract is pulled." My grandpa smiled. That was the side of my grandparents they usually kept hidden. The sadistic side that enjoyed torturing people.

"Then you will be free to marry someone else. You should have children by now," my grandma said matter-of-factly.

Judith winked at me.

"What's your problem with her?" I asked Judith. "You would willingly have her killed then marry her leftovers?"

"It's personal. She went after me first. You don't know what kind of person she is." Judith huffed.

"So basically, I marry her, or she dies?" I asked my grandparents. Judith wasn't worth any further conversation.

"Not exactly. We are still investigating. If she is found guilty, she will hang whether or not you marry her. If the investigation takes longer than five days, you will marry her this weekend. Rules are rules, and we don't want you to suffer." My grandma snuffed out her cigarette.

"Even if it means you have to marry a homeless. Still can't believe Brian bought you one of them." My grandpa rolled his eyes.

"Why did you guys allow the homeless to enter?" They had always despised the lower class.

"That's not your concern." My grandma stood. "Now, if you'll excuse me. Judith, Corbin will walk you out. Try not to steal anything."

Fuck. I should have never come here. Now, not only did I have to marry Ava, I have to make sure my grandparents didn't kill her.

CHAPTER 16

Ethan (Day 2)

SCARS LINED HER SKIN. THAT WAS ENOUGH TO anger me. Then I saw the BB. It was intentional. Either she carved someone's initials into her, or someone else did.

She wrapped the sheet tighter around her body. I wanted to rip it from her. She should never hide herself from me. Was she scared of me?

"I got time." I crossed my arms.

"Huh?" She blinked.

"You said the letters on your hip were a long story. I'm listening." I ground my teeth. No matter the story, I wanted to hurt someone. It was bad enough that she wasn't a virgin, now this.

"Another time. I would much rather return the favor of what you did for me." Her voice was sultry and seductive. Her eyes went to my belt. My dick twitched.

"Tell me, or I will hunt down every person you have ever met and carve my name into them." I stepped closer. Her scent wafted toward me, I wanted to take her right there.

"Geez. So serious. Fine, my ex did it." her voice caught in her throat.

Anger flooded through me. "Why?"

She mumbled.

"Speak up, Peach." I grabbed her arm.

"I tried to leave. He wanted me to have a constant reminder." Tears swelled in her eyes.

I grabbed her and pulled her into me. She clung to me. Whatever strength she had been hanging onto was gone. Ava cried.

He would pay. I would cut his hands off and serve them to her. He mutilated her for his own enjoyment. I would mutilate him for her enjoyment.

"What's his name?" I pulled her tighter into me. She needed to know nothing would ever happen to her again. I would protect her with my life. She was mine.

"No. I don't want you going after him." She pulled back.

"You still love him?" Jealousy stung. It was a new emotion, and I didn't like it.

"No. It's not that. I don't want anything to happen to you." She used the sheet to wipe her tears.

I laughed. She couldn't possibly think this asshole could touch. Men like him were weak. They prayed on women because they thought them weaker, they weren't.

It actually surprised me that someone like her allowed an asshole like that to carve into her. She was a strong independent woman. I shook my head, maybe that's what made her that way.

If he did that to her, there had to be more. I wanted to know it all. He would pay for every single thing he did to her.

"Really, it doesn't matter. Can we move past this?" She gave me pleading eyes. Her beautiful brown eyes pulled me in. I would give her whatever she wanted.

"You really want to move past it?" I asked. I had an idea to help her move on.

She nodded.

I scooped her up and left the room. When I unlocked the door, she gave me a knowing look. Yeah, I locked it in case she let me touch her. She had. Fuck, she tasted so sweet. I wanted more.

We left the spa quickly. I barely gave her a chance to get dressed. She was gonna love my idea. Hopefully, if not, she could always say no.

Multiple times on the way, she asked where we were going. The way her face lit up melted me. She was so excited and giddy. I really hoped this wasn't a letdown.

She tried to hop out of the car as soon as we stopped.

"I will open the door. Don't move," I demanded.

I ran around the car and made her cover her eyes before helping her out of the car. She made some remarks about being just like my nephew.

So to be different, I picked her up. She was light and easily fit in my arms. It's where she belonged.

Once inside, I set her down in a chair. The familiar buzz filled the room. She wouldn't be the only one in the chair today.

"Open," I said.

Ava did as she was told and looked around. She scrunched up her face. Instead of happiness, she looked confused.

"You don't like it?" I asked. Shit, I thought this was a good surprise.

"It's not that. It's... well, why are we in a tattoo shop?" She kept staring at the artwork on the wall.

"You said you wanted to move on. Ice here is the best. He can cover that scar with any tattoo you like." I pointed to my tattoo artist. He was a little strange with his bright blue mohawk, but he was the best.

"Anything? Like two pink fists?" She smiled. That was the look I had been hoping for.

"Yes, and I'll even get a matching one." What's one more tattoo?

"Really? Why?" Her face dropped. "What happens when the marriage contract is up?"

"What do you mean?" I couldn't make the connection.

"If we have matching tattoos. I mean, can I still leave when the marriage is up?" She looked anywhere but at me.

"Of course, I would never make you stay with me." Anger coursed through my veins. I would make sure she never wanted to leave me.

Once she was satisfied there were no strings attached, she got ready for her ink.Ice did a quick freehand to make sure it was what she wanted. She squealed. "Here's to another bad decision."

I assumed I was her other bad decision. She would realize how wrong she was about that. I was the best thing that ever happened to her, well I would make sure I was.

Ice instructed her to lower her pants. I moved my chair to make sure he didn't get handsy and no one else got a glimpse. He shook his head but didn't remark. On the way over, I texted him to explain and to make sure he was free. He said for me, he was always free.

The buzz of the gun filled the air. Ava squeezed her eyes shut. Then the gun hit her skin. She relaxed her eyes. Her mouth parted. At first, it looked like shock. No, I was wrong. It was ecstasy.

The pain turned her on. A moan escaped her lips. Ice turned to me and grinned. I knew what he was thinking, it was the same thing I had been thinking about since I saw her. Oddly enough, I wasn't jealous. Having him turn her on got me hard. What did that say about me?

He continued to work on her as she gripped the arms of the chair. Each time he would hit a new spot, she would moan.

I could barely take it. She had to be soaked. I wanted to taste her again. I couldn't wait to have her. Fuck, my dick pressed against my jeans.

After he was done with her, I got in the chair. I had to think of anything but her so my dick would go down. Ava watched me the whole time. She kept licking her lips and staring at my dick. I should have let her return the favor when she offered.

"Tattooing you was a pleasure." Ice turned to Ava when he was done with me.

"I love it." Ava smiled at him.

"Time to go." I grabbed her hand and pulled her out of the shop.

I wanted to take her in my car. Patience was never my strong suit. Why would I need patience when I always got what I wanted? *With her, I have to take my time.*

My phone buzzed.

DAD

We need to talk.

I clicked the phone off and took Ava home. He was the last person I wanted to deal with. He was probably making sure I was getting married, so our inheritance didn't get fucked with. He always viewed me as a screwup.

"Thank you," Ava whispered.

"Anytime, Peach. Now tell me his name." I grabbed her hand and brought it to my lips.

"Brad Busby." She averted her eyes. There was something she wasn't telling me.

"Where is he now?" There had to be a reason she still seemed scared. Maybe he was still around. Lurking in the shadows. I would kill him.

"Not sure." Her eyes never met mine.

"Peach!" I tucked her pink hair behind her ear. "You're safe."

"Two years ago, he left for Tentokesee. Felix and Sandy think they might have seen his tent recently. I doubt it." She continued not to look at me.

I wanted to rattle her. She was safe with me. How did she not understand that? I would serve this Brad to her on a platter.

"Okay, now tell me how you were going to return the favor." I pulled her in for a kiss. From the corner of my eyes I saw my father walk into Tristan's house. Fuck.

"Ya know. Do what you did for me." Ava ran her tongue across my bottom lip.

"No, I don't know." My lips grazed hers.

"Like the same but for you." Her cheeks reddened.

"Say it, Peach. What were you gonna do for me?" I loved how nervous she got with dirty talk.

"I planned on sucking your cock." She giggled and hopped out of the car.

"Peach, you are gonna get it!" I called out to her.

She turned and stuck out her tongue. Then she ran into the house.

I chased after her. Inside she stood frozen. I almost ran her over. Then I saw what stopped her. My father was standing there, glaring at her.

"Ava, if you will excuse us." I kissed the top of her head.

She nodded and walked away. Damn, she had a killer strut.

"Get rid of her." My father jerked his head back toward where Ava was walking.

"She just walked away. What did you need?" I didn't have time for this.

"Not what I meant, son. I will not have a Moore marry

some homeless person. Get rid of her and find someone else."
My father tried to stare me down.

"No." I pushed past him and went to shower. Ava had me
so worked up I needed to cum.

CHAPTER 17

Ava (Day 2)

Ava,

I owe you an apology. My last letter may have been interpreted as cruel and cold. I assure you that is not me. Since we are to be wed and there is no way to get out of it, I checked, we should get to know each other.

I am not sure what type of timeline you have with your other suitors, and I don't care. There will be a car to get you tomorrow at six p.m. If there is a conflict, make other arrangements for said conflict.

Best,
Adam Gould

Grr. I tossed the letter. That was an apology letter? It was worse than the first. Demanding I make other arrangements! Who did he think he was? Mr. Gould had no right to just send for me when he pleased. I didn't know him, and already I didn't like him.

I opened the drawer in the nightstand and grabbed the paper and a pen. He wasn't the only one who could send letters. I would let him know where he could shove his demands.

My heart sank. I froze. In the nightstand next to the previous death threat was a brand new one. Blood was spread along this one as well. Three words were scribbled on it.

Leave or Die.

He snuck in again. Brad had managed to get in and out of the mansion twice undetected. Ethan said I was safe. I would never be safe from Brad. If he could easily get in my room, he could kill me in my sleep.

What was I gonna do? There had to be some type of security system, like a deadbolt or six armed men outside my door. Like it or not, I was going to have to tell Ethan. There had to be something he could do.

Leaving the letter in the drawer, no way was I getting blood on my hands, I went in search of Ethan. I slammed right into someone. Ouch.

"Ava! I'm so sorry. Are you okay?" Dottie wrapped her arms around me.

"Dottie, hi. I'm fine." I squeezed her back. Things had been so crazy the past two days I hadn't even spent any time with her.

"I just wanted to check on you. See how you are adjusting to this." Dottie was always the mother.

"Shouldn't I be checking on you? I dragged you into this." Fuck. I was a terrible sister for not checking on her.

"Yeah, dragged us all to this mansion. It's terrible. Ha. Joseph is just the sweetest boy. They have cooks and fresh sheets for the bed. I never slept so well." She waved away the thoughts. "This isn't about me. You are the one that agreed to marry three men. How are they?"

Something changed in Dottie. She had a happiness about her I had never seen before. It was like someone took her worry from her. "How's mom?" She had to be better, or Dottie would still be anxiously by her side.

"Amazing. Tristan provided around-the-clock nurses for her. She will be properly medicated and taken care of." Dottie linked her arm in mine and started walking.

"Oh, I can't see her now. Um... I have somewhere to be." As much as I wanted to see her, I had to deal with Brad and his letters.

"That's okay. She will be ready when you are." It's like she knew part of me was nervous about seeing her, afraid the move was too much for her to handle.

"Before you rush off, tell me about these boys. Give me something." Dottie pulled on my arm.

"The quick notes. Tristan is very nice and stand-off-ish. Adam sends me letters. I haven't actually met him yet, not that I want to." I sighed. "Then there's Ethan. He is wonderful, but I can't tell if it's an act. Like, why is someone like him into someone like me."

"Not everyone is Brad." She pulled me in for a hug. "Oh, and I love the new wig."

"It's not a wig. Ethan took me to get it done. Do you like it?" I twirled a little.

"It's very you. I love it." She fluffed my hair.

I gave her a hug and turned to leave. Two steps down the hall, and I turned back to her. "How's Felix and Sandy adjusting?"

"They have four walls and a bed for the first time ever. It'll be a while before they come out. Just don't walk by their door. It's the most I've ever heard Sandy talk. All dirty, dirty things." Dottie shook her head and smiled.

"Good for them. I'll be by tomorrow to see mom." I turned and left.

I wanted to warn her to keep an eye out for Brad. He was getting in and out somehow. The chances of him hurting Dottie or anyone else were pretty slim. It was me he wanted. If the letters persisted, I would tell her.

Hopefully, Ethan could do something about it. Yeah, I should fight my own battles, and in normal circumstances, I would. I couldn't win when it came to Brad. He was stronger, smarter, and more cunning than me. He had a cruel, evil streak about him.

Shit, I couldn't drag Ethan into this. I got myself into this situation. As much as I wanted to pass my problems off, I couldn't. There had to be a way to deal with Brad. I needed a plan.

Steps before I got to Ethan's bedroom, I stopped. This was my battle. I had to keep telling myself that so I didn't run to Ethan. Maybe this was another bad decision, or maybe telling him was. Either way, I was sure I would make the wrong choice.

"Peach?" Ethan asked from behind me.

I jumped.

"You okay?" He turned me to face him.

No, my ex is sending me threatening letters, and I'm afraid he is gonna find me and kill me. "Yeah, just hungry." I shrugged.

"Let's go out to eat." He pulled me into him and wrapped his arms around me.

Tell him. Tell him. "Like a restaurant?" I tried to smile.

"Oh, yes. Exactly like that." He kissed my forehead. "You sure you're okay?"

No, I'm not. "Yeah, I just don't own anything fancy enough to wear."

"You do in your closet." He winked.

I scrunched up my face.

"Haven't you looked in there?" he asked.

"No." Since the second I got here, I had been too busy to really even check out my room.

"Go look." He turned me around and slapped my ass. "Be ready in thirty minutes. It's getting late."

I ran to my room. The closet had everything. Shoes, dresses, tops, handbags, I mean everything. I walked, yes walked, into the closet. There was an array of colors, but pink dominated. I died. There was no other explanation. This couldn't be real.

Not only was there every article imaginable, but it was also organized. Shoes and handbags were at the back. Dresses and skirts to the right. Tops, pants, and jackets to the left. I started shifting through them. Thirty minutes was not enough time.

If something were too big or small, I would have to take it to Dottie for alterations. She was a wiz with a computer and a needle. She tried teaching me how to sew once. I just kept stabbing myself. It wasn't fun.

A bright pink dress caught my eye. The light hit the dress, and it shimmered. I pulled it off the rack and held it up to me. It was low cut with a slit up the side. *Please fit.*

Oh, it fit. It was perfect. The dress hugged my curves and accentuated my breasts. I went to the mirror in the bathroom to check it out. My hair blended right into the dress. Other than that, I loved it.

I went through my bags and found some bobby pins. Once my hair was up and in a twisty style, I started on my makeup. I kept looking at myself in the mirror, something was off. Panty lines. The dress was so tight it showed my underwear. I slid them off. Since the tattoo had plastic over it, I wasn't worried about it rubbing.

Ethan came into the room as I was slipping on my heels. Damn, they accentuated the dress. I turned around, and my mouth dropped. He was in a full tux. He spiked up his hair slightly, it looked perfectly messy. He was so sexy I wanted to straddle him.

"Wow." He pulled me into him and kissed me.

After a dizzying, amazing kiss, he led me outside. The last thing I expected to see was a bike. Not just a bike, a beautiful, sleek black motorcycle. I looked around for the car. He couldn't expect me to ride on that.

Ethan got on and tapped the space in front of him. Nope, not happening. He revved the engine. No. He had to be kidding.

"Just slide on here." He patted the space in front of him.

"No. My dress will ride up." I crossed my arms.

He winked at me. "I know."

"It's dangerous." It was a bad idea to get on.

"It is, but I have a helmet." He grabbed a helmet from behind him and handed it to me.

Ugh. Great, I did my hair for nothing. I put the helmet on and clasped it under my chin. I really shouldn't have gotten on the bike. Did I listen to myself? Nope. I hiked up my dress while trying to keep my pussy covered. Of course, I had to take off my underwear.

As soon as I was straddling the bike, Ethan wrapped his arms around me. He kissed my neck as his hands traveled down my body. He pulled my dress up further, exposing my pussy.

With one hand, he rubbed my clit, with the other, he revved the engine. Fuck. I was soaked. My pussy was throbbing. I was getting the seat wet. He revved the engine again.

"You gonna cum on my motorcycle?" Ethan nibbled my neck.

"If you don't stop, I'm gonna," I panted.

"I don't plan on stopping. Do you want me to stop?" He pulled his hand away.

"No, please," I begged.

Ethan grabbed my hip and shifted me forward, so my pussy was directly against the leather seat. He moved my hips, so I was grinding the seat. My juices made me glide back and forth. He revved the engine. The vibrations slammed into me.

"Fuck, I'm gonna cum," I moaned, grinding harder against the seat.

"Peach, cum all over my seat." He revved the engine one last time.

I exploded. My body was on fire. He continued to grind me against the seat until the last of my orgasm faded.

"Good girl, let's get something to eat." He hit the gas, and we sped off into the night.

CHAPTER 18

Ava (Day 2 into 3)

Even under my bed with all the lights on, I couldn't sleep. Every time I closed my eyes, I saw Brad. After a few hours I crawled out from under the bed.

Dottie's room was only a few doors down. We shared a room up until two days ago. She was used to my nightmares. No matter how often I thrashed or screamed, she slept through it.

I knocked softly on her door. Nothing. I tried again. Nothing. After a few more times, I gave up and turned the knob. It was unlocked. Phew.

All the lights were on. Dottie was curled up in a ball on her bed. Soft snores filled the room. I tiptoed in and crawled into bed with her. She rolled over, put her arm around me, and pulled me into her.

I slept. Not well and not for long, but I slept. Dottie got out of bed early. Like the sun hadn't come up early.

"Why are you up so early?" I mumbled, pulling the covers over my head.

"Joseph wants to swim before school. He is really good." I didn't need to see her to know she was smiling.

"You really like him, don't you?" I pulled the blanket down, might as well get up.

"I do. He calls me Aunt Dottie."

"That's awesome." I got up and headed to the door before she asked me to join her.

"Give the kid a chance. Like it or not, you are gonna be his step-mom, and I will not let you be one of those evil ones." She gave me the stern mom look.

"I'm not good with kids. What if I lose him? Or forget to feed him?" I backed up, getting closer to the door and further away from the conversation.

"That's not gonna happen," she sighed. "Well, not again."

"I gotta run. Love you." I turned and left.

Had I known I was gonna be a step-mom, I probably wouldn't have entered the auction. Kids scared me. Thankfully I didn't know. Putting myself up for sale was the best, bad decision I had ever made.

Last night Ethan said he had some meetings with his dad all morning. I would have to find a way to entertain myself for the day. I had no problem with that. I planned on taking a long hot shower and then figure out the blow dryer. Maybe after that I would mix some powders and make a new blush. There were also all the clothes to try on. Yeah, I could definitely entertain myself.

I opened my bedroom door and screamed. Blood, so much blood.

People ran. My head spun. I couldn't hear. Someone shook me. I stared at the blood. I was being pulled away. I needed to see.

Whoever was trying to move me stopped. I stepped forward. A ringing sounded in my ear, or was it someone yelling at me? I didn't know,

Someone shook me again. I flinched. They stopped.

I entered my room. Blood squished between my toes.

Blood dripped from the walls. Blood covered every piece of furniture.

There was one spot on the wall that wasn't drenched in blood. In thick black letters was printed.

Leave. You don't belong here, Murderer!

My heart pounded in my ears. I looked around. Felix, Sandy, and Dottie were on the other side of the door. They stood staring. Felix was saying something, but I couldn't hear him.

Ethan appeared behind them. He pushed them out of the way, and scooped me into his arms. We were walking away. Ethan was shouting orders. I couldn't understand what he was saying. Blood dripped from my feet.

I looked behind us. Joseph was running toward Dottie. *No! He couldn't see that.* She saw him and ran to him. She grabbed him before he reached my room. Felix slammed my door shut.

Ethan carried me away.

Water splashed my face. I didn't move. Ethan climbed into the shower with me. When did he get naked? The water turned crimson.

How much blood had gotten on me? I looked down at my hands, they were red. Had I touched the wall? Maybe.

Soap slid over my body. Ethan washed me. The water was warm, but my body was numb.

So much blood.

The words.

Brad.

He was coming for me.

My time was up.

A towel wrapped around me. Ethan carried me to a bed,

probably his. He joined me on the bed and pulled me onto his lap.

"It's okay. I will find who did this. They will pay." He rocked me.

It was time to tell him.

"I know who did it," I whispered. My voice cracked with each word.

"Who? How?" He pulled back to look at me.

"Brad, he has been leaving me death threats. They are in my nightstand." I took a deep breath. I would not cry.

He chuckled. "Your ex?"

"Yes. Why are you laughing?" Maybe telling him was a bad idea.

"He can't get in here. It had to be one of the staff." His jaw twitched. "Or Felix. Maybe he is jealous."

"Felix is like a brother. Besides, he has been enjoying his new bed with Sandy. It couldn't be the staff. Few people know I'm a murderer." Tears spilled. I tried to keep them in. I couldn't.

"Peach, there is no way you are a murderer. What did you do? Step on a bug?" He wiped my tears away.

"I am. I wish I wasn't, but I am," I sobbed. "I killed my father."

"Peach, I don't believe that for a second." He kissed my forehead.

"He would hurt my mom. One day I had enough." I closed my eyes, trying not to relive that moment.

"That's protecting your mom. Not murder. Just like I'm going to protect you."

Knock. Knock.

"Come in," Ethan called out as he pulled the sheet over me.

One of Tristan's servants stepped in. I had seen him around the mansion but didn't know his name.

"Sir, we checked the cameras. No one has been in or out. We are still checking, but right now, we have no information." The man looked anywhere but at Ethan.

"It was Brad." I sat up. The sheet dropped.

Ethan growled and pulled the sheet back up. The man turned around. Damn it, I didn't mean to flash him.

"Thank you, Daryl," Ethan replied.

"You're welcome, sir. Should we find this Brad person?" Daryl asked, still not looking.

"No, that won't be necessary," Ethan said.

"It's him," I snapped.

Ethan tucked my hair behind my ear. "Okay, Daryl, look for a Brad Busby and bring him in."

"Yes, sir. Shall I inform Mr. Miller?" Daryl asked.

"Yes, and let him know everything is under control and Joseph is safe. Also, please tell my father our meeting will have to wait until tomorrow." Ethan dismissed Daryl.

"Go have your meeting. I'll be fine." I tried to pull out of his grasp.

"I'm not letting you out of my sight until the culprit is caught." Ethan pulled me tighter.

"Then it looks like you are going on a date with Adam Gould and me." I snuggled into him.

Adam Gould may be rude and had no manners when it came to letters, but he was punctual. At precisely six o'clock, a car pulled up in front of Tristan's mansion. A giant of a man got out and opened the door for me. He was the biggest man I had ever seen and had crazy hair sticking out in all directions. I was about to ask if he was Adam when the man spotted Ethan.

"Ethan Moore!" He grabbed him and pulled him into a hug, lifting him off the ground. Since Ethan was over six feet tall, I was impressed.

"Bri, put me down." Ethan wiggled his legs.

"Oh, sorry." Bri dropped Ethan.

I cleared my throat.

"Wow, Miss Palmer, you are prettier than your picture." Bri did a half-bow.

"You've seen my picture?" My cheeks reddened.

"Yes. We can't be late. Mr. Gould would be distraught." Bri opened the car door.

I slid in first. Ethan and Bri exchanged a few words before he got in. I gave him a questioning look, and he waved me off.

"How do you know Bri?" I leaned in to ask so Bri didn't hear us.

"We had a run-in." He patted my hand, clearly ending our conversation.

The entire way to wherever we were going, probably a restaurant, I imagined what Adam must have been like. His looks didn't matter to me. Even if he was deformed as Ethan said. It was how he had been acting so far that bothered me. He sent letters and demanded I go out with him tonight. Yes, I was about to be his wife, but that didn't give him a right to order me around.

My stomach turned. The letters. Both of the letters from Adam arrived at the same time as the death threats. With all the blood in my room, I hadn't checked to see if there was another letter from Adam. Had he sent the threats? He could have been trying to scare me into leaving Ethan and Tristan so he could have me to himself.

As self-centered as that sounded, it could have been true. He bought me not knowing two others did the same. He could have wanted a wife all to himself.

I squeezed Ethan's hand. If Adam did send the letters and were dangerous, I would be safe with Ethan. Hopefully.

We pulled up to a mansion, which was almost the same size as Tristans. Unlike Tristan's, this one was old. Brick was falling, vines climbed up the walls, the windows were covered in a film, and everything was unkempt. I wasn't one to judge, it was just different. I guess part of me thought all mansions were sparkly and new. At least the ones that were inhabited.

The inside of the house was the complete opposite of the outside. Everything was immaculate. The foyer was spotless and had a spiral staircase. All the walls were void of any artwork. It must have been so clean because there was nothing to make a mess. Did anyone even live here?

Bri directed us to a dining room. Instead of one long table like I expected, it's what Tristan had, there were multiple tables. Each table had a different tablecloth and an array of chairs. Whoever designed this had an eclectic taste. I loved it.

"Boss thought you would like a restaurant atmosphere." Bri waved his arms. "Do you like it?"

"I do." I smiled at Bri. I had thought we were going to an actual restaurant, but this was adorable.

A man in a suit and bow tie scuttered over to us. He had a napkin draped over his arm. He escorted us to a table and pulled out my chair. When he placed the napkin in my lap, Ethan scowled.

After the wine was poured, a man in a tux entered the dining area. A mask of sorts covered the right side of his face. It almost blended in with the other half of his face. The subtle difference was the movement. He gave a smile, and only one-half moved.

Even with the mask, he was handsome. His blonde hair was pulled back into a low pony. His green eyes sparkled when the light hit them. He was clean shaven, and somehow, it made him look older. Normally that had the opposite effect. The tux was snug against his chest, showing he was built like a heavy weight fighter.

Aside from the slight limp and the mask, he didn't appear deformed. Maybe it wasn't Adam.

"Ethan." He stuck out his hand.

"Adam." Ethan shook his hand. They both stared into each other's eyes, jaws twitching. Their knuckles whitened.

"Hey, I thought you didn't know him." Ethan had told me he didn't actually know Adam, he had just heard rumors.

"Things change." Ethan finally released Adam's hand.

"Yeah, like coming over here and demanding I don't marry Ava." Adam ground his teeth. "As if I wanted to."

Ethan shrugged as if that wasn't a big deal.

It was then I decided Adam probably didn't send the letters. Yes, he was an asshole, and I didn't like him very much, but he didn't seem cruel. The only motive I thought he had was to have me all to himself, it was obvious he didn't want me at all. I didn't completely rule him out, but Brad was my number one suspect. Now I had to find out if Adam was still a suspect or off the list completely.

"More importantly, I am Adam Gould. He took my hand and brought it to his lips. The mask bumped my fingers, it was cold and rubbery.

"Ava Palmer." I pulled my hand away. The mask didn't bother me. He did.

"Shall we?" Adam raised his wine glass. "To our wedding and the wedding night."

I wasn't positive, but I was pretty sure he winked at Ethan.

CHAPTER 19

Adam (Day 3)

THAT WEASEL MANAGED TO SHOW UP FOR MY DATE with Ava. I wanted to pound his face in. He had a lot of nerve to crash this. Since he wanted to be here, I would constantly remind him that I would also be fucking Ava. It was purely to piss him off.

Ava blushed when I brought up our wedding night. Shit, had I embarrassed her? Probably. This had to be weird for her.

"Those letters you sent me were odd." Ava glared at me. She was ballsy and beautiful.

In person, she was even more stunning than her picture. She smiled, and her eyes sparkled. Her hair fell around her shoulders in pink waves. The black dress was so low cut I could almost see her belly button. Fuck, she was gorgeous and knew how to dress.

"They were straight to the point," I scoffed.

"The blood made a nice touch." She rolled her eyes and pursed her lips.

"Blood?" What was she talking about?

"Each letter you sent me had a second one. Just a few words and smeared with blood." She interlaced her fingers.

"Peach, it wasn't him. Bri gave the letters from Adam to CeCe and she placed them in your room." Ethan grabbed her hand. "Had they been covered in blood, she would have given them to me."

"You knew he was writing to me?" Ava pulled her hand away.

"You are mine to protect, of course, I knew." He grabbed her hand again.

"Blood? What is going on?" I slammed the table.

"Someone sent her death threats. It's being handled," Ethan growled.

How many people wanted her dead? Judith was trying to get her executed, and my grandparents were trying to help. Now, this. What kind of a person was Ava? Most normal people didn't have people after them. She had multiple. I had been positive I needed to protect her from being hung, but now I wasn't so sure. What if she was the problem?

As the servers came out with our meal, I debated telling her about Judith. If she were the problem, a hanging would be for the best. It was better than my grandparents bleeding her out. Did Ava deserve to die? I didn't know, maybe it wasn't my place to interfere.

"So, how does this work?" Ava stared at the lobster on her plate.

"This marriage or the food?" I asked.

"Both." Ava stabbed the lobster with a fork.

"Let me." Ethan took the plate from her. He pulled the meat from the tail shell. Then he dipped a piece into the butter and brought it to her lips. She sucked on his finger as he put the food in her mouth. Ava moaned as she continued to suck on his finger.

Fuck, my dick hardened. Watching her suck Ethan's finger was so hot. I wanted those lips around my cock. Shit, I would have taken watching her suck his cock. They continued as if I wasn't there. He would feed her, and she would suck his finger, going deeper each time. If they didn't stop, my dick was going to break my zipper.

I cleared my throat.

They both turned to look at me. Ava's face was beat red when she realized they weren't alone. "Sorry," she mumbled.

"How would you like this to work?" I didn't trust her, and I wasn't sure what type of person she was, but we were going to have to get married. Unless my grandparents found proof she hacked the auction system.

"I would like to only be married to one person." She smiled at Ethan.

If she didn't want multiple husbands, why would she hack the system?

"Well, that's not possible," I snapped. "You have to follow the rules of the auction. So how do you want to do this?"

"What are my options?" She finished her wine, and a server refilled it.

"Stay here once a week so we can perform our duties or I can come to you." My dick twitched. Fuck the thought of fucking her once a week excited me.

"So now I get the choice? In your letter, you said you would send for me." Her words were bitter. She didn't like me. That was fine, I didn't like her either.

"You aren't coming to our place. What do you think is gonna happen? We all fuck her at the same time?" Ethan's words were laced with jealousy.

"Don't you think that should be her decision?" I nodded toward Ava. "If she wants to sit on my face while you slide your cock inside her ass, that's up to her."

"No, 'cause you aren't gonna fuck her." Ethan glared.

"Or, if she wants to be bent over her bed while I ram my dick inside her and she sucks your cock, that's her decision. Oh, and don't forget, your ex-brother-in-law will be there too.

Maybe we could all fuck each one of her tight holes. Would you like that, Ava? Do you want three men pleasing you at the same time? Is that why you hacked the auction system? Is that your fantasy?" My dick was on the verge of breaking through my pants. Yeah, I said it to piss off Ethan, but I loved the thought of it.

"She didn't hack the system. And you aren't fucking her!" A vein in his forehead bulged.

"If I don't, she dies. Do you want that?" I left out the part where she might die anyway. Just because he said she didn't hack the system didn't mean I believed him.

"Or I kill you and end this." He stood.

"Excuse me. I'm right here! I entered the auction, and you two and Tristan bought me. So, like it or not, we all have to deal with this." She placed her hand on Ethan's arm. "I don't like this either."

She turned to me. "I'm not positive you didn't send the bloody letters. I don't like you, and I can tell you don't like me. I'm not really sure why you bought me, but you did. I'm not willing to die. So, that means once a week we fuck. I would feel more comfortable if you came to me."

This conversation kept spiraling. I was stuck with this woman for the next five years. Yes she was beautiful, but there was something dark about her. Even if it was just that everyone wanted to kill her. I was torn between letting my grandparents hang her and fucking her senseless.

"You will wear a condom every time. And if she wants me in the room, so she is more comfortable, then I will be there." Ethan was making demands he had no right to make.

"No, she needs to be on birth control. No matter which one of us gets her pregnant, we would all be stuck for eighteen years." Five years I could survive. I couldn't survive eighteen. Judging from the glares, she gave me, neither could she.

"I don't want kids, so I agree with Adam." She averted her eyes.

What woman didn't want kids? That was another strike against her.

"If that's what you want, Peach." Ethan bent down and kissed her cheek.

"Hey, if you want to watch me fuck her, that's fine." I shrugged. "When will the vow exchange take place?" I asked.

"In four days. At our place." Ethan accentuated each word. I had a feeling he was trying to make me jealous.

"Myself, Bri, and my grandparents will be there." Having my grandparents, there was probably a bad idea. I didn't care. I loved them, and since this would be my only wedding, I wanted them with me.

"You are not having the owners of the auction there!" Ethan tossed his wine glass at the wall. He overreacted, why?

"Uh...your grandparents...uh...own the auction." Ava gulped loudly. Neither one of them wanted them there. Interesting.

"Yes, and they will be there. I'm not someone you want to piss off. Now, if you'll excuse me, I have better things to do." I stood and left.

Bri, would take them home. I wanted to give Ava the benefit of the doubt in regard to Judith's accusations. Then she showed up with Ethan Moore. It seemed like she was very much into him. Maybe she had rigged the auction so he would buy her.

Then there were the threats. She had a lot of people after her, which meant she wasn't well-liked. I was going to find out exactly why.

When Bri returned, I sent him out to find Judith. I didn't care for her, but maybe I had misjudged her. I had to find out what she knew about Ava.

It took him a few hours to locate her. She had an address, but she didn't show up there until eleven. He told me that, at first, she flipped out. Refused to go with him. Then he mentioned my name, her face lit up. Judith grabbed a bag and left with him.

I had fallen asleep on the sofa when they finally showed up. Hearing a woman's voice in my house jarred me awake. I sat up, wiping the drool that coated my cheek.

"Mr. Gould." Judith stuck out her hand.

I grabbed it. My saliva-filled hand squished into hers. She laughed and rubbed the saliva off on her jeans. Heat rose to my cheeks. Fuck my life.

"Your goon said you need me." She stared into my eyes.

"His name is Brian," I growled. I didn't like when people called him anything but his name.

"I didn't mean anything by it." She sat down and crossed her legs.

"I'm gonna be blunt with you. I don't know much about Ava Palmer. You seem to know her. Tell me everything you know." I leaned forward.

"Well, she's a manipulative little bitch. She uses her looks to get men to fall for her. Then she crushes them. Not to mention what she does to her friends. As soon as she doesn't need you anymore, she disposes of you." Judith uncrossed her legs and leaned closer to me. "Ava Palmer is a terrible person."

Her rant didn't actually tell me anything aside from the fact that she hated Ava. I already knew that from my grandparents' house. What I wanted to know was why. What specifically happened? I ran my hand across my face. Fuck, I didn't have my mask on. I grabbed it off the coffee table.

"You don't have to do that on my account. We all have scars." She pulled up her sleeves. Marks ran up both of her arms.

"What's that from?" Despite what she said, I put my mask on.

"Fighting mostly. That's how I first met Ava. She showed up at the ring all prissy and in pink. Everyone misjudged her. We all thought she was so sweet. I was even friends with her." She looked off into the distance as if she could see her past.

"What happened?" This was the information I wanted.

"My manager, Brad, who was also my best friend. I secretly loved him but never told him. Maybe that's my fault. Anyway, he took one look at her and fell in love. At first, all three of us would hang out. Then she started sleeping over at our place." Judith clenched her fists.

"You two lived together?" How did she live with this guy and not tell him how she felt?

"He had a tent. I didn't. I was sleeping on a bench. He offered a spot in his tent. And she would come over and hook up with him while I was right there!" She sounded like she was jealous. It didn't seem like Ava was a terrible person.

"So you hate her because she hooked up with a guy you liked?" I rolled my eyes.

"I know how it sounds, but it was so much more. She had him kick me out of his tent. Then she turned everyone against him, so he had to leave town. Even if I could never have him, I didn't want him to leave." She looked like she was on the verge of tears. "Then there was the nickname. I was called Two hits Judith. Then she started calling me Big Booty Judy, and that name stuck."

"How did she turn everyone against him?" I wasn't convinced this wasn't just jealousy.

"She convinced people he was hitting her. Total bullshit. Her marks were from fighting, same as me."

"I would like to meet this guy. Is he still out of town?" I would send for him if he was. Maybe he could shed some light on Ava Palmer.

CHAPTER 20

Adam (Day 4)

JUDITH SPENT THE NIGHT. I WASN'T TOO KEEN ON the idea, but Bri insisted. He was too tired to drive her back.

In the morning, we had breakfast. Neither Brian nor I were good cooks. Luckily Judith was. She cooked a feast of eggs, bacon, potatoes, and pancakes. It was amazing. Normally for that type of food, Brian would have to send out for it.

It wasn't until after we finished our meal that I realized my mask was upstairs. Not once did Judith stare at my face. Maybe she was right, we all have scars. It was nice having company in the house. Since I corrected Judith on what to call Brian, she was overly pleasant to him. I could tell from the smile on his face that he liked her.

"So what's the plan?" I asked through mouths full of food.

"Brad will be at work. He's a server at La Temp. You can't call him by his real name. People are still out for him because of Ava. Her best friend Felix is a fighter. No way could Brad defend himself." She hissed when she mentioned Felix.

"Why couldn't Brad defend himself? And what do I call him?" The more I talked to Judith, the more I wondered if she was telling the truth about Ava.

"Call him Vernon. As for him defending himself, you'll see." She grabbed her plate, then Brian's, and lastly mine. Why would she clean up after me if she was a bad person?

A few minutes later, we were out the door and heading to La Temp. Judith told me not to bring the mask, but I did. She may have been comfortable with my face, but most weren't. When we arrived at the restaurant, she had us sneak in the back when we arrived at the restaurant. I didn't bother to tell her my sister owned the restaurant, and we could have walked through the front door.

Brian wanted to go and see my sister, Tara. I told him she probably wouldn't be there and that it would take longer if he went. He would have wanted to see who was there and how everyone was. It would have taken too much time.

Tons of servers and cooks moved about the kitchen. Since I had last been there, most of the workers had changed. I kept asking if each one was Vernon. She kindly told me to be patient and wait. It had been so long since I went anywhere that all the people and noise were jarring. The odd thing was no one gave me a second glance. Even though that was nice, I was still pissed to be outside. I spent six years inside. Since Brian bought me Ava a few days ago, I had already left the house twice. I was starting to hate Ava Palmer.

Judith elbowed my side and pointed at a server. "That's him."

I'm not sure what I expected, but he wasn't it. He looked like a movie star. His black hair was gelled back. When he saw Judith, he smiled at her. His teeth literally glistened across the room. I wasn't into men, but if I was, he would be my type.

He set the tray down and came over to us. With his left arm, he pulled Judith into a hug and kissed her cheek. Her face reddened.

"Vernon, this is Adam. Adam, this is Vernon." Judith introduced us.

I stuck out my hand to shake his. "Nice to meet you."

He put out his left hand. "Sorry, bro, my right arm doesn't work."

"Oh, what happened?" That would explain why he couldn't defend himself.

"I used to be a fighter. Took a hard hit to the shoulder. It hasn't worked since." He slapped his other arm to accentuate his point.

"Vernon, this is Adam Gould, the man who bought Ava. Well, one of them," she hissed.

Anger flashed across his face, or maybe it was jealousy. I wasn't sure. Either way, he composed himself quickly.

"I just have a few questions, if you don't mind." I adjusted my mask.

"Sorry, I can't help you. I haven't seen Ava in years." He dropped his head as if the thought pained him.

"It's more about your previous relationship with Miss Palmer," I stated.

"Not much I can say. She was wonderful." He averted his gaze. I could tell he was hiding something.

"Tell the truth," Judith snapped. "She can't hurt you anymore."

"Fine, but not here," he whispered and looked around.

I left Judith and Vernon to look for the manager. When I found him, he pulled me in for a hug. It was my cousin Herby. I wasn't surprised Tara hired him to run it. He was meticulous and very business savvy, which was why he let me pay him to take his server.

Vernon tried to finish his tables, he didn't want someone else to do his work. I respected him for taking pride in his work, but I still made him leave. In a few days, I would be married to Ava. I had to know more about her.

Inside my house, Vernon/Brad seemed shy and scared, as if the place bothered him. Maybe he had never been in such a big house. Perhaps he was scared of me. Actually, that made more sense. Ava had people after him, and I was about to marry her. He had to have thought I was up to no good.

"H...h...how...c...can...I help," Vernon stuttered.

"What was it like to date Ava? I asked. When he stared at me, I added. "I'm trying to figure out if she's a good person."

His eyes glossed over. "She is. Well, she was. Maybe she changed. When I was with her, everything was perfect. She made me feel special. Like I was the only person alive. We spent every second together. She even had me manage her in the ring. I hated leaving Judith, but she needed me."

"Then what happened?" I asked.

"I don't want to talk bad about her." He looked around as if Ava was gonna pop up any second.

"It's okay. I won't tell her." I assured him.

"Oh, it's not that. I just don't like talking bad about her. I still miss her. My heart will always beat for her. If I could just see her one more time." He put his face in his working hand. Judith wrapped her arms around him and stroked his hair.

It was obvious Ava broke his heart. He was distraught and yet still wanted to see her. What kind of pull did she have on him?

"Maybe I could arrange a meeting if you tell me the truth. I want to know everything that happened between you and Ava." I leaned back, ready to hear his side. Then I would decide if I was really gonna set up a meeting between him and Ava.

Judith stroked his right hand. He looked at her. She nodded as if giving her approval. He took a deep breath and turned to me.

"Before I start, please understand it's not Ava's fault. She had a worse upbringing than most. Please don't blame her." He stared at me, waiting for a reply.

"I won't," I lied.

He nodded and then began his story. "I was working as Judith's manager a few years back. I used to be a fighter until I lost function in my arm, so I knew how to teach the moves. Judith mostly fought at a place called The Underground. Then one day, Ava walked in. She was different from anybody I had ever met. She was all in pink and had a killer smile.

Everyone wanted her, but she fixated on me. I fell in love, hard. That's when things went bad. She was different when no one was around.

She would look at me without seeing me. Calling me her father and attacking me. I would try to calm her, but there was only so much I could do." He pointed to his left arm.

"Go on. It's okay." Judith coaxed him to continue.

"Then I found out what she did to her father. I was terrified. I tried to leave. She carved my initials on her hip. I felt horrible. She needed me, and I was trying to get away. So, I stayed.

Ava would hurt herself. Sometimes it was cuts, other times, she would bash her head or punch something, including me. I think she did it to feel something.

People started noticing. So she blamed me. I think it was better for her than the truth. That's when I had to leave. Now I'm back under a false name so her friends won't find me." He wiped the sweat from his forehead.

"Geez. What did she do to her father?" I asked, not sure if I wanted the answer.

"She killed him!" Judith shouted. "She's a monster."

"If she's a monster, it's not her fault. She was made that way." Vernon looked down. "Despite all that, I still love her."

CHAPTER 21

Ava (Day 4)

THE SUN BEAT AGAINST MY SKIN DRYING OFF THE water from the pool. Luckily the plastic covering my tattoo hadn't budged. I wasn't the greatest swimmer because I learned in the ocean against the waves. A pool was different, you didn't have to try so hard to stay afloat.

I rather enjoyed it. Joseph banged on Dottie's door at seven in the morning to go swimming. I was in no mood to wake up that early, he didn't care. He had the day off from school and wanted to spend the entire time in the pool. Dottie begged me to go with them.

"Ava, watch!" Joseph shouted from the diving board.

I waved to let him know I was. The little twerp did a backflip into the water. Okay, that was cool. "Nice job!" I yelled.

"See, isn't this fun?" Dottie slapped my leg as she came to sit next to me.

"It's not bad. The kid is cool." I nodded toward Joseph.

"What about the pool? Way different from when dad taught us in the ocean," she laughed.

"Yeah, swim fast, or a shark is gonna get you." I mimicked what our dad used to say to us.

"Or, If you drown, I'm not saving you." Dottie mimicked his other saying.

The door to the back patio slammed open. Dottie and I turned. Ethan and his dad were in the middle of their meeting, and also turned. He kept his word that I wouldn't be let out of his sight. Even last night when I insisted I sleep in my sister's room. He slept in a chair in the corner.

Two nurses steadied a woman between them. My stomach turned. It was my mother. Yeah, I was being childish. I had been avoiding her for days. The move was hard on her. It was something else that was my fault.

The nurses brought her over to Dottie and me, then set her down. She smiled at us, "What a beautiful day."

My mom's hair was curled and fell around her shoulders. She had on loose white pants and a matching white button-up. Her eyes lost the haze they had for years. She appeared content.

"It really is," Dottie beamed.

"How's Joseph doing?" My mother looked toward the pool.

As if he heard his name, Joseph climbed out of the pool and ran toward my mom. "Grandma Carrie."

She wrapped her arms around him. "How's your time? Did you speed up on the dive?"

"Still a little slow. I'm working on it." He bounced from heel to heel.

"Come on. I'll time you." She stood. The nurses steadied her as she got up.

What the heck? It had only been a few days. I counted on my fingers. Four. It had been four days, how did I miss so much?

Once my mother was out of earshot, I turned to Dottie. "How?"

"Isn't it wonderful?" Dottie clapped her hands.

"How?" I watched as my mother pulled out a stop watch and yelled, 'Go!' Joseph dove into the water and swam as fast as he could. My mother cheered him on. It wasn't the same woman I grew up with.

"Doctor Ameer said it could be the proper medication or it could be Joseph." She leaned in closer. "You still can't mention dad, but she is getting better."

"Why is she having trouble walking?" A nurse kept her hand on my mother's back.

"The medications. Dr. Ameer said that will go away and soon she will be good. Not perfect, but good. I think it's Joseph to be honest. The first night he went into her room and told her all about swimming. She looked right at him and said she wanted to see him swim." Dottie smiled so wide, she showed all of her teeth.

This was a miracle. If for no other reason than this, I would owe Ethan and Tristan my life. They gave my mother her life back. It was something I took when I killed her husband.

I leaned back and watched my mom and Joseph. He did laps, and she cheered him on. After a few minutes, Dottie got up and joined them. She shouted and clapped with them.

Soon after, Felix and Sandy came into the backyard. They walked right past me and over to my sister and mom. They didn't even see me, I doubted they were even looking for me. I had been busy since I got there.

As Joseph did with everyone, when they got there, he jumped out and hugged them. Sandy lifted him in the air and twirled him around. It was surreal to see them all so happy. Tears stung my eyes. It was something out of a novel.

I looked over to see Ethan. He had stopped his meeting with his dad and was watching Joseph with my family. I laughed, soon to be 'our family.'

wiping away the tears I saw Mr. Moore, Ethan's father. He was the only one not looking at the pool. He was looking directly at me. His eyes drooped as he plastered a scowl across his face. I quickly averted my eyes and turned my attention to the pool again.

"So this is the famous Ava Palmer that has my Ethan all flustered," a voice said behind me.

I jumped. When did someone else come outside? I turned to see a tall, beautiful woman with long braids past her breasts. Her eyes were the color of honey, and her teeth were blindingly white. I stood and stuck out my hand. Really, I just wanted to see if her skin was as soft as it looked.

"Sorry to startle you. I'm Tasha, Ethan's best friend." She shook my hand. Yup, it was as soft as it looked.

"Hi, I'm Ava. Wait, you knew that. How did you know that?" I realized I was still holding her hand and released it.

"Ethan told me. He said the atmosphere at Tristan's is different. He was right." She nodded toward the pool.

"I don't know how it was before, but this is wonderful." I fussed with my nails. Hers was perfectly rounded. I should have done mine like that instead of more squared.

"It wasn't like this, and Ethan wasn't like this. He's happy. That's an emotion I didn't think he was capable of." She placed my hand on her knee. "Thank you."

Yup even her knee skin was soft. I didn't know how to respond to her. How did I begin to explain to her how happy he made me? In four days, he flipped my world upside down and fixed it. Fixed me.

Felix and Sandy came over to join us. Good, maybe they could help me. I was having trouble speaking around Tasha.

"Hi, I'm Felix, and this is my girlfriend, Sandy. We're Ava's family. So are those two." He pointed to my mom and sister. "I guess soon, Joseph will be our family too."

"That's just wonderful. I can't wait for the wedding." Tasha clapped her hands together. "Ava, what are you gonna wear?"

My heart sank. My closet was ruined. The blood had destroyed all of my clothes. I had nothing to wear. Ethan had CeCe grab me a few items to wear until he could get more, but nothing fit for a wedding.

"Not sure yet, but we are gonna find her something wonderful." Felix stepped in and spoke for me. After years of doing it for Sandy ,he had become a pro at it. And I was thankful for it.

"Oh no. That won't do. I could come by tomorrow with my tailor Frizzo. He is wonderful. I would do it tonight, time is of the essence, but I'm going to a fight." Tasha pulled out her phone and started clicking away.

Felix, Sandy, and I all looked at each other. They both had to be thinking the same thing I was. Maybe, there was an explanation. Maybe, I heard Tasha wrong.

"Did you say fight?" Felix asked.

Tasha looked up from her phone. "How does noon sound?

"Huh?" I scrunched up my face.

"Noon. Frizzo can fit you in. Said he will make you a dress fit for a princess." Tasha went back to her phone.

"Fight. You said you were going to a fight tonight." Felix's eyes grew wide.

"Oh, that. A few of my friends heard about a place that does fights. Like in a ring. Totally boring, but one of the girls going is so hot." Tasha fanned herself.

"All of those places closed down a few weeks ago," Felix said. He was like me, fighting was a part of us. If the rings were open again, we were gonna go.

"No, I don't think so." Tasha clicked furiously on her phone. After a few dings, she held it up to us. "See, they are all

134

open. We are going to Peaks, but if it's lame, the others are open."

I stared at her phone and read the message a few times. The rings were open. I could fight. Yes! I could hug Tasha.

Felix pulled Sandy in for a hug and kissed the top of her head.

Tasha looked at both of us like we had lost our minds. She couldn't possibly understand why we were so happy about fights being open. In her words, 'they were boring.'

"So anyway. Do you have a theme for your wedding? Oh, and what are your colors?" Tasha was waving her hands around like the colors would appear in the sky.

"Uh...no..." Fuck, why hadn't I thought of that? I assumed it wouldn't be like a real wedding. It even had a different name: Vow Exchange. This was terrible, I had so much to do and no time to do it.

"Don't stress. I will be around to help with all of it." She tapped away on her phone again.

"What are you doing here?" Ethan asked from behind me.

"Me?" Tasha pointed to herself. "I came to meet your new bride and help with the wedding. Your dad called and told me about it."

"So my dad happens to call the woman I used to fuck? He used you to upset Ava." Ethan's voice was a steady roar.

Do not get jealous. You will not get jealous. Everyone has a past. "Did you come here to upset me? Or try and hook up with Ethan?"

"Oh no." Tasha grabbed her chest. "I would never. I'm happy for Ethan. I don't want to upset you, and I don't want to fuck Ethan. Or any man ever again, for that matter. I'm sorry, I'll go." She stood.

I grabbed her hand. "No stay. I believe you. Plus, I need help with this wedding."

Tasha appeared genuine. Ethan's dad may have called her

to cause problems, but I truly believed she came with good intentions. Besides, if she had nefarious intentions, she would have coffin-shaped nails and not rounded ones.

"Are you sure? I don't want you to be uncomfortable. Especially in your house." Tasha remained standing as if I was going to send her away at any second.

"Absolutely. Now sit. Let's talk about colors." I turned to Ethan. "Can we do it all? Like bridesmaids and flowers?"

"Whatever you want. I would even wear pink." He pulled my hand from Tasha's. I hadn't realized I was still holding it. Ethan kissed my hand.

"Nope, I will be the only one with pink." I pointed to my hair.

"That works too. Since you all seem to have a ton to talk about, I'm going to handle some business for Tristan while he is still away." He shook his head. "He's trying to acquire land to build a baseball stadium."

"We will be fine." I gave him my most innocent smile.

"Don't let her out of your sight!" He pointed at Felix and Sandy. Then he waved to his dad to follow him and left.

I tried to suppress a grin. With Ethan busy, it would be a lot easier to sneak out and hit up one of those fights. My veins pulsed with the anticipation of being in the ring again.

Tasha excused herself to talk to Ethan's dad for a moment. I don't know what they were discussing, but Mr. Moore had a scowl on his face.

"We need to go to those fights," I whispered.

"Then let's go." Felix went to stand.

I grabbed his hand. "Stop. We can't just go. Ethan has been keeping a close eye on me since the blood in my room. He wouldn't be cool with me going to fight. At least not now." When Brad was caught, I would make sure Ethan knew I would still fight.

"So what do we do?" Felix asked.

"Wait for the opportunity to sneak out." I shrugged.

CHAPTER 22

Ava (Day 4)

TASHA CLICKED AWAY ON HER PHONE. A FEW minutes later, a few of Tristan's servants came into the backyard carrying a glass table and chairs. CeCe handed Tasha a pad of paper and a pen. Dottie joined us, and my mom stayed by the pool timing Joseph.

"CeCe, can you bring us a tray of sandwiches?" Tasha stroked CeCe's hand. "Oh and please make sure one is a tomato and salami for Joseph."

She had a certain finesse about her. Even CeCe blushed when she touched her hand. Tasha was lovely and sweet and seemed unaffected by her elite status. I could care less that she was once with Ethan. Yeah, I was a little jealous for a second. But now she was a new friend.

"Okay, I don't have too long. Maybe a few hours. I can clear my schedule for the next few days. The wedding is on Sunday, right?" Tasha was already scribbling away on the paper.

"No, Saturday," I whispered. Would there be enough time to get it all done?

"Yikes, okay. I have thrown galas in less time. We can do this. Do you have an invite list?" She chewed on her pen.

"Um, everyone here?" Who else would there be?

"This is the wedding party. You need guests. When you walk down that aisle, you want all eyes on you." She reached out and caressed a lock of my hair. "Not that that would be hard. You are stunning."

"So, who do we invite?" This was way more complex than I was prepared for.

"All of New Boston." She waved her hands in the air. "It'll be the greatest event since the Cartright wedding. Oh, they married a homeless person too. Maybe we can play off that."

"Ava has everyone here that she would invite. Why don't we ask the grooms who they want to invite." Dottie scooted her chair closer to Tasha and looked at her paper.

"Great idea!" Tasha pulled out her phone again. What was she doing, texting them? "You're marrying three, right? Who is the third?"

"Aside from Ethan and Tristan, there's a man named Adam Gould." I looked down. Adam should have never bought me. I didn't like him, and he obviously didn't like me.

"Gould? Gould?" Tasha tapped her chin. "Oh, I know his brother Zack. Talk about amazing in bed. If Adam is hung anything like his brother, you are in luck."

Heat rose to my cheeks. "I have no desire to be in luck with Adam."

"Well, you have to sleep with him, so hope it's enjoyable." Tasha looked at her phone. "Okay, Tristan said his secretary will send over a list."

Felix glanced at me and looked toward the door. We had to find a way to sneak out. Tasha was so excited about planning the wedding, I wasn't sure she would let us go. At least not until she had to leave. Which meant there was a high chance

Ethan would finish up and come back. He would not be cool with me wanting to go fight.

"Ethan said he will make a list." Tasha's phone dinged. "His father said let's not try and embarre...nevermind. It doesn't matter what he says."

"What did he say?" Dottie asked.

"Let's not embarrass Ethan by inviting people." Tasha grabbed my hand. "Don't let him get to you. He is old school. He doesn't see the world changing."

"Changing?" I didn't get what she was talking about.

"Yeah, you have to see it. Our ancestors suppressed the poor after World War Four. Pushed them onto the streets. They tried to eradicate them all." Tasha gripped my hand tighter. "But the homeless are rising. It began when you guys started making tents to live in. Then when elites took pity on you guys and started bringing back apartments. It scares Mr. Moore."

"First, how do you know all that?" I pulled my hand away. I knew some of our history, everyone did. But Tasha appeared very knowledgeable. "Second, why would that scare him?"

"I'm a history professor at Bale University. I know, I don't look it. Anyway, it scares him because the homeless have the power to shift the economic status of people. Let me not even get into the government part." Tasha tapped her paper. "Wedding stuff. Let's plan this, shall we?"

Never would I have guessed she was a professor. I inspected my bubblegum nails, no one would expect me to be a fighter. I tried to push aside what she said about Mr. Moore. He had billions, it shouldn't have mattered what a few homeless people had. No matter what happened economic wise, he would remain on top.

Sandy stood and went to the bathroom. Thirty seconds later, Dottie stood and followed her. I debated going with them so I could fill Dottie in on our plan.

"Do you plan on wearing white? I know it won't be a for sure thing until you meet with Frizzo, but a general idea would be cool." Tasha went back to planning as if she never spoke of war and economics.

"That or maybe a champagne color." I wanted something neutral, so my hair really shined. If I had time, I would borrow or make some jewelry to accentuate the dress. Oh, I could pick some flowers for my hair. When I was little, I read Cinderella, and that was exactly how I felt.

"Okay, good. We could do any color for the bridal party, and it wouldn't clash." Tasha checked her phone." Okay, Adam said, just his grandparents and a guy named Brian. Bummer, I was hoping Zack would come and I could get a little wedding night action as well. Not that I'm interested in men anymore, really I would just be recycling him."

"You have Adam's number? Can I see your phone?" I had some things to say to him.

"Yeah, from Zack. Here. Just clock on his pic, type, and hit send. Sorry, I'm sure you know how to work it." She handed over her phone.

I didn't know how to use it. Dottie was the tech-savvy one.

ADAM

> You could always not show up. Love, Ava.

And miss our wedding night? Never. Don't you have your own phone?

> Don't need one.

How else would you tell me how much you want my cock?

Ugh, I couldn't believe I had to marry him. I had high

hopes for him. They were crushed when I met him. Especially since he might have sent the threatening letter. Brad was the number one suspect, but how would he get in?

"Do you need a phone? Ethan could get you one. Shoot, I could." Tasha took back the phone.

"No, I don't talk to anyone." I chewed my lip.

"Except us." Felix stood to take the tray of sandwiches that had just arrived. "Sit with us, CeCe, eat."

"Oh no, Mr. Felix. I ate already." She averted her eyes. "Joseph! Come eat. The pool will still be there when you're done."

Joseph hopped out of the pool. My mother had a towel in her hands, waiting for him. She wrapped it around him and dried him off. This version of my mother never existed for Dottie or me. Not even before I killed her husband.

The nurses helped her over to the table. Joseph dragged his chair to be right next to my mom. He grabbed a salami and tomato sandwich and gave her one. She took a huge bite, and he did the same.

There were days Dottie would beg her to eat. She would claim she wasn't hungry, even when her stomach grumbled. Now for Joseph, she ate. No problem. This kid was a true blessing, even if he was a kid.

"So, we are doing wedding stuff?" my mom asked through chews.

I nodded.

"Joseph, you are gonna be a handsome ring bearer." She ruffled his hair.

"Grandma Carrie, did you have a ring bearer?" Joseph looked up at her.

Shit, she can't mention my dad without a meltdown. Where was Dottie? She was better at this. How was I gonna help?

"No, Sweetie. I had a small wedding. This will be my first

big wedding with a bridal party, flowers, and dresses." She took another sandwich.

Wow! No meltdown, not even a hint of one. Granted, she hadn't mentioned him, but she mentioned marrying him. Still, I couldn't wait to tell Dottie. If she ever came back.

"This will be the biggest wedding ever. I'm Tasha, Ethan's friend. I'll be helping your daughter with her wedding." Tasha shook my mom's hand.

"I'm sure it'll be lovely. I think Joseph should be in a little suit." She smiled at Joseph.

Dottie and Sandy came back from the bathroom and joined us for lunch. Dottie sat and winked at me. Oh, Sandy must have clued her in. Good, she could help sneak us out.

"Tasha, I was thinking of projecting scenes on the walls like nature: waterfalls, mountains, sunsets." Dottie leaned in and grabbed a sandwich.

"Hmm. I don't know if we can put that together fast enough." Tasha scratched her chin.

"Oh, I can. Moore Tech has everything I need. Ethan has allowed me in there, he said I might even earn an internship there. Anyway, I can show you how to do it after lunch." Dottie smiled.

"Perfect. Oh, if we can get pics when they were kids, we could project those too." Tasha scribbled on the paper.

"We don't have pictures," I mumbled. I didn't know any homeless person that had pictures.

"That's okay. I have some other ideas." Tasha tapped her temple with the pen.

Tasha spent the rest of lunch scribbling away on her paper. Every once in a while, she would ask a question and then go back to her writing. I had no clue a wedding was so much work. On the streets, you would go to a free judge, and they would document that you took your vows. That was it.

I read about massive weddings with fancy ballgowns and extravagant updos. Now, I would get to experience it.

Once lunch was done, CeCe rushed out and cleared the table. Again, Felix tried to get her to sit down and relax. She refused.

My mother, her nurses, and Joesph went back over to the pool. He dove in, and my mom cheered him on. Dottie waved to them, said goodbye to us, and asked Tasha if she was ready to see the projectors.

Tasha hugged all of us and promised to be by in the morning. I thanked her. She was absolutely fantastic. Before she came over, I would make sure to have a list of ideas for her. She had done so much work already I wanted to contribute.

As soon as they were gone, Sandy pulled out a pair of pink shorts, a matching tank top, and sneakers. That must have been what took her and Dottie so long in the bathroom. They grabbed my clothes, so I wasn't sneaking out in a bathing suit.

Felix rubbed his hands together. "You two ready?"

CHAPTER 23

Tristan (Day 4)

MY PHONE BUZZED.

TASHA

Hey Love, I need a list for your wedding invites.

Why?

I'm planning your wedding.

Why?

Because Ava Palmer is a lovely woman.
List. Now.

Fine, my secretary will send it over.

"Wedding? How could you get married and not invite me?" Lisa gasped.

Lisa moved around the kitchenette in the hotel room. We

were twenty minutes from the rehab center, and I couldn't get her to go. The first excuse was she wanted a nice meal before we went. We were currently on the fifth nice meal.

When I got her in the car, I questioned her for hours about the letter. She swore she didn't send any letters to anyone. Nor had she been inside my house. It wasn't until Daryl informed me about the blood in Ava's room that I believed Lisa. She couldn't have done it while she was with me.

"Why would I invite you?" I was losing my patience with her. The only thing saving her was the medication the doctor had given her. It suppressed the cravings and the inevitable detox.

"I'm your mother-in-law," she said matter-of-factly.

"You are the woman who gave birth to my late wife. That's it." I grabbed a beer from the fridge.

"If that were true, you wouldn't have spent the last few years taking care of me." She turned on the stove for the water and added oil to another pan.

Maybe she was right. I did feel an obligation to make sure she was alright. I hated her for abandoning her kids and for spelling her dead daughter's name wrong. I hated her for passing her demons onto her daughter. I hated her for depriving my son of a grandmother. I hated her for many reasons. Despite all that, I still felt responsible for her.

"Now, after some clams linguine, we should take a walk. Explore the city. Lisa chopped up some garlic. For spending the last twenty-five years on the streets, she was a good cook, phenomenal even.

"No. We are going to the rehab center." I took a long pull from the bottle and slammed it on the table. "It's time."

"I'm not ready yet." She turned to me with pleading eyes. "This is the first time in years I've been out of the fog. I wanna see a city with new eyes."

She pulled her hair back into a low pony. It was brushed

and shiny. When we left the hospital, it was a tangled mess that frizzed out all over her head. Lisa tried to get the knots out herself and ended up crying on the floor. She looked so much like her daughter that I had no choice but to help. Took me three hours and a bottle of baby oil to detangle her hair.

"Why did you agree to come? You have no desire to get help," I snapped. She kept making excuses, and I was tired of it.

"You think I want to be like this? Years of my life passed in a blur. For most of my life, I've been so high I don't remember anything. I lost everything. I lost a daughter I didn't even know. My son doesn't recognize me. I saw him once, he walked right past me. Had no clue who I was.

Did you know I used to cook? Mitch bought me a restaurant. It was never a success. Running a restaurant was hard. I just wanted to cook for people. Now, all I cook is my next hit. If you mix it with cherry drink mix, it makes a better high." Lisa held onto the frying pan. Her tears splashed the pan. Oil splattered and got her in the face. She jumped back. The pan tumbled to the floor.

I dashed over and yanked her back. A glob of oil narrowly missed her bare foot. Fuck.

"Go clean up. We will go out to eat." I pushed her toward the bathroom.

While she was in there, I started on the kitchenette floor. Oil had splattered everywhere. An entire paper towel roll later, and I got the floor cleaned up.

Buzz. Buzz.

Ugh. What did Tasha want now?

I clicked open my phone. Ethan was calling. The meeting!

"Hey, I'm with Aiden right now," Ethan said the moment I hit answer.

"Good. What does he want for the land?" I had no time

for pleasantries. Lisa could come out of the bathroom at any moment.

"Mr. Miller, you don't seem focused. Are you sure you are committed to running a professional baseball team?" Aiden asked.

"Mr. Cartright, my focus is my concern," I snapped. He had no right to question my commitment.

"Since I'm selling you the land, it's my concern. Since I am the only person in New Boston that owns enough combined acreage to build a baseball field, it's my business." Aiden's voice was calm even though his words were laced with poison.

"Your real estate business retains my law firm, so we both have something to lose if the deal goes wrong." Yeah, I would threaten him if need be.

"No need for threats. All I'm saying is, bringing baseball back to New Boston is a big deal. I want it to be a success," Aiden growled.

I hadn't realized Aiden was so passionate about baseball. "Fine. I'm committed. Now, what do you want?"

"You to be here for the deal. Since that won't happen, I'll settle for a few conditions," he said.

"Spit it out." Lisa could come out of the bathroom at any second.

"Forty percent of the profit. Two sections that are free for the homeless, and my brother Derek to manage," Aiden replied.

"No, what's the dollar amount?" I wasn't giving him part ownership.

"Bro, that's why I called. He doesn't want any money." Ethan grabbed the phone. "It's your call."

"Fuck." I didn't have time for this.

"Tristan, do you think we can stop at the store? I need panties," Lisa called out.

I tried to cover the mic.

"Dude, a woman? You took off for a woman? If Adam hears about this, he'll tell his grandparents," Ethan whispered.

"Adam?" What was he talking about?

"I'll explain when you get back, too many ears. Be back before the wedding," Ethan snapped.

"Chill. Put Aiden back on." This conversation was falling off the tracks.

"Decide," Aiden demanded.

"Thirty-five percent. One section for the homeless. I'll only deal with Derek if Jason is around to keep him grounded." It was well known Derek didn't take anything seriously.

"Deal."

"Ethan will work out the paperwork. I'll sign it when I get back." I clicked off the phone.

Lisa was sitting on the sofa, arms spread wide, smiling at me. She was causing me way too much trouble. This was supposed to be a simple drop-off. Not a babysitting trip.

She jumped up and clapped her hands together. "Ready?"

I sighed and grabbed my keys off the table. One more day. I would give her one more day. If she didn't go to the rehab center tonight, I would leave her here. She had been enough of an interruption. Missing the meeting was bad enough, I couldn't miss the wedding.

Not to mention I missed Joseph. I tried to never be away from him for too long. At times when it was unavoidable, we texted all day long. He filled me in on how well his swimming was coming along and how much he loved Ava's family.

Lisa grabbed my hand and pulled me outside. I yanked my hand away. This wasn't some fun family outing.

I clicked open my car to drive her to the heart of the city to a restaurant. She took my keys and locked the car, then walked right past it. I shouldn't have been surprised that she already had a place in mind. It would be someplace that took forever and would potentially stall her going to the rehab until tomorrow.

No one paid attention to us as we walked. She appeared to be a normal older woman walking with her friend or son. At my request, she wore long sleeves to cover her tattoo and track marks. Her face was still pockmarked, but she had enough makeup to cover that up. The only thing she couldn't fix were her teeth. They were broken, brown, and barely stayed in her face. If she completed rehab, I would get her into a good dentist.

She turned a corner and kept walking with determination in her step. How did she know where she was going? I had assumed she looked up close restaurants, but we had been walking for a few minutes. Fuck, was I allowing her to go to a drug deal?

"Where are we going?" I grabbed her arm and spun her around.

"Relax, Tristan, it's a surprise." She grabbed my other hand and looked into my eyes.

Her daughter had the same eyes. Big brown eyes as dark as the demons hiding inside them. When I first met Ashley, I had drowned in those eyes. I fell hard for her. Believed everything she told me. Even when she said she didn't need help, I listened. She got worse, and I didn't force her to get help.

Now, her mother was looking at me with those same eyes. I couldn't save Ashley, maybe I could save Lisa. "No, we are not going to some drug deal. You are getting the help you need. I will toss you over my shoulder if I have to."

"Oh, stop. We aren't going for drugs. I promise after this, you can take me to the rehab as long as you promise me something." Lisa kept a hold of me.

"What?" Her games were getting old.

"You call me daily. Visit me every week. And once I"m clean, I get to meet my grandson." Tears swelled in her eyes.

"I call twice a week and visit twice a month. Before you meet Joseph, you need to be clean for six months with no blocker medication. Nothing." I wagged my finger at her.

"Deal, now let's go. You are gonna love this surprise." Lisa turned and skipped down the street.

I had no intention of keeping the deal. There was no way she would be able to stay clean. She spent more than half her life high, she wasn't going to change now.

Lisa took a left, and a huge stadium stood in the distance. It was home to the Carolina Sharks.They were currently ranked number two in the professional baseball league. I took Joesph to a game last year. He just kept asking to drive to the beach for a swim.

Lisa did a little jig and waved both of her arms at the stadium. What was she doing?

"I've seen this place before," I sighed.

"Well then, let's go watch a game." She linked her arm in mine.

"Lisa, we can't just walk in. You need tickets." I looked at my watch. "The ticket office is closed and we aren't gonna pay a scalper two times the price of what a normal ticket would be."

"It's a good thing I'm Lisa Moore of Moore Tech. You know who provides the tech for all the security cameras and the jumbo screen?" She closed-mouth smiled.

"Moore Tech." I knew the answer, but how did she?

"Exactly. Of course, I didn't know that until I called. The manager was honored to give me two tickets on the first base-line." She skipped toward the entrance.

"When did you call?" I asked.

"While you were crying on the phone about buying land." She walked over to a security guard. "Lisa Moore."

"Ma'am, right this way. He escorted us inside and directly to our seats.

A minute later, a server came over to take our drink order. Lisa ordered us both sodas. I tried to protest, but she made a good point. If I was drunk, I couldn't drive her to the rehab center.

The game was amazing. Lisa asked questions and cheered when it was appropriate. She seemed genuinely happy, and it made me wonder when the last time she was happy. It had me hoping she stayed clean and got better.

Cameras floated in and out of the crowd. At one point, I had to swat one away. It got in our faces and plastered it on the jumbo screen. Instead of hiding from it, Lisa waved. Ugh. Luckily, they wouldn't show this in New Boston.

After a close game, the Sharks won. Lisa cheered louder than anyone in our section. An older gentlemen tried to her her number. I asked if he wanted to lose a hand, he didn't, so he left.

"Okay, you can take me to the Center." Lisa wrapped her arms around me. "Thank you for never giving up on me."

CHAPTER 24
Ava (Day 4)

"No, you aren't fighting in my club." Von furiously shook his head.

"You gotta be kidding," I snapped.

"Kid, you may be a fan favorite, but you ain't worth me being strangled by my own intestines." Von rubbed his neck.

"That doesn't make any sense." Felix scratched his head.

"Those elites came by a few days after her fight with Judith. Told me to close up shop until they gave the okay. Paid me a lot of money. Anyway, when they called and said I could open again, there was one condition." Von was extra fidgety.

"What was the condition?" I ground my teeth. The elites were Ethan and Tristan. They did this, why? Why stop me from fighting? A few days after my fight would have been before the auction. They hadn't even bought me yet, why would they stop me from fighting?

"The condition was never to allow you to fight again. If I did, they would strangle me with my insides." Von stepped away from us. "I like my insides."

"Those fuckers!" I couldn't believe they did that. Ethan

had told me The Underground might remain closed forever. This was what he meant. It would remain closed for me.

Two other places told us the same thing. I wasn't allowed to fight. Ethan was clever. He hit up the major rings. The ones that paid the most and had 'no death' rules we off-limits for me. Looked like I would have to see if Ethan got to the more sketchy places.

"Let's check out Ton-tons." I bolted down the street.

"Are you crazy?" Felix caught up to me. "They don't have death rules. They won't stop a fight if you're getting your skull stomped in."

"I need to fight." This was my thing, and Ethan was taking it away from me. It wasn't fair.

"Let's go to Peaks. I'll fight. Then tomorrow, you can talk to Ethan. He can tell Von to let you fight. It's safer." Felix grabbed me seconds before I walked into Ton-tons.

"Fine, but I will fight. No man gets to tell me what to do." I ground my teeth. I dealt with that from Brad for far too long.

We headed into Peaks, and it was crowded. Men and women were everywhere. I looked around for Tasha and her friends. Even in a crowded room, she was easy to spot. They were in the VIP section. It was a bunch of cushy recliners up high surrounded by glass with a personal server. From her viewpoint she would never see me. Not that it mattered. She didn't know Ethan would flip if he knew I was here. Not that I cared. He couldn't control me.

Felix and Sandy took off to sign up for the next available match. Von was the only owner I knew that prescheduled his fighters. Even then, he would switch things up if he thought he could get more money. Peaks owner Tree, just put anyone in that she wanted. She loved Felix, so he would probably be up next round.

Tree had a thing for men. All men. She wouldn't even allow

women to fight. I always thought it was because she couldn't bat her eyes at them and get them to grovel at her feet. Not that Felix ever did, but he was respectful and helped her around the club. Brad, on the other hand, she hated him. Tree was one of the few people who saw him for who he was. He fought for her before he became a manager. Then when he started managing me, he tried to convince her to let women fight. It was a nasty argument that got him banned for a little while.

Ugh, why was I thinking about Brad so much? The memories kept flooding back, and none of them were good. I shut my eyes to try and block out the memories, and one of the worst words played out in my head.

Rain drizzled down, leaving a misty dew on us. Brad shook his hair, and it flung water on my face. I laughed as I tried to wipe it off with my wet t-shirt. When that didn't work, I gave up, pulled off my wig, and tossed it in my gym bag. I didn't want it to get ruined.

Brad and I had just left Von's place. I had been matched up with someone twice my size, and I won! It was marvelous. I was still an amateur, yet I was doing well.

"Ya know I could manage you." Brad clasped my hand.

"That's not fair to Judy." I looked down. I didn't want him to think I didn't like his idea.

"Do you not want me to manage you? Would you rather Felix did it?" He pulled his hand away and sped up down the sidewalk. "I'm so stupid. I shouldn't have said anything."

"That's not it. Dottie manages me. You know I would rather have you than Felix." I spun him around to face me.

"Maybe we can talk to Big Booty Judy. If she doesn't mind, then I can help Dottie manage you." He averted his eyes. I knew he was worried I would say no.

"Stop calling her that." I playfully slapped his arm. "Okay, we can do that."

"What, she has a huge ass." He smiled. "Since you said yes, I have a surprise."

I hadn't actually said yes, but that's how he took it. Years later, I found out he told Judy and Dottie, I begged him to manage me. At the time, I thought he was being sweet and that his surprise was romantic.

We walked for a while in the rain. My bag was soaked and grew heavier with each step. I wanted to ask Brad to carry my bag, even for a little while. Since he had told me to leave it at Von's I knew what his answer would be. Had I known we would be out in the rain for so long, I would have listened to him.

When I was about to tell him I needed a break, he stopped. We were at a rickety old building covered in moss. Years ago, it may have been something special. Now it had a wall missing and bricks crumbling. During the war, a bomb must have hit it. The place was totally unsafe.

Brad pushed the fence back and ducked under the barbed wire. He couldn't be serious. No way did he think I was gonna go in there. Then he smiled. Even in the darkness, his smile glowed. I couldn't say no. Maybe I could have, but I wanted him to think I was cool.

A guy like him should have never been interested in someone like me. Everyone loved him. He was hot, kind, and always tried to help people. At least, that's how I used to see him.

"Isn't this dangerous?" I grabbed the fence to steady myself. Metal sliced my palm. After the fight I had, it just added to the cuts and bruises.

"Yes, you scared?" He led the way to the building.

Of course, I was scared. That didn't stop me from following him. We entered the building and climbed over tree roots to get to the stairs. Brad easily maneuvered himself through the rubble. With my bag slung to my back, I had a little bit of trouble. A few times, I slipped and scraped numerous parts of my body. I *inspected my nails. A few were chipped and broken. Fuck. I would have to shorten them all to match.*

After a few flights of stairs, he led me into a room. It had been cleared of debris and looked cleaner than anywhere else in the building. Candles littered the floor. Well, like five. A lantern was in the corner.

Brad made me wait while he lit the candles, spread out a blanket, and sat down on it. It was beyond romantic. I joined him on the blanket. He peeled off his wet t-shirt and tossed it to the side, then winked at me.

Woah. The candles, secluded area, the blanket, he couldn't think. I was a virgin. This was not about to happen. I stood to leave, and he pulled me back onto the blanket.

"Brad, I'm not ready," I whispered.

"Huh?" he gasped. "Ready for what?"

"Sex." I hated telling him no. We had talked about sex, I wanted to wait until marriage.

"Oh. This was to celebrate being your manager. I took off my shirt because it was wet." He pulled a flask from his pants and handed it to me.

"I'm sorry." I took the flask and took a sip. We barely drank, but every once in a while, it was fun to have a few sips.

"You know, I'm waiting until you are ready." He pulled a second flask out. "Take off your shirt, so it dries."

I listened to him and laid it onto the floor next to me. From the sound of rain pounding against the window, I didn't think it mattered. Our clothes were gonna be soaked when we left.

Brad got up and pulled another blanket from the corner. "It's freezing. I have to get out of these clothes."

"Aren't we gonna get wet when we leave?" I pointed to the window.

"Not if we wait it out." Brad took off his pants and boxers.

I had never seen a man fully naked, but I knew the concept of getting hard and shrinking when it was cold. He must have been really cold.

"Like sleep here?" I took a gulp from the flask so I would stop looking at him. Warmth filled my throat. It was pure moonshine.

"Yes, Judy is always in my tent. This way, we could have the night to ourselves." Brad finally sat down and covered himself with the blanket.

"Oh. I hope my sister doesn't worry." At least when I slept in his tent, my sister knew we weren't that far away. This place was secluded. We were all alone. A chill ran up my spine. I shouldn't have been scared to be alone with Brad. He was a good guy. I gulped down more of the moonshine.

"Come here." Brad pulled me into him and wrapped the blanket around both of us. "You gotta take these pants off. You're freezing."

I didn't want to. I had never been naked with Brad. We did some over the clothes stuff, but that was it. Instead of listening to my gut, I listened to Brad.

We stayed under the blanket finishing our flasks. My head spun. I was no longer cold. Brad's face swirled in and out of focus. The room was spinning. I grabbed onto Brad. He moaned in my ear. Huh?

Hands were all over me. I pushed. Brad was on me. I fought him. He didn't stop. I begged. He continued. He grabbed my face. His tongue slid down my throat, silencing me.

Darkness faded in and out. "Ava," he whispered.

"Ava."

I blinked.

The sun shone through the window.

"Ava." Brad touched my face.

I flinched.

"Ava." He turned my face toward his. "I love you."

"How can you say that?" Tears leaked from my face.

"I wasn't sure until last night. Then we made love." He kissed my nose. *"I was surprised you wanted to.*

What? My mouth dropped. That wasn't what I remembered. His hand held me down. The smell of moonshine. I looked over at the flasks. They were empty. Maybe he was right. Maybe we got drunk and made love.

"Ladies and Gentlemen, in this corner, we have Bambo the Rambo." Tree waved her hand toward a short, stocky man with bulging muscles. He growled.

"And in this corner, we have Feisty Felix." It wasn't the most creative name, but it worked.

The crowd cheered. Tasha slapped her friend and pointed to Felix. She jumped up and down while clapping. She really was fantastic.

"Supporting your boyfriend?" a voice whispered in my ear.

I froze.

The hair on the back of my neck prickled up. Bile rose. I held my breath.

"I don't get a kiss?" he asked.

I turned to him. He looked the same. I'm not sure what I thought he would look like. Maybe sad. I guess I hoped everything he did to me would eat away at him. That he would look affected by it. Although I knew better.

"Brad." I tried to keep my voice steady.

"Not even a hug?" He grabbed my arm. His fingers dug in.

Just like that, I was back to the scared woman. Tears stung my eyes. He had control again. "Brad."

"I love my name on your tongue. Want me to make you scream it again?" He squeezed tighter.

"I'm...I'm...getting married," I whispered.

"I heard that. It doesn't matter. They will never want you." His nails pushed into my arm.

"Please, Brad." I tried to pull my arm away.

159

"Look at you begging. You're pathetic. Do those losers who bought you know what you are?" The whisky on his breath crept up my nose.

"You're drunk, Brad. You're hurting me." I pleaded. He had broken through the skin. Blood dripped.

The room was filled with people, but no one paid attention. They were all cheering for the fight. I yanked my arm again, and he squeezed tighter. Fuck. I had to do something.

"Hurting you? You destroyed my life. Judy loves me, yet I can't love her back because of you. Because I love you." He pulled me closer to him. Our bodies were touching. "I came back for you and you enter a marriage auction. It's supposed to be me and you."

"It was never you and me." Tears dripped down my face.

His expression changed. His eyes dropped. He released my arm but kept his hand over the nail marks.

"Are you okay? Sorry, I bumped you. You took a nasty fall," he said loudly, accentuating his words.

A hand touched my back. I flinched.

"Hey girl, I didn't know you like fights." Tasha wrapped her arms around me. "You okay?"

"Yeah, she fell." Brad tipped his head to her. "I must run. It was a pleasure."

I opened my mouth to protest. Brad had already weaved his way through the crowd. I should have chased after him, bashed his head in. Told him enough with the death threats.

"Wow. He is hot!" Tasha squeezed my shoulders. "So cool you are here. I saw you and texted Ethan. He is on his way."

Fuck.

CHAPTER 25

Ethan (Day 4)

I PACED THE ROOM. MY FATHER SAT THERE watching me with his judgmental eyes. We had been arguing for the past few hours. Since my grandfather passed, there was no one to mediate between us. All decisions for Moore Tech had to be agreed upon. There was one, in particular, we couldn't agree on a resolution.

"You haven't even met her." I racked my hand across my face.

"I don't need to. She is seventeen," he retorted.

"She is highly intelligent and knowledgeable when it comes to technology. If we give her the proper training, she can become a great asset for Moore Tech." I flopped into my leather chair.

My father didn't understand the long-term goals. If we acquired someone like Dottie now, she would be loyal to the company. He only saw her for her economic status.

"I will not have a homeless person in my company or my family." He slammed his hand against my desk.

"And there it is." I ground my teeth. "This isn't about Dottie, this is about Ava."

"Do you have any idea what that will do to our reputation?" he asked.

"Ha. If your wife abandoning us and becoming a drug addict didn't tarnish our reputation, this won't," I quipped.

My father walked around the desk and grabbed me by my shirt. I stared him down. We were the same height. Had been since I was a teen, and that was the last time he laid his hands on me. Until today.

I latched onto his wrist and jammed my middle finger into his pressure point. He immediately released me. This could have been an excellent opportunity to educate him on what happens when someone touches me. Had he been someone else, I would have.

"Calm down, son. This is getting us nowhere." He sat back down as if he didn't attack me.

"Look, the bottom line is Grandpa forced me into a marriage. I chose Ava. End of discussion." I adjusted my tie.

"Like always, you make decisions just to piss me off." He opened his folder. "Can we get back to this? I don't have all night."

This was by far the most unproductive meeting to date. All we had to do was pick candidates for the Moore Tech internship. Three hours later and we hadn't agreed on anyone.

"Here is the deal. We need four. You pick two, and I'll do the same." I scratched my chin. "To make it interesting, we make a bet. Whichever person has a trainee drop out first owes the other a million."

My father pursed his lips. I had given him an opportunity to prove I was making a bad decision. In order to do that, he would have to allow a homeless person to take a position at our prestige company. If Dottie succeeded, she would be the first at any Tech company in America. My father was debating on if it was worth the risk.

After five minutes of silence, he sighed. I had him. He glared at me and nodded.

My choices were easy. Dottie Palmer and an eighteen-year-old kid named Manny Moon that just got accepted to Bale University. My father chose two nineteen-year-olds with perfect GPA's and stellar resumes. He didn't look beyond the paperwork to see the person. Not to mention his two candidates had highly connected last names. One was even Tasha's cousin.

"Finally." I clapped my hands. "If you'll excuse me, I have to go to the security room."

"For what?" My dad placed his folders in his briefcase.

"Not that you care, but someone is threatening Ava. I'm checking the cameras to see if someone has managed to get in. I'm also deciding where to put new cameras." I had told Ava her ex couldn't get in, but I didn't believe that.

The man was cunning. I sent Daryl out to find this Brad Busby. He came back empty-handed. He even checked the location where Felix said the tent was, it was gone. Brad either left or was hiding. I believed it was the latter.

I would scour every hour of footage to find out who was getting in and how. As an extra precaution, every square inch of this house would be equipped with new cameras. Whoever was threatening her would lose their life.

"I'll go with you. It's always fascinating to see our tech in action," My father followed me out of the room. "You know we could get the drones like they use at the games. Then we can program them to activate when they sense movement or heat detection."

I inclined my head toward him, acknowledging his well-thought-out idea. It had actually surprised me he was being valuable and not a hindrance. Knowing him, it was to observe his technology in a real-life application versus the sports arenas they are usually in.

Tristan's security room spanned the length of the house and was located in the basement. He had twenty-four house surveillance and had separate dormitories for each of his staff members on his security detail. Everything was meticulously placed and well-kept, as if they had a separate cleaning crew from the rest of the house.

The section that I was interested in had a wall covered in multiple television screens. They covered every square inch of the grounds. I glanced at the screens. Joseph was diving into the pool. He was really going to need to take a break from the water. Members of Tristan's staff mulled around and went about their day-to-day duties.

Ava wasn't on any of the screens which only meant she was inside the house. Tasha probably requested they take the meeting inside where she would have more table space. It was lovely that she was helping Ava, even if I was skeptical about her motives.

"What can I help you with?" Sam, the security guard, asked when he realized I was behind him. He wasn't very observant, considering that was the sole requirement of his job.

"I need footage from every day since Ava moved in." I crossed my arms.

"Particularly anything that shows someone entering or exiting that doesn't belong." My dad sat in the chair next to Sam. "Also, I would like to install more cameras inside the premise. Who is in charge?"

"All decisions like that gotta be run through Mr. miller. He has given you guys permission to review footage but nothing about installing anything." Sam sat up, straightening his spine.

I was on the verge of breaking his fingers when my phone buzzed.

TASHA

So cool you guys are here, come say hi!

Where???

Peaks. Are you not with Ava?

Aren't you planning the wedding with her at Tristans!

That was till I had to leave. Maybe that's not her.

Send a pic now!

Tasha sent a somewhat blurry photo. Ava's pink hair was a dead giveaway. Her back was to the camera, but whoever she was with was facing the lens. He had dark gelled-back hair and darker eyes. His hand was wrapped around her upper arm, which I was not fond of.

Led permeated my stomach. Rage shot through my veins. Without knowing it was him, I knew it was him. I would bathe in his blood. Not just because he carved his name into Ava but also because he had his hand on what was mine.

Brad would die.

"Pull up footage from the last hour," I ordered. As much as I wanted to rush out, I had to make sure there wasn't a mistake.

"Looking for anything in particular?" Sam clicked away at his computer.

"Ava leaving," I fumed.

Sam tapped on the screen. A recording of Ava played. Felix, Sandy, and Ava walked out of the mansion and down the driveway. I checked the time stamp. Two hours. They left over two hours ago, and I hadn't noticed. Fuck.

Tasha, I'm on my way.

If she was in danger, it was my fault. I should have never left her out of my sight.

"Sam, pull all the footage and send it to my laptop. I must go." I had planned on staying here and watching them, but now I couldn't.

"Son, I'll check them. Go." My dad patted my back.

Odd. There was no time to ponder his impromptu change in behavior. Ava needed me.

My tires screeched in front of Peaks. I charged inside and found the nearest bouncer. I tossed him against the wall before he had a chance to blink. He wasn't a competent bouncer.

"Lock the door," I demanded.

"Huh?" he stammered. Piss trickled down his pant leg and hit my shoe. I dropped him. Not competent at all.

A swollen version of him wobbled over to me. He hefted up his belt several times as he approached me. I looked down at the man who had pissed himself. I couldn't have two scared bouncers.

"Sir, I need you to put the place on lockdown." I raised my hands to appear less threatening.

The moron pointed a stun gun at me. I did not have time for his incompetence. I charged him and grabbed him by the neck. While I had him swinging, I searched his waist for his radio. He gurgled something incoherent.

With his radio in hand, I clicked the side button. "This place is on immediate lockdown."

"Who is this?" a woman's voice asked.

"Ethan Moore! Any more questions?" I asked.

"Ethan, baby, it's me, Tree. You heard him. Everyone lock it down," she bellowed. "Anything else I can help you with?"

166

"I'm looking for someone, so no one leaves till I say so." I clicked off the radio and looked at the man gasping for air and the one covering his wet spot. I clicked the radio again. "You also might want medical assistance for your two slobs that guard the front door."

CHAPTER 26

Ava (Day 4)

SIRENS BLARED THROUGH THE CLUB. I COVERED MY ears which didn't do anything to dull the noise. *What the fuck!* Tasha had invited me to her VIP section to watch the fights. I figured since Ethan was on his way, I might as well be easy to find.

Felix won his fight, which because of Brad, I hadn't seen any of it. Felix and Sandy went to the locker room after and hadn't come out yet. Which meant he was probably entering another fight.

The next few matches I didn't pay attention to. Brad found me here. He had to have followed me. There was no way it was a coincidence. He found me and was letting me know.

The sirens continued. What was going on? Tasha linked her arm to mine and pulled me to my feet.

"I have to find Felix and Sandy!" I shouted.

Tasha pointed at her ears.

"Felix and Sandy!" I shouted.

She pointed at her ears again and shrugged.

Everything went silent. I couldn't hear. Tree stood in the

middle of the ring with a microphone. Her mouth was moving, but all I heard was ringing in my ears.

I went to leave when Tasha yanked my arm. She shook her head then pointed at my seat. What was she trying to tell me?

Before I could figure it out, a tall man with tattoos on his hand entered the ring and stood next to Tree. Ethan. Shit. He grabbed the microphone from Tree.

The ringing in my ear dissipated while he was speaking.

"...leave unless I have given you permission," Ethan roared into the mic.

I was close enough to see the blacks of his eyes, the scowl spread across his face, and the twitch of his jaw. He was pissed.

"Miss Ava Palmer, approach the stage," he demanded.

I stood still.

"Miss Ava Palmer." He searched the crowd.

I took a step back and hit the chair. Fuck.

"Ava, what are you doing?" Tasha whispered.

"Not going up there. Have you seen his face? He looks like he wants to torment and torture someone." I shook.

"So you want to make it worse?" She nudged me.

"Damn, Grim Reaper doesn't scare me as much," I mumbled.

"You have till I count to three!" He held up his fist.

What could he possibly do?

"One!" He ticked one finger up.

He was being ridiculous.

"Two!" He ticked up his second finger.

I shuffled down the aisle. Tasha let out a sigh of relief. I was pretty sure Ethan would never do anything bad to me. That didn't mean I wanted to test that theory.

As I walked toward the ring, every head turned in my direction. This was not the type of attention I wanted when I was in the ring. I enjoyed cheers and hollers.

Ethan locked eyes with me. The darkness faded from his

eyes. He handed the mic to Tree and strode over to me. As I grabbed the rope, he grabbed my hand. He pulled me into him. His hand was in my hair. His lips crushed into mine. I was spinning. He deepened the kiss. Everyone faded away. It was just us.

I wrapped my arms around him. He kissed me as if air wasn't important. Breathing didn't matter, only we did. Hunger fed the passion. My hands gripped him. His hand tightened around my hair, keeping me steady.

"Ladies and Gentlemen, Ethan Moore and his fiancé, Ava Palmer," Tree announced over the mic.

"Yea!" Tasha screamed.

Everyone else joined in. The club clapped and cheered. That was the attention I craved, being loved. That was why I enjoyed fighting so much. It was standing in the middle of the ring while everyone cheered for you. Now, I was getting the same attention for kissing my man.

Ethan pulled away and cupped my face, "You okay?"

"I'm fine." I choked back the tears.

"I will find him." Ethan pulled me in for a hug and kissed the top of my head.

I didn't ask how he knew or who he was talking about. Somehow Ethan knew Brad was here. If we were lucky, Brad wouldn't have had the chance to sneak out before Ethan showed up. When it came to Brad, I didn't have much luck.

"We are gonna search every person here until we ascertain him. Then, I'll execute him." A growl started in the back of his throat. "When we get home, I'm going to bend you over my knee and spank you for putting yourself in jeopardy."

My pussy throbbed. I wanted him to do that immediately. Why wait until we go home? He had to have realized that wasn't a deterrent.

"I want to fight. You can't stop me." I crossed my arms.

"We can dispute that later. I don't want you to get injured

like you already did." He pointed to my arm. "What owner allowed you to fight?"

"Huh?" I hadn't been allowed to fight because of him.

He grabbed my arm and removed the scarf that Tasha had tied around it. I had completely forgotten about it. The nail marks from Brad.

"That wasn't from a fight," I whispered. I don't know why I was afraid to tell him, but I was. Maybe because it proved him right that I shouldn't have left the house.

"Where did it come from?" The growl in his throat grew louder. If werewolves were real, I would have been convinced he was about to shift.

"Brad." I averted my eyes.

Ethan turned and grabbed Tree by her shirt. She was three times as wide as him, and he moved her like she was a feather. A smile hit the corners of her lips. If I was the jealous type, that would have bothered me...a lot.

"Order every person in this room to line up." He released her.

Minutes later, bouncers wrangled everyone into the room. Felix and Sandy came in and lined up. Ethan instructed the staff the bring them and Tasha over to us. It was amazing how quickly everyone moved about without any complaints.

"Ava, we are going to inspect every person here." Ethan grabbed my hand. "If Brad is still here, all you have to do is nod. I will rip his soul from his body. I have distributed his picture to my security. It's blurry, but it should be enough. We will locate him."

We weaved in and out of the crowd. Every male with dark hair was pushed to their knees, so Ethan knew I got a good look at them. Felix, Sandy, and Tasha stayed close to us. They all knew what he looked like, so they acted as extra sets of eyes.

Two hours later and we had checked everyone three times. Brad must have snuck out before Ethan arrived. Everyone was aggravated and begging to go home. After breaking a radio and a few doors, Ethan agreed.

True to his word, Ethan had me bent over his knee in his bedroom. He had a grin the entire walk to his room, so I knew he wasn't actually going to spank me. At least not hard.

"Drop your shorts." Ethan licked his lips.

My pussy throbbed. I pulled off my shorts and bathing suit bottom in one swoop. I was already soaked.

Ethan sat on the edge of the bed and patted his lap. I skipped over to him and laid across his knees. He let out a growl as he rubbed my ass. Fuck. My heart raced. My body was on fire. I bit my lip, waiting for him to begin.

His firm hand gave me a little pat. I moaned. He hit me again, slightly harder this time. I wiggled my ass. He slapped a tad harder. The smack vibrated my pussy.

"You have been a bad girl." Another smack.

"I told you I wanted to fight." Yeah, I was purposely trying to piss him off. This role-play was hot.

"I told you that you don't need to fight." he slapped harder. That one stung. "Do you enjoy defying me?"

If this was the punishment, then yes. "You don't control me."

He smacked my ass so hard the noise echoed in the room. My pussy dripped. "You are mine, Peach."

I reached my hand between his legs and grabbed his cock. He was rock-hard. My being defiant was turning him on. "You don't own me."

He ran his hand along my pussy. Fuck. I bucked my hips up, begging for more. He slapped me again. This time my pussy juices made the noise louder. "You are so naughty."

I unzipped his pants. He moaned. Ethan was about to

learn how naughty I could be. Freeing his cock, I gasped. My mouth was not going to fit around that. I licked the tip.

"Fuck, you gonna be a good girl and wrap that pretty mouth around my dick?" Ethan intertwined his fingers in my hair.

"You gonna let me fight?" I swirled my tongue around the head of his dick.

"No." He pushed my head onto his cock.

I wrapped my lips around his shaft. He barely fit. Bobbing up and down, I sucked hard. Every time I ran my tongue along his tip, he moaned. Never had I been so turned on sucking a cock.

He pushed down harder. I gagged. "That's right. Be a good girl and choke on my cock."

The door creaked open. I didn't care, there was no way I was stopping. I jerked his shaft, and I sucked. My hand didn't fully grasp his dick. There was no way my pussy could handle it.

A finger slid up and down my slit. I moaned against his cock. Fuck, please make me cum. He spanked me again, hard. Ouch. My ass stung.

"You like that pussy, brother?" Ethan asked.

Huh? I pulled back and turned my head. Tristan was standing behind me. My mouth dropped.

He stuck his finger in his mouth. "Mmm, she tastes so good."

CHAPTER 27

Tristan (Day 4)

THE PLANE SHOOK AS IT LANDED. I HATED FLYING. No matter what anyone said, it was unsafe. Had I not left Lisa my car, I would have driven back. She begged me for it.

On her twenty-eighth day of being in the program, she would get weekend leave. Lisa promised she would only use it to go into town. Did I trust her? No, but I wanted her to succeed. She deserved a chance.

Daryl waited for me outside the airport. He didn't ask any questions. He had a jist of what was going on, but I didn't give him all the details.

"Update me on the house." I climbed into the backseat. Mostly, I was asking about Ava, but he didn't need to know that.

"Joseph has grown quite attached to Ava's family. His dive time has gotten faster, and his hitting average has gotten lower. It's not my place, but his heart isn't in baseball." Daryl drove off and headed for home.

I cleared my throat.

"Right, anyway. There have been no leads on who is

threatening Ava. Tonight she snuck out and went to fight," Daryl kept both hands on the wheel.

"Is she okay?" Anger flooded my veins. What was she thinking?

"Not sure. Ethan brought her home, and her arm was bandaged." Daryl pulled into the driveway.

"Did Ethan say anything?" I clenched my fists. How had he not informed me of this?

"I didn't ask, I was on my way to get you." Daryl stopped the car.

I hopped out and stormed into the house. Yes, the marriage was for Joseph's benefit. That didn't mean I wanted her harmed. The entire time I was gone, she was on my mind. It was solely because I was worried about her. Someone had been sneaking into my house and threatening my fiancé. That was not allowed. Whoever it was would pay with their life.

Controlling my breathing, I went to Joseph's room first. No matter what, he would always be my first priority. He was snuggled up in his bed, sleeping. I tucked the covers around him and went in search of Ava.

Dottie jumped out of bed when I opened her door. "Hello?"

"Is Ava in here?" I asked.

"Nope." She had been sleeping but kept the light on.

"Sorry." I shut the door.

Ava wasn't with her mother either. She didn't even budge when I opened her door. I tried Felix and Sandy's room. It was locked. After a few minutes and lots of giggling, Felix came to the door.

"Hey, you're back. What's up?" He kept the door closed enough so I couldn't see into the room.

"Where's Ava?" I stepped back.

"With Ethan, I think." He shrugged.

As I walked away, I heard Sandy say, 'Get back here, big daddy.'

Ethan wasn't in his office. I sighed, this late at night, he would be in his room. He never slept, and as far as I knew, neither did Ava. At least I wouldn't be waking them. Once I made sure Ava was alright, I would get some sleep. Hopefully.

I opened the door. Fuck, I should have knocked. It hadn't crossed my mind that they would be doing anything. The wedding wasn't till this weekend, so I assumed Ethan would wait.

Ava gagged on Ethan's cock. She stroked it as she sucked. My dick pressed against my zipper. I should have turned around and left. I didn't belong here.

Ethan pushed her further onto his cock. I stepped forward. Her bare ass was red, as if he had just spanked her. My hand twitched.

It would be fine to watch. Soon she would be my wife. I made an agreement I wouldn't fuck her. Watching was different.

Ethan locked eyes with me. He grinned. Of course, he would be cool with me watching. He pointed to her pussy.

She dripped onto his pant leg. Fuck, she was so wet. I ran my finger along her pussy.

She moaned.

Shit, I shouldn't have done that. I wanted more.

Ethan spanked her hard. "You like that pussy, brother?"

Ava turned to look at me. I should have left. Her eyes glowed with desire. I needed to taste her.

I stuck my finger in my mouth. "Mmm, she tastes so good."

"Do you want him to lick that pussy while you suck my cock?" Ethan asked Ava.

I tried to leave. My feet wouldn't move, I needed to hear her answer.

"You wouldn't be mad?" Ava looked up at him.

That was enough for me. I dropped to my knees.

"Not at all. Be a good girl and cum for Tristan." Ethan pushed her head back onto his cock.

Ava lifted her ass up to give me better access. I dove in. Fuck, she was sweet. I licked her slit as she moaned. I grabbed her hips and lapped her up. The last time I tasted a pussy was too long ago. Ava was perfect.

Every time I made her moan, she gagged on Ethan's cock. I needed to fuck her. No, I couldn't. This was far enough. I released my cock. With one hand, I gripped her hip, with the other I stroked my dick.

I wouldn't fuck her, but I had to cum. With each one of her moans, I pumped my dick. Shit, I was already so close. Slowing down, I concentrated more on her. She rocked her ass up and down, moving in rhythm with my mouth.

Ava's moans grew louder, yet still muffled by Ethan's cock. I had never shared a woman before. It had 't occurred to me how intoxicating it could be. Hearing Ava choke on another man's dick was driving me wild.

"You gonna swallow my cum, Peach?" Ethan moaned.

"P...pl...please," her voice was garbled.

Shit.

I sucked her clit between my lips. She reached her hand back and grabbed my hair. I sucked harder. Ava was getting close.

Pumping my dick quicker, I ate Ava. Part of me didn't want her to finish. I wanted to keep her on edge. Leave her in ecstasy for a while. She gripped my hair tighter. Her moans grew louder.

It was time to give her release. I flicked my tongue against her clit. Her body tensed I didn't stop.

"I'm coming!" she shouted.

Ava rode out her orgasm on my face. I picked up the pace

of stroking my cock until I was about to cum. *I could shove my dick in her and cum inside her tight pussy.*

I stopped myself from standing. Grabbing her ass, I pumped out the cum. It hit the floor. Once I was done, my stomach turned. I shouldn't have done that.

"You ready?" Ethan asked.

I stood and stepped back. Ethan pushed Ava deeper onto his cock as his eyes rolled back. She gagged. He moaned and released her.

Ava stumbled backward. Cum dripped from her lip. I hardened again.

No.

She licked her lips.

Fuck.

I stepped back again.

This had to stop.

I put my dick away and turned to leave. This was wrong, but fuck, it felt marvelous.

"You don't have to leave," Ethan called out to me.

"I just came to make sure Ava was okay. I heard she was bandaged." I gripped the door knob. "She is more than okay."

"There was a run-in with my ex," Ava whispered.

"I'm handling it," Ethan grunted.

I nodded and opened the door. Sighing, I shut the door and turned. "Ava, I'm sorry. I crossed the line. I shouldn't have done that."

She stood there in only a top. Her pussy was uncovered and begging for more. Fuck, I wanted her.

"We are both marrying her in a few days. It wouldn't be wrong for us to both have her." Ethan grabbed her by the neck and kissed her. "You are welcome to join us."

"What happened to your possessiveness?" I asked. Ethan was clear that Ava was his, yet he was trying to share her.

"Oh, I am. She is mine, but watching you please her

turned me on," Ethan stroked her hair. "She deserves the world, and we can give it to her."

Would it be so wrong? This wasn't about love. It was a sexual desire. A need to bury my cock inside her pretty cunt.

"That was fun. We could do more of that." Ava chewed on her lip.

I looked at the bed. She had been so scared her first night here. Sleeping under the bed with her hadn't been about desire, that was about caring for her. I wouldn't allow myself to fall for her.

"I'm sorry. This was a one-time thing." I opened the door and left.

CHAPTER 28

Adam (Day 5)

BOOM. BOOM.

I jumped out of bed. The house didn't rattle, so it wasn't a bomb, At least not one that hit the house. Rubbing the sleep from my eyes, I looked out the window. Still nighttime.

Bri barged into the room in his boxers. "Someones' here."

Huh?

Knock. Knock.

"Oh, it was knocking, not something exploding." My dreams had turned a normal noise into something unnatural.

Brian waved me on as he went to the front door. Since he hadn't bothered to get dressed, neither did I.

Years I went without anyone disturbing me. One week of Ava and my life was flipped upside down. I had to find a way to get rid of her, or this would never end.

The cuckoo clock by the door rang four a.m. Seriously, what was wrong with people? I flung open the door before they could knock again.

"Help, we had nowhere else to go." Judith had her arm around Brad's waist.

Blood and mud were smeared all over Brad. I could barely

tell it was him. As if on cue, the clouds opened up, and rain poured down.

I didn't have time for this shit. I wasn't some rescue clinic for the homeless. Judith gave me big pleading eyes. Nope, I pushed the door.

Brian grabbed the door and flung it all the way open. In one fell swoop, he picked up Brad. He carried him into the living room and set him on my sofa. Great, the blood was never gonna come out of the fabric.

Judith knelt in front of Brad, stroking his hair. "It's gonna be okay."

"What happened?" Brian pulled a blanket from the chest in the corner and tossed it on Brad.

"Ethan Moore stabbed me," Brad groaned.

"Why would he do that?" I asked him, then turned to Brian. "Call Nurse Damar and tell him to come here." I didn't want a dead homeless person in my house.

"Why else? Ava. I went to Ton-tons to check out the competition for Judith. Ava was there. I tried to escape." Brian coughed.

"He hunted him down and stabbed him." Judith wiped away a tear. "Brad had to crawl to me. I had to take him somewhere."

Taking him here seemed a little odd to me. Even though I couldn't stand Ava, she was my fiancé. Her enemies were knocking on my door, asking for help. How did they know she wasn't here?

"Risky coming here." I sucked my teeth. If Ethan did stab him, he should have disposed of him.

"I didn't want to bother you. Judith insisted." Brad groaned.

I got up to get him some towels. He was a mess and destroying my sofa. I didn't want blood to drip onto my rug.

Brian hadn't kept up with the laundry. Probably because

of how busy our week had been. I went to the laundry and grabbed a few dirty towels.

When I walked back in, Judith and Brad were whispering.

"Why did you say Ton-tons? You were at Peaks," Judith whispered.

"Uh. Can we trust him? No, so we can't tell him the truth," Brad whispered back.

I cleared my throat and entered the room. Why would where the interaction take place matter? Judith took the towels and began to clean Brad. Her eyes glowed when she looked at him. She was still in love with him. Brad glared at her, the feeling wasn't mutual. The second he noticed me looking at him, his face softened.

Brian entered the room. "Damar is on his way."

"Thank you. Can you get pants and a shirt for me?" We hadn't gotten dressed. "And yourself."

"Oh, sorry, Miss Judith." Brian covered his privates and left.

Nurse Damar was so quick to show up, I had just tossed my shirt on. Damar walked in without knocking. As soon as he saw Brad, he opened his bag and got to work. "What happened?"

"We were at The Underground when a man stabbed me." Brian grabbed his side and pulled his knees up to his chest.

Damar disinfected his wound while Judith cleaned the mud off of him. Brian squashed around, getting drinks and cookies. Washing down a chocolate chip cooking with a rum and coke at four in the morning wasn't my idea of breakfast, but it worked.

Ring. Ring.

There was no way someone was calling me in the middle of the night. I wanted my secluded life back.

Ring. Ring. Brian handed me my phone. "It's Grandpa."

Seriously?

I grabbed the phone and walked away. "It's the middle of the night."

"The world doesn't stop, Adam," my grandfather said.

"What can I help you with?" I asked.

"It's me who can help you," he replied.

"And?" It was too early for his mind games.

"I have a friend inside Miller Manor, he has given me some valuable information." He paused for effect. "There is a rumor that Tristan Miller plans to never touch Ava Palmer."

"What's your point?" I was too tired to try and connect the dots.

"Let me make this simple, Adam. Get proof, and your grandmother and I will let you out of the contract."

"What?" My head spun. "How? That doesn't even make sense." I knew the contract. Tristan not fucking her wouldn't help me.

"Tristan Miller is in the process of acquiring land I want. If you can get proof that he won't touch her, I can use that to get him to back down. As a thank you, we will let you out of the contract." My grandfather whispered into the phone as if someone would overhear him.

"Wait, I beg you to let me out of the contract, and you say no. Now, you want something, and the tables turn." I sucked my teeth and pinched the brim of my nose.

"Yes." He had me, and he knew it. "I need video and audio of him turning her down."

Shit. Let me add this to the list of issues Ava Palmer had caused me. "I'll get it done."

"Good, they sign the deal Friday. I need it before then. Grandma said she loves you." He hung up the phone.

Did he say Friday? There was no way. A day. He was giving me a day.

I stormed back into the room and paced. They were all concentrating on Brad. He groaned at all the right times. Judith fawned over him at every moment she could. A few times, Damar pushed her out of the way so he could sew Brad up.

Something was off, and it wasn't just my grandparents having me blackmail Tristan. It was Brad. I wasn't sure why, but I didn't buy his story. Out of pure curiosity, I would find out what really happened.

"Brian, do you still have that friend that drives limos?" I had a plan.

"Yeah, you don't want me to drive?" He averted his eyes.

"It's not for me." I assured him. "Brad are you up for working tonight?"

"The cut is pretty deep," he whispered.

"It's not that deep." Damar cut the thread he had used to sew him up. "I can give you pain meds to ease the pain."

"Perfect, I need you at work. I'll call Tara and put you on." I pulled out my phone to text my sister.

"What do you need?" Brian asked, defeated.

"I'll be there with Ava and her other men. I need you to bug the table and wear a camera." I wanted as much proof against Tristan MIller as possible. I would goad him into admitting he wouldn't fuck Ava. As an added touch, I was gonna bug the limo that took them. Before I went to sleep tonight, I would be out of the marriage.

"Her men? Ethan would attack him again," Judith gasped.

"Not with me there." There was another reason I wanted Brad there. I didn't believe Ethan stabbed him and let him live. I wanted to see how Ethan, Brad, and Ava interacted together.

Damar stood and collected his things. "You're all set." He nodded toward the door for me to walk him out.

As soon as we were out of earshot, Damar whispered, "Something's up."

"What do you mean?" I knew that, but how did he?

"The cut looked self-inflicted with his right hand." Damar opened the door and left.

CHAPTER 29

Ava (Day 5)

FEATHERS FLOWED AROUND MY WAIST DOWN TO MY ankles as I twirled in the dress. Frizzo brought several options for me to try on. So far, I hadn't wanted to take off the first one. Somehow it fit perfectly. The thin straps and bust were flawless. I had wanted a champagne color, or so I thought. This was true white.

"Frizzo, you have outdone yourself." Tasha kissed him on the cheek.

"You didn't give Frizzo much to work with, but Frizzo says a blank canvas is better than a broken one." Frizzo kissed her back. He was over six feet tall and as thin as a broomstick.

"I love it." I twirled, ignoring his quip about me being blank.

"Would you like to try on another?" Tasha asked.

I looked at Dottie and Sandy. My mother was busy with Joseph.

"Do you feel like this is the one?" Dottie took a sip of wine.

Tears filled my eyes. It was so real. I was marrying Ethan. I couldn't believe how badly I had misjudged him when I first met him. He was perfect, dreamy, and sexy.

"Still weird you have to marry three men." Tasha sat beside Dottie. "I mean, cool and all, but the glitch was weird."

"Yeah, but it's only five years, right?" Plus, the glitch gave me Ethan.

"Unless one of them knocks you up. Frizzo could never handle that many men." Frizzo fussed with the feather. "I mean, okay, Frizzo did once, but that was in college."

"I'm on birth control. I couldn't handle Adam for that long. He is such an ass." I grabbed the wine from Dottie and chugged it.

"What's his deal anyway?" Dottie took the glass back. "He is odd. One minute he is saying dirty things to you, and the next letting you know he can't stand you."

"I think the filthy things he says are to get under Ethan's skin, not mine. They have some sort of history, I just know it." I chewed my lip. Adam was a jerkface.

"Miss Palmer, a package has arrived for you." CeCe entered the room with a small box.

It was wrapped in pink with a white bow. Stuck under the ribbon was a note.

Speak of the devil.

Ava,

Something so you can tell me how much you want me. Something to wrap around that pretty throat. And something for that little pussy. A limo will pick you up at six tonight.

Adam

I wanted to chuck the package at the wall. He was such an

arrogant asshole. Ethan would flip if he saw the note. Luckily he wasn't allowed in the room while I picked out my dress.

With all the threats I had previously received, I expected the box to be filled with blood. I still wasn't convinced Adam wasn't involved. Surprisingly the first thing in the box was a cell phone. I tapped the screen. It was a picture of his dick as the background. Damn, it took up the whole screen. I tilted the screen down, so Dottie didn't see.

The next was a pearl necklace. I smiled. Dick pic aside, the necklace was beautiful. I looked in the box to see what he sent for my pussy. The only thing left was a thin chain with a silver heart charm. Huh? Did he send two necklaces?

Tasha grabbed the note and the box. Dottie held up the pearls. They had two strands, and one hung from the middle of the first.

"Those are underwear, Sweetie." Frizzo pointed at the pears.

"Huh?" Dottie and I asked simultaneously.

"He's right. See, for your pussy." Tasha pointed at the note. "The pearls rub against your clit. Cum in an instant."

Dottie dropped the pearl panties and stepped back. My face was on fire. Adam had a lot of nerve. He couldn't expect me to wear those.

Buzz. Buzz.

ADAM

Like my gifts?

No. You have a small dick.

You won't say that when you're riding it.

You are so vile.

So? See you tonight. Bring your men.

I set the phone on the table.

"That's a huge dick!" Dottie gasped.

I sighed. "Can you just take it off my background?"

Dottie nodded and started clicking away at the phone.

"Can Frizzo get back to what Frizzo does best?" Frizzo took the necklace from the box and clasped it around my neck.

The heart sat right above my breasts. It was beautiful. Adam had good taste, even if he was a jerk.

Dottie grunted, "He has it locked. I'll have to take it to my room to try and hack it. Come by later and pick it up." She got up and left.

"No. No. Frizzo must fit her for a bridesmaid dress." Frizzo stomped his foot when he realized Dottie had left.

"I'm sure you can do it without her." Tasha grabbed his shoulders.

"Of course, I can. I'm Frizzo." Frizzo ran around the room going through the trunks he had brought over.

Hours later, Frizzo announced he was done. Sandy had a light purple dress that hung to her calves. Dottie had a navy blue dress that complimented the purple one. It was going to be the perfect day.

Tasha insisted on me staying with her to make other decisions. Weddings took a lot of work. "I'll be back. I want to see if Dottie fixed the phone." I also wanted to check my room to see if there was another bloody letter.

Ethan had me moved into another room. Even after my room was cleaned, I couldn't be in there. Since I got a letter from Adam, I had a feeling there would be another threatening note covered in blood.

I raced down the hall. If Ethan found out the fitting was over, he would come looking for me. I didn't want him to know Dottie was hacking my phone to remove a dick pic from

Adam. He may have been fine with Tristan eating my pussy, but he didn't like Adam.

Bam. Ouch. I ran smack dab into Mr. Moore.

"Are you homeless and blind?" he spat.

"Neither are a negative!" I shot back.

"Well, you are." He adjusted his suit jacket.

"Your son doesn't think so." I turned on my heels.

"Ha, if you only knew the reason he's marrying you." Mr. Moore chuckled down the hall.

I froze. What did he mean by that? Bile rose. I had been falling so hard I hadn't stopped to think why he was marrying me. Did Ethan not feel the same way about me?

Wiping a rogue tear, I went into my room. I would figure out what Ethan's dad meant, but first, I had a few things to do. I scanned the room. Yup, lying on my bed was a single piece of paper.

You had a chance.

It had to be Adam. I wasn't sure what his endgame was, but I was sure it was him. The only other explanation was Adam and Brad were in cahoots together. It was unlikely, but not impossible. Brad had a way with people, they all thought he was fantastic.

I tossed the note in the drawer and headed to Dottie's room. Somehow I would find proof Adam was behind the threats. Maybe that would be enough to get me out of the contract with him. Threats had to be considered physical abuse and against the contract.

"Any luck?" I asked Dottie when she opened her door.

"Yeah. It's off there." Dottie shut her laptop.

"I need another favor." I grabbed the phone off her desk.

"Of course. Oh, I got the internship for Moore Tech. I

know getting married wasn't an easy decision for you. And you have to be married to all three men, but thank you. I never imagined such a life." Dottie hugged me.

I chewed my lip. Her speech made what I was about to ask even harder. "I need you to investigate the glitch. Find out who set it up for me to be purchased by multiple people. I also need you to see if any of the servants know why Ethan bought me." I didn't want to prod. The marriage auction changed my life for the better. I should have looked at it as a blessing and moved on. I couldn't.

"Why? Look at it as a good thing and move on. I see how you look at Ethan. If the glitch was intentional, it could ruin everything. So what? Why does it matter why Ethan bought you? He did, and you two are happy. Leave it be." Dottie sighed.

"Don't you think it's odd I met Tristan and Ethan at a fight with Judy? Then, a week later, the fights closed down." My stomach turned. "I get invited to the auction, then the kicker, there's a glitch. Tell me this is all coincidence. Not to mention Brad is back in town."

"It could all be a miracle. A gift from fate." Dottie shrugged.

"Do you really think that?" I asked.

"So it's odd. Ask Ethan about it," she said.

"I would, but what if it's true and he lies." I flopped onto the bed. It shouldn't have bothered me, but it did.

"Look, I get it. The whole thing is hinky. Maybe they did set it up, maybe Adam is in on it. Who cares? They helped us. If I look into it, there is a chance the auction board will find out. Then, no marriage, and boom, we suffer. Everything gets ripped away." Dottie racked her hand across her face. The worry that had been gone for days was back.

I should have let it go. The glitch was the best thing that happened to me. Well, If I exclude Adam. He was the part that really bothered me. If it was just Ethan and Tristan, I could ignore the coincidences. It wasn't. In two days, I would also be marrying Adam. That was a problem. He was awful.

"If we can find the glitch, we could tie it to Adam. Then I would get out of the contract with him." I didn't want to marry that asshole.

"So you want me to track down the glitch and recode it, so it links to Adam?" Dottie tapped her chin. "You'll let your suspicions of Ethan and Tristan go?"

"Well, I still wanna know why Ethan bought me." The rest was a great plan. Unless Ethan and Tristan were in cahoots with Adam, if they were, I didn't want any of them.

"No. That's the deal. I'll pin the glitch on Adam, no matter if it was random or someone did it. You marry Ethan and Tristan and let the conspiracy theory of them two go." Dottie stuck out her hand.

"Deal," I lied and shook her hand.

CHAPTER 30

Ava (Day 5)

AT PRECISELY SIX O'CLOCK, A LIMO PULLED UP IN front. Tristan and Ethan were both in black suits that accentuated their muscles. Tristan stayed a few feet away from me. Every time I looked at him, he looked somewhere else.

Tristan didn't even want to go. He figured Adam had a trick up his sleeve, and that was why Adam told me to bring them. Ethan agreed and said that's why they had to go. My stomach twisted, Adam was definitely up to something.

A tiny man with blue-black hair scuttled over to the passengers side of the limo and opened the door. I had expected Brian to come pick us up. He was actually a very sweet man, and I was a little sad he wasn't there.

"Something's up," Ethan whispered as he helped me into the limo.

As soon as we were in, my phone buzzed.

"What's that?" Ethan cut his eyes at me.

"Adam sent me a phone." I clicked it open.

ADAM

Did you wear the pearl panties?

No

"He sent you a phone and underwear?" Tristan moved next to me to read the texts. "Odd."

"Yeah, I don't like it. One minute he is being nice, the next, he is being an ass." I could get whiplash from his mood swings.

We are gonna have fun.

Doubtful

Listen to my instructions, and you will.

I tilted my phone to Ethan so he could read it. Although Adam's words were playful, my skin crawled.

"I think this is some sort of setup. Do as he says." Ethan's voice was below a whisper. Was he afraid someone was listening?

Ready?

Sure

Tell one of them to lick that pussy of yours.

What? I dropped the phone. Why would that be his instructions?

Tristan picked up the phone. His eyes widened as he read the text. I couldn't tell if it was excitement or horror. He handed me back the phone without a word.

I'm waiting.

I took a deep breath. "Ethan, lick my pussy."

My dress had a slit up the side that allowed me to spread

my legs slightly. I pulled it up the rest of the way. I had on a sheer pair of pantyhose and no underwear. I grabbed the pantyhose to pull them down.

Ethan grabbed my hand. "Leave them on, Peach."

He knelt between my legs and pushed them further apart. My pussy throbbed. His mouth hovered above my center. The heat from his breath was so close. I scooted forward some. He backed up, so he was still close but not touching.

> Anything?

> Yeah, what do you want, a play-by-play?

> Excellent idea.

The phone buzzed. Adam was face-calling me. What the heck? Did he think he was gonna watch me while Ethan ate me out? My pussy twitched at the idea.

I ignored the call.

> Answer.

"What's his game plan?" Tristan asked.

"I think I know. Here isn't the place to discuss it. All three of us need to do what he says." Ethan rubbed his mouth against my center.

"Fuck." I moaned,

Buzz. Buzz. Adam called back.

I answered as Ethan sucked my clit through the pantyhose. Shit, I was on fire.

"Look at that pretty face. Is he making you feel good?" Adam's face appeared on the screen.

I nodded.

"Aim the screen at your pussy." Adam demanded.

I did as he said. My face was red. This was a mixture of humiliation and sexualness. I hated him, but I didn't want this to end.

"Rip her pantyhose." Adam's voice hastened.

Ethan happily obliged, exposing my pussy. Cool air grazed my lips. A shiver ran up my spine.

"Ava, you ready for a dick in your mouth?" Adam asked.

Ethan dove into my center. I gasped. His tongue flicked up and down against my clit.

"Yes," I moaned. I wanted to suck Ethan's cock.

"Tristan, pull out your dick," Adam smiled.

We all froze. He knew. I didn't know how, but somehow he did. The other day Tristan ate me out, and hadn't been able to look at me since. He made a deal that he wouldn't have sex with me. Somehow Adam knew about it.

Tristan grabbed the phone. "How about you worry about where your dick goes and not mine."

Shit, he was gonna get us caught. Even if Adam knew, he had no proof. Tristan was about to give him the proof he needed.

I glanced around the limo. A few spots glistened. Cameras. That was his plan. He was gonna record Tristan turning me down. I had to do something. Ethan wasn't gonna like this.

"She is about to be our wife. I'm just making sure you can satisfy her." His eyes turned down, and his smile widened. Yup, this was a setup.

I bent down to Ethan and whispered," I'm sorry."

"Huh?" He scrunched up his face.

While Tristan argued with Adam, I unzipped his pants. He may have been mad at Adam, but he was rock-hard.

Before I could stop myself, I wrapped my lips around his cock. Ethan growled. Tristan gasped.

"You wanna watch me suck him? Is that it?" I grabbed the phone from Tristan.

I pulled the tip into my mouth and sucked hard. Tristan grabbed my hair to stop me. I sucked harder. Fuck he filled my mouth. My heart raced.

Tristan's fingers dug into my hair. I felt the moment he decided to stop fighting me and push me further onto his dick. I gagged.

Pulling back, I looked into the phone. "Happy? Did that prove your point? Tristan and I will be very sexual in our marriage. We still have time to consummate the marriage. Which we will and I will enjoy it. Unlike when I have to be with you. I will despise every second with you."

I jerked Tristan while I glared at the phone. "And I will never suck your dick."

To push the point home, I gave Tristan one last suck and let go.

"Wait," All three of them yelled.

I froze. What was wrong?

"I mean, you already started." Ethan grinned.

"Why stop?" Tristan grabbed my hair.

"Be a good girl and make him cum," Adam demanded.

I rolled my tongue over the tip of his dick. He moaned. Wrapping my lips around him, I sucked. Blowing him as Ethan watched was surreal.

Giving Tristan pleasure made me so wet. I pressed my legs together as I slid my tongue up and down his balls and then up to his tip. His dick was so big, I couldn't fit the whole thing in my mouth.

I stroked and sucked. He groaned and pushed my head down. His dick hit the back of my throat. My makeup ran down my face.

"That's it, suck him." Ethan came behind me and reached his hand between my legs.

"Good girl, suck his cock." Adam growled.

Oh shit, he was still on the phone. Tristan took the phone

from me. He must have angled it better because Adam groaned in approval.

Ethan rubbed my clit, and I bobbed up and down on Tristan. It wasn't long before the vibrations came. I was so close. Ethan slid a finger inside. Fuck, so close.

Tristan's legs tensed. He pushed his hips up and started fucking my throat.

Explosions erupted through my body as Ethan fingered me. I gasped as warm liquid hit my throat. Tristan shot hit load into my mouth. I swallowed every last drop.

When we were done, I leaned back into Ethan. He wrapped his hands around me and kissed the top of my head.

It took me a minute to catch my breath. By the time I did, the limo had come to a stop. I peeked out of the window expecting to see Adam's mansion. Instead, it was a restaurant with the words La Temp highlighted above.

I took a deep breath. My makeup was ruined. There was a hole in my pantyhose. I still had the after effects from the orgasm. There was no way I could walk into a restaurant.

"The reservation is under Adam's property. See you inside." Adam hung up the phone.

He was such an asshole. I dug through my purse for my mirror and makeup bag. If I had to go in there and play nice, I was gonna make sure I looked hot.

After doing the best I could, I got out of the limo. Tristan and Ethan linked their arms in mine. This time Tristan kept his eyes on me. I didn't know if he had changed his mind about our no-sex agreement. He had been clear that we wouldn't do anything sexual, but it seemed he was slowly changing his mind.

Butterflies fluttered in my stomach. Could it really happen? Ethan, Tristan, and Me? Was it so far of a stretch? They both bought me. Tristan hadn't planned on having a relationship with me, but so far, there had been two sexual encounters.

"I don't think testing Tristan was Adam's only plan," Ethan whispered. "Stay on alert."

"I don't get it. Why buy me and then try so hard to get out of the marriage?" I shook my head.

"Not sure, but we will find out." Ethan opened the door for me.

"Why did you buy me?" I might as well take Dotties' advice and just ask.

"Cause you looked so good knocked out," he laughed.

I slapped his arm. "I'm serious."

"Name?" A woman in a black suit approached us.

"Adam," Tristan sighed.

"Last name?" The woman snickered.

"How many Adams could you have?" I asked.

"A lot. Without a last name, I can't help you." She tapped the clipboard.

"Property," I sighed.

"Reservations for Adams Property right this way," she giggled. "Sorry, he's family. I think he's funny."

Real funny. How would she feel about him if she knew he just watched me blow a man and get fingered? I rolled my eyes. I forgot to take my pantyhose off. I would have rather had none on than these with a big hole.

The woman brought us over to a table in the middle of the room. Ethan held out the chair for me.

"Is there a bathroom?" I asked instead of sitting.

"Yeah, and it's free." The woman pointed to the back of the restaurant.

Ethan started to walk with me.

"It's fine. I'm just going to the bathroom. Adam isn't going to jump out and attack me." I kissed his cheek.

He looked reluctant but went back to the table. Tristan

hadn't followed me but hadn't sat down yet, either. They both watched me.

I turned to actually watch where I was going. The restaurant was filled. Chatter flowed from every table. A little girl ran around screaming as her father chased her. It was all so normal.

For most of my life, I lived on the streets. Being dressed up in a fancy restaurant was never a possibility. It was a dream. I smiled as I turned the corner.

Ouch.

I was in such a daze I walked into a wall. Stepping back, I rubbed my forehead.

"Ava," a familiar voice crawled up my spine.

No! I turned to leave.

He grabbed me with both hands and slammed me against the wall. I had walked into Brad, not a wall. Tears filled my eyes. This was bad.

I opened my mouth to yell. His hand was on me, silencing me. Struggling against him was no use. He was stronger than me.

"Did you think you could hide from me?" He licked the side of my face.

Tears fell down my face. His eyes blackened. There had to be a way to get out. Ethan and Tristan were so close.

"We are meant to be together. How do you now see that?" Brad rubbed his body against mine.

Vomit filled my throat. His lies never stopped. He said those things to make me believe him. To get me back so he could go back to controlling me. He didn't actually want me. None of it mattered, I would never escape him. Brad found me here at a restaurant. I was now positive he had sent the letters. I didn't know how he got in, but he did.

"I love you, Ava. Leave with me. These guys are using you. We have a past, and we can have a future. Remember the first night we made love?" His hand that wasn't on my mouth ran up my leg. He rubbed my pussy through my dress.

My skin crawled. Tears rolled faster. I pushed against him to get away. He rubbed harder. I tried to knee him, but I couldn't get my leg up high enough.

"What do you say?" he leaned back slightly to examine my face.

I slammed my head into his.

"You bitch." He slammed me against the wall. "Fine, I'll slit your throat, then fuck your corpse."

He was pulled away from me. Ethan and Tristan slammed him into the opposite wall.

I leaned forward, gasping for air.

"Fuck, Vernon. What's wrong with you?" Adam blocked my view.

Vernon? Who was that? I looked around. No one else was in the little hallway.

"Hey, I know this wasn't the deal, but she tossed herself at me. What was I gonna do?" Brad laughed.

I ground my teeth. Everything that came out of his mouth was a lie. *Deal? With Adam?* I should have known. This was all a setup by him.

My vision blackened. I tossed punch after punch at Adam. I screamed and yelled. Adam grabbed me and held my arms by my side. "Shh. I'll explain later."

Tristan and Ethan were already dragging Brad from the restaurant.

"Careful, my arm doesn't work," Brad cried out.

"He's lying," I called out. I was the only one that knew his secret.

Years ago, he injured his arm during a fight. He knew if he kept fighting, he would be killed. He was good, but not good enough. To stay out of the fighting ring but get money for coaching he said his arm was immobile. According to him, the clubs would expect him to still fight if his arm was in workable condition.

I didn't learn his secret until the first time he held me down. All these years, I never told a soul. Even when Judy accused me of not being kind enough to him. Of not helping him more. She had no clue he would use both of his arms to hold me down and rape me repeatedly.

"Are you okay?" Adam pushed my hair back.

"Touch me, and I'll kill you." I spat.

"What deal?" I had to know.

"To be your server. He wanted to see you. I wanted to see your reaction to him." He shrugged.

"Did it satisfy you? Was my reaction good enough for you? What is wrong with you?" First, you demand I suck Tristan's dick, then you bring me here with my asshole ex. Why do you hate me so much?" I ground my teeth. He was a monster.

"I was satisfied watching you orgasm. I can't wait to see it again on our wedding night." He stepped closer, but not enough to touch me. "As for your ex, that was a test. You passed."

"Fuck you." I ripped the necklace off that he bought me and tossed it on the ground.

CHAPTER 31

Ethan (Day 5)

AVA LOOKED BACK AT ME, WATCHING ME. I LICKED my finger, which still had her juices on it. She grinned and walked to the bathroom.

The idea of her going anywhere without me bothered me. Someone was after her. So far, I hadn't found any leads. My father examined all the tapes and hadn't found anything.

Ava was convinced it was Brad or even Adam. I had dismissed her accusations. Neither would have a way of getting inside the mansion. Then Brad found her at the fight. There was a chance I had misjudged him.

I still wasn't convinced Adam had done it. His objective was to get out of the marriage Brian had arranged. Aside from that, I didn't see him as evil. There was also the fact that his burns were from trying to save a life. An evil person doesn't do that.

Even the limo ride wasn't evil, it was about getting out of the marriage. Somehow he knew Tristan had no plans on consummating the marriage with Ava. There had to be some kind of compensation for proving it. My conjecture was he would get out of the contract. That backfired, and I got to observe Ava pleasing Tristan. *What a night!*

"She'll be fine." Tristan sat and leaned back.

"Bro, you don't get it. Someone is out to get her." I paced.

"Complimentary red wine?" A waitress poured four glasses of wine. So Adam planned on dining with us.

"You really are falling for her." Tristan smiled and took a sip of wine.

"Don't act like I don't see how you look at her. It's the same way you used to look at my sister. " I slumped in my chair. Very seldom did I discuss my sister.

Ashley was always troubled. That's what my father called it. I just knew her as different. She was haunted by things we couldn't see. The last time I saw her, I knew it was the end.

"I'll be back tomorrow." I kissed Joseph's button nose.

"Never change." Ashley pulled me into a hug. "Don't let being an elite hinder you."

"Hinder? Being on top is the best. I'm gonna ride my bike around until I find a hot piece of ass." I smirked.

"Being on top is lonely." She scooped up Joseph and walked away.

That night she was gone. We were left with her ashes, and Adam was left with burns over most of his body. He had just happened to be walking by when she set an abandoned house on fire.

"I think about her all the time. I feel like I'm betraying her," Tristan whispered.

"She left you. She left all of us," I sighed. "It's time to move on. It's okay to want Ava."

"Can you believe it's been six years since she took her life?" Tristan looked down.

Adam plopped in the chair beside Tristan. His mask was firmly in place. His blonde hair fell in his face. The smug look he wore needed to be removed by force.

"Where is our blushing bride?" He grinned.

"In the bathroom cleaning up from me making her cum. Something you will never do." I leaned forward.

"Nice try with your whole setup, But don't worry, I will be fucking her." Tristan clenched his jaw.

"Hey, just making sure." He checked his watch. "Where is the server?"

"She came by with wine." I lifter my glass. "Hasn't come back."

"She?" Adam sat up.

"Yes?" I furrowed my brow.

"How long has Ava been gone?" Adam stood and scanned the room.

"A few minutes. You know how women are." Although I kept my voice calm, I got up and started toward the bathroom.

"Fuck. I put her in danger." Adam took off running,

Tristan and I ran past Adam. He was fast, but his limp impeded his speed. We reached the back of the restaurant and turned the corner. Brad had his hands on Ava. She was against the wall with his body pressed to hers. Tristan and I pulled him from her and slammed him into the opposite wall.

Anger coursed through my veins. I turned to inspect Ava. Tears flowed from her eyes. Brad would die for this.

"Fuck, Vernon. What's wrong with you?" Adam stood between Ava and me.

Vernon? Did he not know who this was? Had Adam been a pawn?

"Hey, I know this wasn't the deal, but she tossed herself at me. What was I gonna do?" The scumbag laughed.

Tristan and I led him out of the restaurant. He cried something about his arm, but I couldn't hear with the blood rushing in my veins.

We got Brad outside and against the brick wall. His grin dropped.

"Call Daryl to get us and make sure Adam takes Ava home. He hurts her, and I will kill him." I instructed Tristan. I didn't want Ava alone with Adam, but I didn't have much of a choice. I had to deal with Brad.

"How are you getting into Tristan's mansion?" I lifted Brad off the ground.

"What are you talking about?" Brad looked around. He kept his composure pretty level, even with the tremor in his voice.

"The notes! How are you getting in and threatening Ava?" I shook Brad.

"Sir, I don't know what you mean. I love Ava," Brad whimpered.

Tristan tapped my shoulder.

"Adam wants to know which home. He specified that his house is also her home."

I ground my teeth. "His house. No sex till the wedding night." I hated the idea of her at his house. All three of us were supposed to consummate the marriage with Ava. I knew that. I had to accept that, but he wouldn't touch her unless I were there.

Ha. One second I was worried about him hurting her, the next, fucking her. He gave off mixed vibes when it came to her, and I wasn't sure which one bothered me more.

"You know she isn't a virgin?" Brad asked.

"Your little dick doesn't count," I chuckled.

Daryl pulled up and hopped out of the car. He panted as he ran over to the passenger side to open the door. Damn, he had to have sped to get here so fast. I tossed Brad in and climbed in after her.

"I don't want to go with you," Ava whined. She stomped out of the restaurant with Adam.

"Ava! It's not too late. I love you!" Brad shouted.

It took one quick hit to shut him up. Blood poured from

his lips. I clenched my fist. His tooth nicked my knuckle. Fucker.

Ava ran over to the car. "You can't send me home with this asshole!"

Tristan grabbed her and whispered in her ear. She huffed and shook her head. Damn, she was beautiful. It was hard not to give in to her. I wanted to bestow upon her the world. She deserved everything.

"Move and die." I shoved Brad into the backseat.

I took Ava's hand and led her away from everyone.

"Please, I don't want to go with Adam." Ava's lip quivered.

I ran the pad of my thumb across her lip. "Peach, trust me."

"I do. I don't trust him." She pointed to Adam.

"He won't hurt you." I rubbed her arms.

"How do you not see he is an asshole? Adam or Brad are leaving those notes, maybe both. You are taking one monster and leaving me with another." Ava stepped back.

"Adam isn't a monster." I clenched my teeth. She needed to trust me.

"How do you know?" She crossed her arms. "You just met him the other day, right? Or are you lying? You know him, don't you? Don't you? Tell me the truth."

"Yes, okay. I know him. It's not important." I grabbed her arms. "Please, trust me. His asshole demeanor is because he has an issue with me, not you. He won't hurt you."

"I'll go if you promise to tell me how you know him." She kept her arms crossed.

"Fine, but first I need to take care of Brad," I sighed.

Telling her how I knew Adam would dredge up some memories I would rather stay hidden. I close my eyes, now wasn't the time to dwell on that. Ava had to trust me that

Adam wasn't a threat. He hated me, Blamed me for things I had no control over, but he wouldn't hurt a woman.

"Don't kill him." Ava chewed her lip.

"What?" My head spun.

"For three years, he emotionally and physically abused me. I would like to repay the favor." She averted her eyes.

"My little psycho." I kissed the top of her head. "Done."

She reluctantly walked away and left with Adam. I hopped in the back with Brad, who now donned a fresh black eye. I gave Tristan a quizzical look, who shrugged.

"Gentlemen, please listen to me. Ava isn't who she says she is. She is a manipulator. Whatever she told you guys, it's a lie." Brad shook as he pleaded with us.

"Oh really? So she lied about you branding her?" I grabbed him by his shirt collar.

"Yes. She did that to herself. I tried to leave her. She told me she would tell everyone that I did it. I was afraid she would beat me. Ava plays the victim." Tears streamed down Brad's face.

He was almost convincing. If I didn't know Ava, I would believe him. Maybe.

"Lies. Now here is how this is gonna go. Every single thing you have ever done to Ava is gonna be done to you." I grinned,

Brad cried and blubbered. Snot ran down his face. When we got to the house, Tristan and I dragged him down to the basement. Daryl opened doors for us and never asked any questions. We reached the cell, and Brad fought back. It didn't do any good. Both of us were stronger than him. His hits were weak and cowardly at best.

Inside the cell, I had Tristan hold him down. With my pocket knife that was attached to my keychain, I made good on my promise. On his hip, I carved **APMMG**. Ava Palmer Moore Miller Gould.

CHAPTER 32

Adam (Day 5)

AVA SAT AS FAR AWAY FROM ME AS POSSIBLE IN THE limo. She acted as if I would be bothered by it. It was refreshing. I had expected her to try and berate me for having Vernon/Brad at the restaurant.

I expected the interaction to go differently. Brad was supposed to approach the table so I could see her reaction. Then Brad accosted her by the bathroom. At least it proved that Brad and Judith were lying about Ava. I still didn't like her, but at least she wasn't a bad person.

Buzz. Buzz.

TRISTAN

We will be by later to collect Ava, and you can explain what the fuck that was bout.

She can stay the night.

No.

She'll be fine.

> She has trouble sleeping. We will get her.

> You think being in the house you kill her ex in will help her sleep?

> We aren't killing him.

> Even more reason.

"You're sleeping at my place." I scooted closer to Ava.

"No, I'm not." She huffed and turned away from me.

"Don't be a brat." I looked away from her. Ava's beauty was captivating, and I refused to be caught in it.

"Ha. I'm being a brat? Why? Because I don't want to stay at your house? You are in cahoots with my ex. I want nothing to do with you," she spat.

"I'm not in cahoots with anyone." I racked my hand across my face. "What happened tonight was an accident."

"Accident?" she screeched. "An accident is filling your nails too short or applying too much blush. This was on purpose."

Brian pulled into the driveway, and Ava jumped out of the car. I followed after her. Instead of going to the front door like anyone else would have done, she plopped onto the curb. The girl was the definition of a brat. If I liked her, I would have bent her over my knee and taught her a lesson.

I walked right past her into the house. She couldn't stay out there all night. Brian, on the other hand, stayed out there with her. Why did he have to be so caring?

Two hours later and they were both still out there. Rain smacked against the window that I was watching them from. Brian hopped up and darted inside, the rain bothered him. Ava didn't budge. It wouldn't take her long before she was tired of getting rained on and came inside.

Ring. Ring.

"Hi, Grandpa," I answered the phone.

"Got my proof?" he asked.

"Nope. Whoever told you that was wrong." I sighed. "Any luck with the glitch?"

"Wow. It was a reliable source." He seemed genuinely shocked. "As for the glitch, everything points to a genuine mistake."

That was my last chance to get out of the marriage. I was really gonna be stuck with Ava for the next five years.

There was some rustling on the other end, and then my grandmother got on the phone. "Sweetie, maybe look at this as a blessing. We only want you happy, so we tried to get you out of the contract. But really you should give it a try."

"I don't want to get married. Just pull the contract," I yelled. My grandmother didn't deserve my anger, but she was playing games. "You two were gonna pull it if I had proof of Tristan not fucking her. You have the power."

"Sweetie, we were gonna hang Tristan. That's how we were gonna pull the contract. We didn't tell you because you get all heroic," My grandmother spoke in a calm voice like she didn't just speak of murdering someone.

"Look, I gotta go. The wedding is Saturday at Miller Manor." I clicked off the phone.

Rain was coming down so hard I could barely see Ava. Her hot pink hair was a blur. It was maddening. Why wouldn't she come inside?

I shook my head and went outside. She didn't acknowledge me as I sat beside her. Streaks of makeup ran down her face, more so than what was there after her encounter with Brad. Yeah, I was a tad responsible for that.

"Come inside. Stop being so stubborn," I said.

"I used to live in a tent. When it rained, I would sit outside. I loved the feel of the water. It was like the earth was taking a shower. Even when the water was freezing, it was beautiful. My sister would sit with me too. We couldn't hear our parents fighting when it rained hard enough.

Then one day, Brad walked me through the rain into an abandoned building. He raped me while the rain slammed into the window." Ava kept her gaze on the concrete. "Since then, I feared the rain. Silly, I know. He took so much from me. I will no longer allow him to take things away from me. So, no, I will not go inside."

Ava laid back and rested her hands under her head. Ava closed her eyes and let the rain wash over her. I stared at her trying to figure her out. Why did she share something so personal?

"How do you and Ethan know each other?" she asked without opening her eyes.

"Sure you don't want to hear it from him?" I laid beside her.

"I do, but I also want to hear your side. There has got to be a good reason for why you are such a dickhead," she chuckled.

"Short version. He was there when I woke up in the hospital, covered in burns. We argued. He left." My eye twitched.

"Nope, I want the long version." She turned her face to me.

We were so close, I could kiss her if I didn't hate her. "I used to take walks at night. One day I was walking by a building that was on fire. There was a woman sitting in the window. I went in to save her. A beam fell on me.

Two weeks later, I woke up in the hospital. Ethan was there. He attacked me for not saving his sister."

"Sister?" Ava rolled onto her side. "Wait, the letter you sent me."

"Yeah, it was for her." I sat up. "I've had enough of this rain. Come inside or don't."

I stood and headed toward the house. She didn't budge. If she wanted to stay out there and catch a cold that was on her.

"How do you do that?" she called out.

"Do what?" I turned around.

"Switch. One second, you almost seem kind, the next, your cold again." Ava was now standing, shouting into the rain. Her dress clung to her body, accentuating her curves. Fuck, even looking like a drowned rat, she was a vision.

I approached her. Before I knew it, my hands were in her hair. Her lip quivered as I stared into her eyes. Every inch of me wanted her. I could take her right here. She wouldn't protest. As much as she hated me, her body wanted me. I could tell by the shift in her body, by the way she tilted her face toward me. She was waiting for me to make a move.

"Make no mistake, I'm never kind." I let go of her, turned, and went into the house.

CHAPTER 33

Tristan (Day 6)

JOSEPH BEGGED TO STAY HOME FROM SCHOOL. THE mansion was being turned into a wedding venue courtesy of Tasha. Joseph wanted to see everything happen and of course get a few laps in. He was obsessed with swimming, and I wasn't sure how to stop it. He had a future in professional baseball, not swimming.

My son gave me one last pleading look as he got out of the car. I shook my head. He sighed, grabbed his book bag, and headed into the school. For a brief moment, I thought of the homeless children. Did they have any type of schooling? There had to be something in place. Ava and Dottie were intelligent, they had to learn somehow.

As we pulled away from the school, Daryl cleared his throat. He was never one for conversation. When he did talk, it was important.

"Yes, Daryl," I said.

"Sir, it's not my place. I was just wondering how Miss Lisa was doing." He kept his eyes on the road.

"Oh." I hadn't expected that. "She's okay. I got her into rehab, but I don't know if she'll succeed."

"May I suggest something?" he asked.

"Of course." I leaned forward.

"I have this cousin. He doesn't have anything going for him. For the right price, he could go down there and keep an eye on her." Instead of heading straight home, Daryl circled the block.

"Do you think that would help?" There was a big part of me that wanted her to succeed.

"Yes. I've known plenty of people that were addicts. The biggest help is having someone. My father died of an overdose. I would have tried anything to help him," Daryl wiped at his face.

He had been working for me for as long as I could remember. Aside from CeCe, he never spoke of his family. Until today. I didn't know he had a cousin or anything about his father. It made me want to ask more, but he deserved his privacy.

"Can you set him up with a car, phone, accommodations, and anything else you can think of?" I pulled out my phone to transfer money into Daryl's account.

"Yes, sir." Daryl pulled onto my street.

Since his cousin would be down there with her, I wouldn't have to go. There was no way I would be able to get out of the phone calls, but that wouldn't be too much of an inconvenience.

When we finally pulled up to the driveway, Daryl had to park at the end of it. Cars and delivery trucks blocked out the pathway. Tasha had everyone in town setting up. Scaffolding was being set up on the front lawn. I didn't want to know what that was for. Knowing Tasha, she would have gymnastics hanging from it.

Tasha stood by the front door with a clipboard and headset on. I tried scooting by her, but she grabbed my arm.

"Frizzo laid out a tux on your bed. I need you to try it on." Tasha wrote something down, barely looking at me.

"You should be a wedding planner instead of a professor." I smiled.

"I'm good at this, but I love history." She tapped her earpiece. "No, I said no almond milk! Oat milk! Do you know how many people are allergic to tree nuts?" She sighed. "Sorry, Tristan, it's a crisis. Go try on the tux."

I kissed her cheek and headed into the house. People weaved down the hall carrying various items. Two people carried cages with parakeets. Another person chased a peacock around. Tasha really was making this the event to talk about. Good, Ava deserved to be the center of attention.

Ethan charged down the hall. Sweat dripped down his temple. There was no way all the wedding had him nervous, or maybe he realized it was too soon to get married. He was obsessed with her, but marriage was a huge commitment.

"Bro, where would a sewing kit be?" Ethan shoved his hands in his pocket. It was quick, but I was almost positive there was blood on his knuckles.

"How would I know? I've only had to sew Joseph's stuffed animal a few times, and I just ask a servant to get the supplies." I shrugged.

"It's your house. You should know where your stuff is." He leaned in. "It's an emergency."

"CeCe would know." I headed toward the kitchen.

Ethan grabbed my shoulder and spun me around. "Not her. We also need someone who can sew."

"Joseph mentioned that Dottie can and I can a little. Are you gonna tell me what's going on?" I asked. Joseph had texted me that the eye of his stuffed elephant fell off. Dottie sewed it back on for him. According to him, she was the best aunt ever.

"Perfect." Ethan clapped his hands together. Definitely blood on his knuckles.

We found Dottie in her room. She had tech spewed across her bed. A projection of a waterfall played against the wall above her desk. She was fussing with the lens, trying to get the picture to come in clear. Her curly hair fell in her face, and she blew it out of the way.

"Dottie, we need you and your sewing kit." Ethan leaned on the door frame.

"It's in the top drawer." She nodded toward her dresser. "But I can't help. I have too much to do for tomorrow."

"We need you, come on," Ethan demanded.

"Ask Sandy or CeCe, even Frizzo may be able to help you." Dottie blew more hair out of her face.

"I'm not asking. Let's go." Ethan turned and left.

Dottie let out a sigh but followed us. I wasn't sure where Ethan was taking us, but I had a feeling it had to do with our prisoner. After Ethan carved Ava's initials into him, we left him whimpering on the cell floor.

Ethan must have visited him this morning. I didn't know what he needed Dottie for, but it was probably some sick form of torture.

Brad was lying on the floor of his cell. Blood poured from his side. I was pretty sure he was dead.

"What do you need her for?" It was clear he didn't need to torture Brad any further.

"To sew him up. I may have gone a little too far." Ethan ran his fingers through his hair.

"So," Dottie and I said simultaneously.

"So? Ava's gonna be mad. She wanted him to suffer the same way she did." Ethan tossed his hands into the air.

"She wants you to do this to him for three years?" Dottie gasped.

Ethan nodded.

"Well, if that's what she wants, thats what she gets." I opened the cell door. "Ethan, go get cleaned up. Dottie and I got this."

Ethan patted me on the back and left. I wasn't the best with a needle, but I could hold him down while Dottie sewed him. If she had issues, I could take over. It wasn't the first time Ellie the Elephant lost his eyes. CeCe wasn't always around, and I had to do the repairs myself.

"I'm supposed to sew him up?" Dottie pursed her lips.

"I guess so. If it's too hard for you, I can." I held out my hand for the needle and thread.

"No, I just don't think he's worth it." Dottie knelt beside Brad and lifted his shirt.

Brad was covered in bruises. All of his cuts were superficial, except one. A long gash ran from his nipple to underneath his rib cage. Ethan either sliced him or tossed him into the metal bunk. Either way, I didn't think a needle and thread would be enough.

"Dottie, help me," Brad groaned. His eyes were open halfway, and his lips barely moved.

Ava wanted him kept alive, and I wasn't sure that was possible at this point.

"Don't touch him yet. I'll get some gloves and alcohol." I grabbed Dottie before she touched him.

I left Dottie inside the cell with Brad. There was no way he would be able to escape or cause her harm.

At the top of the stairs, Ava was coming down with a tray of food. "What the hell are you doing?" I asked.

"Bringing him food." She held up the tray. There were two dishes with what looked like dog food and a kid's cup filled with water.

"Who made that?" I asked. She was either a terrible cook, or it was dog food.

She shrugged. "I scrapped the pots in the sink. I poured some gravy on it to cover the soap suds."

"Haha. You are a little psycho. I gotta grab some stuff. I'll be back." I leaned to kiss her. Nope, that was a bad idea, I stopped myself and walked away.

Fuck, she was too easy to care for. It was easy to want to be with her. I was pulled toward her even though I didn't want to be.

When I returned with rags, alcohol, gloves, and a proper needle, Ava and Dottie were sitting on the bunk. Gravy was smeared across Brad's face.

Brad groaned as I cleaned up his gash. Ava tried to help, but her hands shook every time she went to touch him. She was still scared of him. No matter how strong she tried to be, it wasn't working. Years of being with him ruined her. She was broken, and I hated how much I wanted to fix her.

CHAPTER 34

Ava (Day 6)

BRAD WAS ON THE VERGE OF DEATH. HIS breathing was labored. I shouldn't have cared, letting him die would be a mercy. I couldn't do it. I wanted him to suffer.

I turned to look at the cell bars. I also wanted him to want me, it made no sense. His approval meant nothing to me. Yet, it did. Being able to turn him down would be the closure I wanted. Not his fake 'I love you' crap. I wanted him to really want me. It was a terrible desire, and I couldn't explain it. I really was fucked up.

Tristan and Dottie worked quickly to sew him up and disinfect the area. Brad reached out his hand to mine. I pulled back. He wanted me to feel bad so I would him and release him. If I touched him, I would break. He had a hold on me, which I had to work on.

"We can handle this," Tristan whispered.

"It's okay. I don't mind staying." I clenched my fists.

"Don't you have a lot to do today?" Tristan wiped blood from his hands.

"Not really. Tasha has people doing everything." I looked

at Brad. In another lifetime, he and I would have been married. Maybe in that life, he would have loved me.

"Dottie, would you give us a minute?" Tristan turned to my sister, who was tying up the thread.

"Yeah, I'm done anyway." Dottie wiped her hand on a towel and went to leave. "Ava, when you're done, I need to talk to you."

I nodded.

Brad grabbed my ankle. I flinched and tried to step back.

"Don't touch her." Tristan grabbed his throat.

"It's okay." I caressed Tristan's shoulder.

Brad gurgled. "Ava, help me."

Shit. Moths fluttered around my stomach. My veins iced over. What was I gonna do? This was wrong, no one deserved to be mistreated this way.

"Maybe we can send him away when he heals," I whispered to Tristan.

It was the humane thing to do. My father raped and abused my mother for years, yet I gave him more mercy than Brad.

Tristan was on me so quickly I hadn't seen him move. His hand was in my hair, forcing me to look at him. Usually, his features were strong, stern, and void of smiles. Now his face softened.

"He has no power over you," Tristan whispered.

I blinked. What did he mean by that? Of course, Brad didn't have power over me.

"He has no power over you," he repeated.

I looked down. No one had power over me. Especially not someone who abused me for years.

"He has no power over you." Tristan pulled my face to his. His thumb rubbed under my eyes, wiping away something wet.

Had I been crying? I didn't think so, yet tears fell from my chin. How did Tristan know Brad still affected me? How did he know a small part of me wanted him to want me?

I had to stop the tears. Tristan was so close. I looked down at his lips. He ran his tongue across his bottom lip.

"He has no power over you. It's okay to let him die. It's even better to torture him." Tristan wiped away more tears.

He kept making me cry on purpose, but I couldn't stop. Crying in a cell with Brad wasn't helping anything. I had to get away.

"Fine, kill him. I gotta go." I stood to walk away.

"I'd rather torture him." Tristan pulled me to him.

Our bodies pressed together. His lips crashed into mine. I opened my mouth to allow him access. He kissed me with everything he had. I kissed him back, not caring Brad was inches from us.

My back hit the wall. Warmth pooled between my legs, I was ready for him. His kiss was intoxicating. In that kiss, I gave myself to him. All thoughts faded away. He grabbed my thighs and put my legs and his waist.

As we kissed, he ground himself into me. I moaned against his lips. Fuck, my body was sizzling. My hand was in his hair, deepening the kiss. His cock rubbed against my pussy. All that was between us was a little bit of fabric. I wanted more. I wanted him inside me. Shit, I needed him.

I reached down between us to grab him. Tristan grabbed both my hands and placed them above my head.

"Not yet, little psycho." He showered my neck with kisses.

"Please." A chill ran up my spine. I didn't need to fuck him, but I needed to cum.

"One more day." He kissed my lips again.

"Please," I begged.

"I can't wait to fuck you. Your pussy is gonna feel so good wrapped around my cock." He rubbed against me again.

"When I'm done, I'm gonna come down here and torture this dumb fuck for ever laying a hand on you."

Brad groaned next to us. That was why Tristan was kissing me the way he was. It was another form of torture for Brad. I wanted to stop him. Tell him that Brad could care less if anyone kissed me. He never cared for me.

"You don't have to do this," I whispered.

Tristan pulled back and studied my face. "What?"

"I mean the kissing. I know you are only doing this to torture Brad. He never loved me. He doesn't give a shit if someone else has me." I looked down.

"This has nothing to do with him. You need to stop thinking anything does." He pressed his lips to my forehead. "This is about you, little psycho. He has no power over you, and you need to realize that."

"Okay, can we go?" I asked. Tristan had never kissed me or talked about fucking me. Yet, here he was in Brad's cell talking about it. The only explanation was to torture him. His crap about Brad having no power over me only reminded me that Brad did.

"Not until you tell me what you are gonna do to me tomorrow." He ground his cock against me again.

"Why?" My voice cracked.

"Because I need something to hold me over," he grinned.

"Oh really?" I rolled my eyes. "Okay, Tristan. I'm gonna ride you while Ethan plays with my tits, and Adam watches."

Ever since the limo ride, I had thought of all three of them. Our wedding night was fast approaching, and I would be with all three of them. I didn't know if it would be one at a time or all three. My stomach twisted. No way I could handle that.

"Good girl." He released me. "Now we can go."

As we walked out of the cell, Tristan stepped on Brad's hand. Brad groaned and mumbled something as we left. I wasn't positive, but I thought he called me a bitch.

I found Dottie a few minutes later in her room. She was playing with some tech machine when I came in. Dottie saw me and dropped what she was doing. Then she locked the door.

"What's up?" I asked.

"I looked into it." She chewed her lip.

"The glitch?" Yes, finally, some answers.

"Yeah, but are you sure you wanna hear this?" She started pacing.

"Of course." How bad could it be?

"Well, it's all a tad much and confusing." She opened her laptop and showed me a few documents. "It took a while, and the only reason I was even able to find out was because I was on a Moore Tech server. You see, the glitch came from Moore Tech."

"So Ethan did it? Why? I thought he wanted me to himself. Why put a glitch that allows others to purchase me?" I tried to read the screen. There were so many numbers and letters mixed together. It made no sense to me.

"That I don't know. But it was set that only a million-dollar buy would get you. My guess is Ethan and Tristan did it, and Adam was an accident." She chewed her lip.

"Why do you think Adam was an accident?" They knew each other. Maybe it was some weird payback for trying to rescue his sister.

"A gut feeling. Nothing I have found has his name on it. Not even the original purchaser lists," she replied.

"But he did purchase me. How would he not be on the list?" I asked.

"He was after the auction. Purchaser 63 was blank, and his name was added after. That's not even the weirdest thing about the auction. Look." She pulled up a screen with the entrant's names.

Judith Blackwell

Bid #1 Purchaser 12: $2,000
Bid #2 Purchaser 20: $40,000
Bid #3 Purchaser 4: $65,000
Bid #4 Purchaser 7: $100,000
Final Bid: Purchaser 0: $0

I blinked and reread the screen. "How?"

"So, I did some digging, and the same glitch that allowed you to be purchased by multiple people prevented her from being purchased at all." Dottie raised her eyebrows.

"Ethan." I suppressed a smile. It was sweet that he did that, but completely wrong. I was gonna have to talk to him.

"Yes. There's more." Dottie clicked away.

"How is there more?" I asked.

"The only reason homeless were allowed in this year was to get you to enter. It all connects—the fights closing down, the homeless in the auction, the glitch. Ethan wanted you and was going to stop at nothing to get you," Dottie said.

"How do you know? It could still be a coincidence." I didn't believe it was for one second.

"Because of this." Dottie clicked on the screen, and an email popped up. "It was encoded, but I fixed that."

Mr. And Mrs. Gould,

I am emailing to inform you that this year you are to allow the homeless to enter the marriage auction. Honestly, it only has to be one, an Ava Palmer. I trust this will not be an issue.

Ethan Moore

"Why did he go through all the trouble to get me? He could have anyone." I pressed my nails into my palms. Ethan was hiding more than the glitch, and I was going to find out.

"I don't know. But let it go. I tried to pin the glitch on Adam, but this is all so sophisticated I can't. Plus, it's all tied back to Moore Tech, no matter how hard I tried to change the codes. You know the truth, now let it go," Dottie begged. "We have a great life. Please don't make another bad decision and ruin it."

I pulled Dottie into a hug. "Don't worry."

Making bad decisions was part of who I was. It wasn't something I enjoyed, and when I tried to make the right choice, I ended up making the wrong one. It was how things always went. Maybe that was why I left Dottie's room and went in search of Ethan to confront him.

CHAPTER 35

Ethan (Day 6)

ADAM BARGED INTO THE HOUSE. THERE WERE SO many people around that no one noticed he didn't belong. He was charging down the hallway right toward me. I didn't have time for his bullshit.

"I need to talk to Brad," Adam huffed.

"That's gonna be a little hard." I grinned. "Why do you want to talk to him?"

"There are some loose ends I would like to discuss with him," Adam replied.

"Like what? You had him come to the restaurant and put Ava in danger. Do you really hate me so much that you would harm her?" I growled.

He was still so angry at me over something that happened six years ago. Yeah, I attacked him in the hospital. Not my finest moment. I blamed him for not saving my sister. It wasn't his fault. He tried to get to her. The fire was too intense. The fire department report stated that she had poured gasoline everywhere. There was no saving her.

"Oh, grow up. I just don't like you or her, for that matter.

Now, where is Brad?" He looked around as if Brad was going to walk up the hallway.

"In a cell, recovering, or dead. I'm not sure." I shrugged.

"I didn't know he was gonna attack Ava. I knew he was lying about his arm injury. But you stabbed him. I kinda thought he would attack you. And well, you don't matter." He adjusted his mask.

"Stab him? I didn't touch him until last night." I cut my eyes at him.

"Really? Huh. The other day he said you found him at the fight club and stabbed him. He really is a pathological liar." Adam scratched his chin. A smirk formed in the corner of his lips. It was as if he admired Brad for being such an asshole.

"Why would he lie about that?" I asked.

I really didn't understand Brad. He was obsessed with Ava, yet left her. It was as if he got a kick out of tormenting her but got bored with her. Ava had told me he took off to manage some other fighter in a different country. I didn't understand why he bothered to come back.

"I think to get mine and Judith's pity. He is a manipulative fuck. Almost had me convinced everything was Ava's fault." Adam looked up and down the hall. "Is Ava around?"

"No. Is that why you really came? You want to see her. To0 bad. You will see her tomorrow." I checked my watch. My father was expecting me.

"Your jealousy is unnecessary. I don't want her." Adam glanced to his right as he spoke, his eyes never met mine.

"If that's what you need to tell yourself. I gotta ask, and only because Ava thinks you have something to do with it. Did you leave her letters?" I asked. If he was lying, I expected him to look anywhere but at me. There was also a chance he would tell me the truth to piss me off. Although I doubted he did it. He may be warming up to her, but he didn't want to marry her.

"Yes, I did, but not the threatening ones that she thinks I did." Adam stared me right in the eyes. "Now that I have provided her with a phone, I don't need to send her any more letters."

"I believe you but if I find out you are lying, I will kill you," I smirked.

"Yeah, go ahead and try. As fun as this has been, I'm leaving." Adam turned and walked toward the exit.

I shook my head and went to my office. Adam was a strange, angry man. He spent so long cooped up that his social skills were lacking. His hate for me was justified, but his pretend hatred for Ava wasn't.

The fact that he was injured trying to save my sister should be enough to like him. I shouldn't blame him. Yet, I couldn't help but be pissed at the man who failed to save her. Adam was the last person to see her alive, and part of me resented him for that as well.

Some day I would sit him down and find out everything that happened with him and Brad. I didn't have the time today, and it wasn't that big of a deal. I was just curious. Honestly, it was funny that Brad pretended to get stabbed by me to get sympathy from Adam.

My father was already in my office when I stepped inside. He had a stack of papers in front of him and a smile across his face. My stomach turned.

"Why do you look happy?" I sat across from him.

"I finally found a solution. Well, Benny did, but no matter." He pointed to the stack of papers.

"Solution to what?" I glanced at the papers. There was a bunch of legal jargon strewed across it.

"The marriage clause. You don't have to get married." He clapped his hands together.

"Oh don't worry about that. I don't mind getting married now." I envisioned Ava walking toward me in a white

229

dress. Her pink hair tied up in braids. Our wedding was so close.

"You can stop that now. You picked a homeless person to piss me off. You aren't marrying her." He slammed his fist down. "Benny is taking care of it."

"How?" I was going to marry Ava, but I was curious about what game my father was playing.

"It was pretty simple when Benny and I put our heads together. Your gramps froze all of our assets because you had one month to get married. So I set up a non-profit organization called New Boston Inc." He waved his hands as if that explained everything.

"So?" I stared at him.

"So? Really, you don't see it." He slid a folder over to me. "Everything was donated to New Boston Inc. Ha. All of our money was donated to an organization that I run."

I shook my head. Leave it to him to find a way around my gramps will. I was doing my part. Had he just waited one more day, we would have our money, and I would have my bride. Not that what he did would make any difference, I would still marry Ava and have my share of the money. Wait.

The folder that he slid over to me was labeled New Boston Inc. I opened it. His name was on every piece of paper. Our funds were transferred to him as CEO of the non-profit.

"You control all of the money?" I knew the answer.

"Yes, now you understand. Marry this homeless whore, and you get nothing." He grinned.

"You would take everything away from me because I am gonna marry a homeless woman. Why are you so ridiculous? If you gave her a chance, you would see that. You have been here all week. Have you not noticed how things are with her around? Her and her entire family are lovely. Shit, even her best friend Felix is a good dude." I tossed the folder at him.

"I have seen her manipulate you. That whore has even

gotten into Tristan's head. You two don't see her for who she really is. She killed her father, and yet you still want her," my father chuckled. "Women are nothing but trouble. You should know more than anyone."

"She isn't mom or Ashley." I walked over to him and grabbed his hand. "Ava isn't them. Stop worrying, dad."

It all made sense. He was using her being homeless as an excuse. It had nothing to do with that. He didn't want me to end up like him, with a drug addict ex-wife and dead daughter. He still blamed himself for their demons and didn't want me in the same boat.

"You are only marrying her for the money." My father shook his head.

"I..."

"What?" Ava asked behind me.

I turned to see her standing in the doorway. Tears filled her eyes as she started to back up.

"Ava, let me explain." I stepped toward her.

"Yes, please explain to her that the only reason you want to marry her is that your grandfather put in the will that you get married in thirty days, or you don't get your inheritance." My father smiled from cheek to cheek.

"Is that true? Is that why you rigged the auction? You set it up for me to be in that auction. Why me? You figured some homeless person would be easy to manipulate? That I would be so grateful that I wouldn't care that I was just some pawn?" Ava cried.

"Stop backing away and listen to me!" I shouted.

My father snickered.

Ava turned and ran.

CHAPTER 36

Ava (Day 6)

"Ava, get back here!" Ethan's footsteps pounded behind me.

I weaved in and out of workers, trying to get far away from him. My brain was spinning. He was marrying me to get his inheritance. How romantic! It was bad enough Tristan married me to be a mother figure for his son. At least he was warming up to me. Then there was Adam, I had no clue why he bought me. Did anyone actually want to marry me?

Workers carried flowers and fabric down the hall. Others had trays of food and drinks. Ha. They were getting ready for my wedding, something I was so happy about a few minutes prior. Now, it was all fake. The whole thing was a facade.

A hand grabbed my neck and spun me around. I was face-to-face with Ethan. The vein in his forehead bulged.

"Let me go," I demanded.

"Not until you talk to me." His grip on my neck tightened.

"Listen to what? The fact that you are only marrying me to get money?" I held back the tears. "Guess what? I only entered the marriage auction for money."

Clap. Clap.

Ethan and I turned toward the clapping. Adam slowly clapped as he approached us. I seriously hated that guy. The part of his face not covered in his mask was turned upright into a wicked smile.

"You finally learned the truth, Ava." He stopped clapping and crossed his arms. "You were a means to an end for him, and you think I'm the bad guy."

"Ha. Coming from you, that's comical." Ethan released me. "You didn't even buy her, Brian did, and now you're stuck with her."

"What?" Heat rushed to my cheeks. My chest sunk in.

"Don't act all shocked. I have made it clear I don't want you." Adam shoved his hair from his face. "At least I didn't pretend like Ethan did."

I don't care. I don't care. The room spun, my heart slammed into my chest.

"Fuck you." Ethan grabbed Adam by the collar and slammed him into the wall.

"What are you gonna do? Beat me? She isn't innocent, either. You think she entered the auction to find true love?" Adam cackled.

"Maybe not, but she found it." Ethan's jaw twitched.

"Don't do that," I said. "Don't act like what we have is anything more than a contract."

My heart sank to my feet. Adam was right, I didn't enter the auction for true love. I entered it to help my family. At the time, it felt like the right decision, even though I rarely made those. Then I started to fall for Ethan, and everything changed. After Brad, I swore never to let my heart get involved with another person. This was why, this pain killed.

"Exactly, this is all just a contract." Adam winked at me.

Ethan swung at Adam. They exchanged blows in a dance-like manner. Neither one of them was paying attention to me anymore. I took the opportunity to take off. By the time they noticed I was gone, I would be far away.

No, I wasn't planning on leaving them. Even though I wanted to, I couldn't. The contract was unambiguous, I would be killed. Not to mention I couldn't leave my family with these people. I had thought Ethan was a good man, he was only in it for the money. He set it up so I would have no choice but to marry him. My dumb ass fell for his tricks.

As I walked down the hall, deciding where to go, Tasha tapped her clipboard, yelling at one of her workers. She was talented but maybe a tad too bossy when it came to the staff. The worker was off to the side, and I could barely make out their silhouette.

"I will try it on, I've been a little busy," Tristan replied.

He stepped out of the shadows. He was the worker Tasha was yelling at. Ha, I wasn't the least bit surprised she had a way with talking to the men. She yelled at them, and they respected her more.

I dipped into the nearest room so he wouldn't see me. The last thing I needed was him telling me how much he didn't want me either. I already knew that, I didn't need a reminder.

Once the door to the room was shut, I sunk down and let the tears flow. How had I been so foolish to think that Ethan and I had something after a week? With all I went through with Brad, I should have protected my heart more. Instead, I allowed him to fool me into thinking I was special.

"What are you doing?" My mother sat up in her bed.

Shit, I hadn't realized this was her room. Probably because I had never gone to see her. It's not like I didn't want to, but this week was busy.

"Sorry, I...uh." I used my shirt to wipe my tears. Mascara smeared my white t-shirt.

"Don't apologize, just get off the floor and come over here," my mother demanded.

I went and sat next to her. She was still in her pajamas even though it was the afternoon. Since Joseph was at school, she didn't have to get up early. He was her reason, and as happy as I was, I was a tad jealous. Not that I should be, he was good for her.

"Do you like it here?" I asked.

"Of course. Joseph is a great kid, and he calls me grandma." Her face lit up.

"Right, but what about the rest? Are you feeling better?" I swallowed. "I mean, before you were...um..."

"You mean, am I out of my psychosis?" she laughed. "Yes, after what we did, I never thought I would feel again. For years I was numb, seeing the world through a haze I couldn't interact with. Now, I feel. Thanks to Joseph, I am wanted. He enjoys it when I'm around. He really is such a good kid."

Tears rolled down my cheek. "We needed you, we wanted you. Dottie and I enjoyed you."

"No, you two only ever needed each other. I was mad at you for years for killing my husband and having me drag the body for six blocks to bury. While I fell into myself, you two helped each other." She wiped the tears from my face. "I never should have put you in a position to have to take care of me."

"I'm sorry," I sobbed.

"Enough of the past. Why did you come in here crying?" She tucked my hair behind my ear and half-smiled.

"I just found out Ethan married me to get his inheritance. I know I shouldn't care, but I thought he was falling for me," I replied. It was the first time I had ever had a mother-daughter moment with her.

"My teenage daughter had to kill my husband to protect me. I am not the person to give out relationship advice," she said. Just like that, our moment was over.

"I know. So, no matter what, I have to marry them tomorrow. I was wondering if you would give me away." I had been meaning to ask her and hadn't gotten around to it.

"Oh, I would. It's just I already told Joseph him and I would walk down together." She averted her eyes.

"Right, right. Um...no biggie." I stood and wiped the tears that wouldn't stop. "Look, I gotta go. I'll talk to you later."

"Okay, don't worry. You'll figure out your boy problems." My mother crawled back into bed and pulled the blanket over her.

I speed-walked down the hall, avoiding everyone. A few times, I had to turn around because a worker looked like they were about to talk to me. I had to get out of there. The mansion was quickly becoming a prison. Ha, people would die for this lifestyle, and I was complaining about it.

Once I was outside, I took off down the driveway and kept walking. I wasn't sure where to go, but I wouldn't be back till I had to.

CHAPTER 37

Adam (Day 6)

I ROLLED AROUND ON THE FLOOR WITH ETHAN. HE slammed his head into mine, damn that thing was hard. Laughing, I pulled back and punched him. A few workers screamed and ran. Apparently, seeing two elites fight was new to them.

Ethan was pulled off of me. I looked to see Tristan tossing Ethan backward. Ha, he deserved that, hitting me because I hurt his feelings. Screw him.

"What is going on?" Tristan looked from Ethan to me.

"Your friend is a maniac. Attacked me because he is sensitive," I panted.

"You need to learn to shut your mouth." Ethan leaned over. "You're just mad that Ava hates you."

"I hate her too." I raised my hands and dropped them.

"Speaking of her, where did she go?" Ethan asked.

"I'm guessing she ran off after you hit me." I ran the back of my hand across my mouth. It wasn't as much blood as I expected.

"Fuck, I gotta find her." Ethan turned and left.

I should have chased after him and continued our fight.

He really needed his ass kicked. Maybe then he wouldn't walk around all high and mighty.

Tristan nodded his head at me and followed Ethan. He never said much to me if he could help it. After the fire, he visited me once. He thanked me for trying to save his wife and told me if I ever needed anything, all I had to do was ask. Since the limo incident, I was pretty sure that offer was over. Oh well, it was a sight to see.

I pulled out my phone and checked Ava's location. It was another reason I sent her a phone, I could keep track of her. The last thing I needed was for her to run away, and then both our lives would be put in danger for not performing our matrimonial duties.

Ava was already over a mile away. I should have learned from the fire not to chase women around. Instead, I kept the tracker open on my phone and went to my car. It was already blocked in by multiple delivery trucks. The wedding would be too much of a show of wealth. I despised everything about it.

Since my car was blocked in, I took off on foot. It didn't take long for my leg to bother me. I really should have listened to Damar and did my PT. Of course, until I had met Ava, I wasn't doing much physical activity. She really did put a strain on my whole life.

I checked the phone, she was already close to the center of town. *What! Was she running? Ugh, at this rate it would take forever to get to her.* I should have called Brian. He would have picked me up and driven me to her. It would have been quicker. Had it not been his day with his mother, I would have. It was part of his routine.

An hour later, I was still chasing her. Luckily she seemed to stop. Since it was the poor part of town, there was no way of knowing where she actually was. I kept going, even though sharp pains shot up my leg.

The street had abandoned house after abandoned house.

Grass was overgrown, and trees found life in the sidewalks. It looked like something out of an apocalypse movie. People strolled up and down the streets as if this was normal. A woman stopped and asked me if I wanted to buy her. I handed her a hundred and kept walking.

According to the phone, she was halfway down the street. I leaned against a house that may not have been able to take my weight. The siding was long gone, and vines crawled in and out of the windows. Ava was close, and I didn't want to be out of breath when I arrived.

"I never thought you would be on this side of town," Judith said. She came out of the alley next to the house and leaned beside me. Her red hair fell down her shoulders instead of the standard tight bun she wore.

"I'm as shocked as you," I replied.

"So, what are you doing here?" She looked up and down the street as if she was embarrassed to be seen with me.

"Trust me when I say you don't want to know." I rechecked my phone, Ava hadn't moved.

"Probably not. Well, I'll let you get to it." Judith crossed her arms and scuffled her feet. "Hey, uh, you haven't seen Brad, have you? I mean, it's not a big deal. I hadn't seen him today, so just wondering if you had."

"Nope. Since we are kinda on the subject, it's best if you and him leave me alone." I didn't want her to think we were friends.

"Yeah. Right, of course. When I see Brad, I'll let him know." She picked at her nails. "Look, I meant what I said about Ava. Be careful, she is nothing but trouble."

I opened my mouth to reply, but Judith turned and went back into the alley she came from.

What a strange interaction. I shrugged. At least now, she would probably leave me alone. I didn't need her showing up at my door in the middle of the night again. Especially when she realized Brad was never coming home.

I found Ava sitting outside the entrance to a fight club. A sign that looked like someone scribbled said Underground. She had her head down and didn't realize I had approached her, or she didn't care.

"When I first met Brian, he was living with his mom. She collects books, so I was delivering some to her." I sat down beside Ava. "Brian just met me and hugged me. That day I hired him as my assistant. His mother was skeptical. She was afraid I would allow something bad to happen to him."

"Why are you telling me this?" Ava asked without lifting her head.

"If I don't hold up my end of the contract, he will also suffer the consequences since he bought you for me. I tried to get out of the contract, but it seems like all my attempts have failed. So to protect Brian, I will do what has to be done," I explained.

"Again, what's your point?" she asked.

"That means you will hold up your end." I rolled my eyes. How did she not understand that?

"Is that why you tracked me down? I had a bad day, I don't feel like talking to you." Ava lifted her head. Her makeup was smeared across her face, and her skin was blotchy.

"Yes. You are going to stop wallowing in self-pity and come back with me." I stood.

"Fuck off," she whispered. "You don't get to tell me what to do."

"I will toss you over my shoulder and drag you there. We are getting married tomorrow. Stop being a brat because no one actually wants to marry you. You entered this for the money. Everyone else had their personal reasons. Get over yourself." I couldn't believe how insufferable she was being.

"I will rip your nuts off. I'll be there tomorrow, okay, with a fucking smile on my face. I just need tonight, okay. Tonight, I am gonna be the homeless girl one last time and walk the streets. Then I will pretend to be the happy bride." She pulled a tissue from her purse and blotted the tears.

"Fine, I'll stay with you out on the streets then. But if we are gonna walk, I need breaks." I stretched my leg.

"No. I don't want to talk to you." She pulled out her makeup and began applying it.

"Deal, no talking. I don't have anything to say to you anyway." I sat beside her, waiting for her to be ready.

CHAPTER 38

Ava (Day 7)

I SHOULD HAVE SLEPT. THAT WOULD HAVE BEEN THE smart thing to do, I really should have slept. Instead, I spent the entire night walking around New Boston. None of it felt real. It was like I was watching the city from above it.

Adam stayed with me, and as promised, he didn't say a single word. I had nothing to say to him, so the silence was comforting. Roughly every hour, I would stop and allow him to rest his leg. He never said thank you, but he would smile every time we sat down.

As the sun rose, I headed back to the mansion. Adam walked me to the door, turned, and left. I watched him go, his limp had gotten so much worse throughout the night. I should have let him rest more. Screw that, he didn't have to come with me. That was his choice.

Tasha charged at me when I entered the house. "Where have you been?"

"I went for a walk," I said. She didn't need to know about the argument between Ethan and me.

"Well, you look like you haven't slept. You have bags under

242

your eyes." She grabbed my hand. "Let's go. We have lots of work to do.

Just like that, I was being whisked away into a fairytale wedding. Tasha had thought of everything. Even a bubble bath to get me ready. Which she had servants ready to give me, and I refused. I could wash my own ass.

The morning went by in a blur. People floated in and out with different assignments from Tasha. Dottie and Sandy stayed with me all morning, getting equally pampered. Dottie didn't seem too thrilled about having her eyebrows shaped, but she remained a good sport.

Our nails were painted, our makeup was done, and our hair was blown out, it was all a dream. A lady even came and massaged our legs so we wouldn't get pains from being on our feet all day, at least, that was her explanation.

It took hours to be pampered, and I loved every second of it. Tasha even had people come in carrying trays of food and mimosas for us. It was beyond fancy. Although I was tired from not sleeping, I was still able to enjoy it. My only complaint was it went by so fast. I think that was because I wasn't ready to marry three men who didn't want me.

Felix walked into the room with a fresh haircut and a tux on. Sandy smiled from ear to ear when he walked in. He smiled back and even did a little spin for her. We all clapped and cheered him on.

"Thank you, thank you." He bowed. "You all look so beautiful, especially you, Sandy. I can't wait to tear you up tonight."

Sandy waved him off as her cheeks turned bright red.

"Ava, I wanted to talk to you. Sandy and I were discussing this last night. Well, I don't want to bring up a sour subject, but, ugh, how do I say this?" Felix scrunched up his face.

"Spit it out," I chuckled. The man always took forever to say what he wanted to say.

"Okay, okay. So, Sandy and I, um think, if you want, I could walk you down the aisle," he said. "It's just we talked to your mom, and she said she would be walking Joseph down the aisle, so I could do it."

Tears swelled in my eyes. "Thank you, both of you. I really appreciate the offer, but there was a reason I didn't ask you. Your job is to walk Sandy down the aisle and apparently tear her up after."

Everyone in the room laughed.

"Yeah, but who is gonna walk you down the aisle?" Felix asked.

"My two feet." I wiggled my toes.

Clap. Clap. "Ladies, it's almost showtime." Tasha stepped into the room.

She had on sleek black pants and a flowy purple top, she was absolutely flawless. I wanted her in the wedding party, but according to her, she was too busy setting everything up.

"Let's do this," I sighed.

Frizzo sauntered into the room and was followed by his entourage of workers. They rushed around, pulling out the dresses and shoes. Felix bowed and left us to it.

I checked the clock, twenty minutes left. My stomach turned, and my skin got all tingly. I lifted my arms so I didn't sweat onto my dress. This was it, no turning back. Not like I was ever able to turn back.

Tasha ushered us into the room leading to the backyard. I peeked out the window. Cocktail tables and benches were everywhere. Tables held ice sculptures, wine glasses, and little hors d'oeuvres. Red, lilac, and green trees littered the backyard. Ornaments and reels of fabric were laced throughout them.

"It's beautiful," I gasped.

"Wait till you see the aisle." Tasha pointed toward the back of the property. "There are huge pine trees that make an aisle.

It's like it was made for this. Plus, Dottie added a magical touch to it."

"Thank you," I whispered. I may be stuck marrying three assholes, but I had people in my life that were amazing. That's what mattered.

"Okay, it's showtime." Tasha tapped her earpiece.

We went to the edge of the tree line. Tasha snapped her fingers, and the music started playing. I looked down, I was almost positive it came from the rocks.

Joseph and my mother entered the trees first. The cute little boy turned around and gave me a thumbs-up. Next was Sandy and Felix, they disappeared into the trees as well. I wanted so badly to peek, but I didn't want all the guests to see me. Brian came up behind us and gave a little nod to Dottie. He had on a tux, and his hair was combed back, the man looked very dashing.

"Bri, I knew you were gonna walk me down the aisle, but can you walk Tasha? I have a different job to do." Dottie smiled at Brian.

"You two know each other?" I asked. When had they met?

"Yeah, he has been by a few times to bring you letters from Adam. We got to chatting, he is so nice." Dottie smiled.

"Thank you, Dottie." His cheeks reddened.

"No, I have things to plan." Tasha averted her eyes.

I grabbed her clipboard and tossed it on the ground. "Go."

Somehow, Tasha listened to me. Her and Brian walked into the tree line and were out of sight.

"I know your little sister shouldn't be the one giving you away, but I'm going to." Dottie put her arm into mine.

"I should have asked." I dropped my head.

"No, I should have offered. I just assumed mom would have gotten over herself and done it," Dottie said.

"Well, thank you. And you are wrong about one thing.

You have never been the little sister. You were always more mature than me," I whispered as we entered the trees.

Two rows of trees made the perfect aisle. They were so tall they blocked out most of the sun. Mason jars and lights hung from all the branches. Chairs weaved in and out of the trees avoiding the roots that popped up. So many people were there that I couldn't make heads or tails of who was who.

At the end was a wooden archway covered in flowers. On the right side, my three men stood looking sexier than I had ever seen them. As much as I hated all of them, I couldn't deny how handsome they were.

A short, stocky woman in a black dress stood under the archway with a binder in her hand. She had to have been the judge. Behind her, there was a white screen the size of most apartment buildings.

Once I reached the first set of chairs, rose petals began falling. I looked up, drones floated above everyone, showering the crowd with petals. The screen behind the judge projected petals floating through the wind. I squeezed Dottie's hand, it was perfect.

As I got closer, the screen turned to tulips blossoming as I reached the end. A dove flew by, and I wasn't sure if it was on the screen or real life. Dottie kissed my cheek and went to sit next to the rest of the wedding party in the front row.

"Ladies and Gentlemen, thank you for attending the wedding of Ava, Ethan, Tristan, and Adam!" the judge shouted into a microphone.

The music stopped.

My stomach turned.

"We are gathered here today for the contractual matrimony of these wonderful people. If anyone has any objections keep them to yourself as this is a binding contract." She giggled and flipped the page in her binder.

"Now, Ava Palmer, do you promise to uphold your end of the contract for the next five years?" she asked.

"Yes," I whispered. *Not like I have a choice.*

"Adam Gould, do you promise to uphold your end?" she asked.

"Yes." He rolled his eyes.

"Tristan Miller, do you do the same?" she asked.

"Yes, happily." He winked at me.

"And last, Ethan Moore, you?" she asked.

"Ava, I want you to know I'm sorry," he said.

"A simple yes would suffice," the stocky lady scoffed.

"Anyway, it's true I got into this marriage because I had to. We all did. That doesn't mean my feelings are invalid." Ethan put his hand on his heart.

"Can we just get this over with?" I ground my teeth.

"No, I need you to know I'm sorry. It was about the money, but it's not anymore. I'll give it all up. Every last dime. I would rather have nothing than not have you." He grabbed my hand.

"Look around. We are getting married. You have me." I pulled my hand away.

"I don't want you like that. I want your heart. I want all of you," he said.

"You would give up all of your money for me?" I asked. Maybe I was wrong about him. If he was willing to give up billions, that meant he did feel for me the way I did for him.

"Yes." Ethan smiled.

A tear rolled down my face. "Okay, you have all of me. You don't have to give up your money, though."

"I love you. And yes, I promise to uphold my end." Ethan grabbed my hand and kissed it.

"Finally," the stocky lady sighed.

Adam pulled a handkerchief from his pocket and handed

it to me. I blotted the tears, hoping my makeup hadn't gotten too messed up.

"You all may kiss the bride." The judge closed her binder.

Ethan went first. He dipped me like they did in the books and took my breath away with his kiss. When he pulled me upright, my head spun. It was dizzying.

Tristan was more gentle and kissed my lips but kept it brief. His eyes shot over to his son. My guess was he didn't want his son watching him kiss someone that wasn't his mom.

Then there was Adam. I wasn't sure what I expected. He wore his mask, so I wasn't surprised it wasn't a full-on kiss, but I had expected more than what he gave me. He kissed my hair, turned and walked away.

It was only five years, right?

CHAPTER 39
Ava (Day 7)

THE GUESTS DANCED AND DRANK AND ATE INTO THE night. I was escorted around by Tasha as she introduced me to people I wouldn't remember. I loved the attention, but it was overwhelming.

For most of the night, my husbands were busy talking to other business people. According to Tasha, the elite's never took a day off, even at weddings, they wanted to discuss business. It seemed a bit exhausting to me.

"Can I have this dance?" Ethan held out his hand.

I took it and entered the dance floor. He held me close as we moved to the beat. Everything was beyond perfect.

"I'm sorry I didn't tell you about the will. I should have," Ethan whispered.

"It's okay. I shouldn't have gotten so mad at you." I laid my head on his chest.

"You had every right." Ethan kissed the top of my head.

"I love you." I looked up at him.

"I love you too." He bent and kissed me.

Everything was perfect. I was dancing with my new

husband, who I was in love with. We had the next five years of our lives to be together. Nothing could get in the way.

"Can I cut in?" Adam asked.

Well, he could get in the way.

"No," Ethan and I said simultaneously.

"Your father would like to speak with you." Adam glared at Ethan.

Ethan sighed and gave me a kiss goodbye. Sadly, Adam stepped in and pulled me close to him.

"Are you excited for tonight?" Adam smirked.

"The wedding? Yeah, it's perfect." I looked around.

"I mean the fucking. Getting railed by three guys has gotta be a thrilling experience for you." Adam winked. "Unless you have already done that."

"Why does everything out of your mouth have to be so vile?" I spat.

"It's what's going in your mouth that I'm concerned with." Adam released me and walked away.

I hated that man so much. Snakes erupted in my stomach. As much as I hated him, he was right. I was going to have to be with all three of them. In a few hours, maybe less. Even if it weren't all at once, it would be one after the other. Crap, how was I gonna handle that?

I went over to the bar and grabbed a glass of wine. I chugged it in one gulp, then I grabbed another one. If I had to be with all three of them, there was no way I could be sober during it.

"Yes, I checked all the tapes. It was that Brad character. He was sneaking in through the sewer system," Ethan's dad said. "And don't worry about the money, you still have your cut. I'll leave you alone about marrying that homeless girl."

I turned around. Ethan and his father were a few feet away talking. His father kept that angry smug on his face even though he was delivering good news.

"Perfect. Thank you, dad." Ethan slapped his dad on the shoulder.

I had known it was him the whole time, but hearing the confirmation made me feel so much better. He deserved to be tortured. I closed my eyes, now was not the time to dwell on him. After all, it was my wedding day.

A pair of arms wrapped around me and squeezed tight. Tristan's cologne of lemon and sandalwood filled my nose. He was being friendly, and in public, odd.

"Well, hello, bride." Tristan kissed my cheek.

"Hello, husband." I turned to face him.

"I wanted to discuss something with you. I know I hadn't planned on touching you. And since then, I have. A lot. Anyway, I know sex was off the table, but with Adam's suspicions, I think it would be best if we did. At least tonight." He bit his lip.

"Yeah, you said in the cell with Brad you wanted to. So, I figured we would." I gulped down more wine. "If you're asking, I'm fine with it." *Not that I know the logistics of it.*

"Perfect. We will all meet you in the main guest room. Neutral ground and all, we figured it would be more comfortable for you." Tristan took a sip of wine and set the glass down.

"Okay, now?" I asked.

"An hour? If we don't sneak away while everyone is here, people will talk. They like to know the marriage was consummated. Especially Adam's grandparents." He grabbed my hand and kissed it. "I really am sorry about giving you mixed signals. See you soon."

I let out a deep breath. One hour, I had one hour. I could do this. I grabbed a full bottle of wine and snuck out of the wedding. Even though I was the one in white, no one noticed. They were all so busy enjoying themself. It was rather magical.

Once in my bedroom, I popped open the wine and began

chugging. Three men. I had to sleep with three men. This was not going to be easy. A little voice crept into my head *if all their attention is on you, it could be rather enjoyable.* I paced and shook out my body, trying to get the jitters to go away. That's when I noticed the package on the bed.

My heart sank. Brad was locked in the basement, could he have somehow gotten into my room? *Stop it, you're being paranoid.* I grabbed the card that was attached.

For tonight,
Knock 'em dead. I hope they are all hung.
Tasha.

I opened the package. It was a very lacy, very risqué underwear choice. Well, it was more of a bra-underwear combination that wasn't much of either. It was black and was missing the crotch and nipple coverings. Damn. I chugged more wine.

After debating back and forth on the underwear choice, I finally put on what Tasha had left for me. Damn, it was a perfect fit. Instead of feeling naked and ashamed, I was sexy and powerful. Yeah, I had to fuck three guys, but they were my three guys.

Before I knew it, the hour had passed, my bottle of wine was empty, and I was wrapped in a robe to cover the scandalous lingerie choice. Well, time to go have some fun.

Hiccup.

I burped to try and release the hiccups, now wasn't the time. I looked at the clock again. It was time. I had to go. I slipped on the heels that I had worn with my wedding dress and walked toward the spare bedroom.

Hiccup. I walked into the room.

All three were sitting there. A fireplace roared in the center of the room. A chaise lounge was on one side, and a bed on the other. The men were in chairs that looked like they had been brought inside from the wedding.

Hiccup. Damn, they are hot pieces of chili cheese fries.

My stomach turned. It was either the wine or the nerves, I wasn't sure. They were all staring at me. I had to do something. I untied the robe and let it slide off my shoulders.

Hiccup.

"Are you drunk?" Ethan approached me.

"No." I stumbled toward him.

"Looks like we will have to postpone, Peach." Ethan smiled.

"Huh?" We had to get it done. *Hiccup.* The room was heavy. Things started to spin. Ethan kept moving.

"We are not touching you until you are sober." He looked down at what I was wearing. "Save the outfit for next time."

"But, what are we supposed to do?" I slipped and fell into Ethan's arms.

He scooped me up and placed me on the bed.

"What do you mean?" Tristan asked.

"Adam's killer grandparents. They are gonna give us the whack." I slid my finger across my neck in case they didn't realize what I meant.

"There will be plenty of fucking tomorrow, and we will stay for a while, so everyone thinks we did it." Adam pulled the sheet over my body. When he wasn't a dirt licker, I really didn't mind him. Well, sometimes.

"Impressive. I thought you were gonna go all rules are rules on us." Ethan slapped Adam's back.

"Not tonight, I have no desire to have sex with a girl that won't remember it." He leaned down and maybe kissed my forehead. Or it was Tristan.

They were all blurring together. My eyes were hazy like a doughnut. I made a lot of mistakes in my life, but marrying them wasn't one of them. The room got heavy.

"Sleep, Peach." Ethan caressed my hair. "We all have the next five years together."

I pried my eyes open. It was still dark in the room and my head was pulsating so bad I thought it would explode. Fuck, why did I drink so much. I glanced over and noticed the nightstand had a glass of water with two pills beside it and a note.

This will help.

Downing the pills, I looked for the men. All three of them were still in the room. I had expected them to leave. Nope, they were all there. Adam was passed out on the sofa, Tristan was in a chair, and Ethan was asleep on a rug in front of the fireplace.

They all looked so peaceful, I almost forgot Adam was a monster. I took a deep breath and slipped out of bed. They had said we had plenty of time for sex, but I also knew the rules. Our marriage had to be consummated. Okay, I was also horny thinking about having all three men.

Amazingly enough, the headache faded to a dull throbbing. Those pills worked in minutes. I tiptoed over to Ethan, he was still in his tux. I slowly unzipped his pants and released his cock. I licked the base and ran my tongue up to the tip.

"Fuck, Peach," he moaned and grabbed my hair.

His cock slammed into my throat, and I sucked him. He moaned, pushing me down further. Now was the time. I needed to feel him.

I climbed on top of him and slid down onto his cock. My cunt was throbbing, he filled me completely. My body was in flames. As I rode him, I felt another set of hands wrap around my body and grab my chest.

Tristan was behind me, playing with my nipples while I rode Ethan. My pussy clenched around Ethan's cock, already on the verge of an orgasm.

"You like that cock?" Tristan asked as he pinched my nipples.

"Yes," I moaned. "I can't wait to feel your dick inside me."

He pulled me off Ethan and pushed me forward. While Ethan lay underneath me, Tristan slid his cock in behind me. He was gentle, slowly sliding in and out.

Ethan grabbed my hair and pulled my face to his. He kissed me while Tristan fucked me from behind. Tingles ran up my skin. Ecstasy was bringing me close.

"I'm gonna cum!" I screamed.

"Shit," a grumble came from the other side of the room.

I looked over to see Adam sitting up on the sofa. He had a smile on the side of his face, not covered by the mask. His eyes locked onto mine and sent me closer to the edge.

Tristan shoved his dick in and grinded against me. My pussy tightened around his cock. He filled me with his cum as I orgasmed on him. I fell forward onto Ethan.

"You aren't done yet, Peach." Ethan smiled and rolled me onto my back.

"But I just..." I stammered.

"And you will come again. First." Ethan looked at Adam. "If you want to consummate, hurry up. I won't have you being the last one with your dick in her."

Adam walked over, unzipped his pants and released his dick. Yup, he was hung. Shit. All three of them were going to rip me open. He slid his cock inside me and paused. His face tensed.

"Neither one of us wants this, there is nothing in the rules about orgasms." He pulled out, zipped up his pants, turned, and walked out of the room.

My mouth fell open. I guessed he technically consummated, but I expected a little more.

Before I could fully comprehend what had happened, Ethan was inside me. His cock was so large I thought my insides were ripping apart. Yet, through the pain, pleasure came. He took his time, allowing me to adjust to him.

I kissed him as he slowly rocked inside me. My breath was shallow, and I had a hard time staying grounded. This was everything. He was everything. I lost myself in the moment.

"I'm not gonna last, Peach." Ethan ground his teeth.

"Me neither." I wrapped my legs around him, pulling him all the way into me.

His dick ground my inside. Vibrations trickled through my body, I was getting closer. My pussy throbbed. His dick slammed into me again and again. Everything exploded. "Fuck me, Ethan."

He rode out my orgasm with his own. We were both panting as he pulled out of me and rolled over. Tristan cuddled up with me and wrapped his arms around me. All three of us fell asleep by the fire. I was sandwiched in between my two husbands, and nothing could have made me happier.

The end.

Note From the Author

Thank you to Everyone who read this book. Your support means everything to me.

This book started off as a standalone. That's exactly how it was supposed to stay, but the characters have minds of their own. There are still issues that need to be resolved. Yes, that includes Adam and Ava. They just can't get along. I'm working on the next book and trying to get it to you guys as quickly as possible.

If you read this book and thought Lisa was completely unbelievable with that tattoo, I wish you were right. Someone very close to me passed away fifteen years ago. Her mother recently changed the spelling of her name. She had decided it was the way she had wanted to spell it. (To that mother: if you ever read this, I hope you never wipe your butt clean and it's always itchy.) Now that I have that out of the way, I hope you all enjoyed the book.

Till Next Time. Muah,
Callie Sky

Also by Callie Sky

The Triplets and The Blonde